Tribal Blood

A Kayne Sorenson Mystery

Thomas Paul Severino

Tribal Blood

A Kayne Sorenson Mystery

Thomas Paul Severino

Copyright 2018

Pollywog Pond Communications, Ft. Lauderdale

tomseverino.com

tomseverino100@gmail.com

Front cover art: *Ute Indians Led by Chief Buckskin (*Public Domain)

Back cover art: *Chipeta or White Singing Bird. Native American Ute Tribe* Denver Public Library (Public Domain)

ISBN: 978-1-7322278-2-8

Thomas Paul Severino

For Gerald

Tribal Blood

Thomas Paul Severino

Also by Thomas Paul Severino

The Kayne Sorenson Mysteries: The Quartet of Blood

Seed Blood

Tribal Blood

Stage Blood

Ancient Blood

The Kayne Sorenson Mysteries: The Quartet of Evil

The Evil Genius

The Shadow of Evil

The Pearl of Great Evil

The Evil League

The Kayne Sorenson Mysteries: The New Adventures

The Crystal Orb

The Flower of Gold

The Amazing Adventures of Rebecca Quinto

The Frozen Diva

The Lost Museum

The Last Maya

Tribal Blood

Native American isn't blood. It is what is in the heart. The love for the land, the respect for it, those who inhabit it, and the respect and acknowledgment of the spirits and elders. – Native American Proverb

A Native American grandfather talking to his young grandson tells the boy he has two wolves inside of him struggling with each other. The first is the wolf of peace, love, and kindness. The other wolf is fear, greed, and hatred. "Which wolf will win, grandfather?" asks the young boy. "Whichever one I feed," is the reply. – Native American Proverb

... more and more, I have this growing feeling that we are encountering a powerful and dreadful evil lurking just beyond our intellectual reach and connected to much that is malicious and deadly. -- Kayne Jason Sorenson, Ph.D.

Prologue

The woman looked carefully at the severed flesh and bone.

Without removing her heavy gloves, she gently knocked a bit of the dried mud from its contours. It appeared to be human. Turning it over in the beam of her flashlight, she guessed it was part of a little finger. Carefully easing her find into a plastic zip-lock bag, she backed carefully out of the culvert.

White River barked excitedly as Susan Chipeta Walker emerged from the large drainage pipe. She had entered and climbed out against the direction of the minuscule water flow. Above, the western skies continued to darken with the promise of snow. A big storm was headed for the Richmond Ridge and surrounding territory. The bounty hunter could feel the changing atmospheric pressure in her bones. Time to head back. She called White River to her.

"Finally got something, pal," Susan said to her buddy. The big dog, aware of something important, barked again, circled her twice, and sat at her feet with frosty breath and tongue dripping. Her mistress adjusted the dog's harness vest with particular care.

Susan moved back to the other side of the drainage pipe, playing the light beam over the ground and the small icy flow that left the opening. She inspected the surrounding area on her hands and knees, careful not to disturb the terrain. She looked in the four compass directions for landmarks that would coordinate with this place on the mountain, speaking softly in the ancient tongue over the spot that yielded up evidence of the dead.

Susan had spent many times with her grandfather and her younger brother on these mountains, learning the tracking skills that were a part of the tradition of her tribe. Together, they tracked both animals and men. Chief Arapeen was often asked by local law enforcement to trace the movement of criminals in the wilderness of Colorado, Nevada, and Utah. She remembered that just before he died, he spoke wise words of encouragement about their work together.

"You have mastered the tracking ways of our people, my children. You both have gone beyond even me in the art of listening to the voice of our earth's mother and her brothers, the air, the water, and the sky. Use your skill only for good, my little Braves."

Susan was 14, and her brother was 12 at the time of the great chief's death.

Pulling her heavy coat closer against the mountain chill, the bounty hunter headed back up the steep slope to her Jeep on the steep road above. White River ran ahead, making sure the way was clear and safe.

Susan Walker wanted to get off the mountain and back to the reservation before the storm hit. As she stepped into the vehicle, she looked up to see a light aircraft heading for the airstrip in the valley below. She thought, *They need to head for cover like the rest of us.*

Susan slowly drove the Jeep further up the narrow mountain road to the turnaround. As she approached, a very large truck suddenly appeared behind her. *Too close*, she thought. *This could be trouble.* She opened the glove compartment and moved the Webley to her lap.

As she came to the turnaround, a broad space that swung out away from the mountain and high above the valley below, the truck rammed the back of the Jeep. The force sent her vehicle dangerously close to the low wall at the edge of the drop-off.

Susan stopped the forward motion of the Jeep, turned the wheels uphill, and set the brake. She jumped from the driver's seat, followed by the enraged White River. Behind her, the light aircraft descended to the landing strip.

"What's going on, asshole? Forget how to drive?" she addressed the two burly men who emerged from the truck aiming with her gun.

"No, I think we are doing just fine. Seems you've been poking your nose into places it don't belong."

"That so?"

As the dog waited for the signal to attack, Susan gestured to each man with the gun barrel. "Since I have my friend here aimed at your nuts," she said to the driver. Looking at his partner, she continued, "And can swing over and take off yours before you can say 'deballed,' suppose you toss that ax handle this way, Bubba."

The larger of the two men dropped the club on the ground. Susan stepped closer and addressed her stalkers.

"Now, hands up, boys."

She reached into the coat of the smaller of the two to search for a weapon. The larger man, suddenly in motion, unleashed a black and silver blade from his belt and threw it into the side of the chest of the Native woman.

As Susan fell, dropping her gun, White River attacked, going for the arms of the would-be killer. Susan rolled onto her back and extracted the blade that had been partially stopped by the heavy padding of her coat.

Immediately, the smaller attacker raised the retrieved ax handle and delivered three sharp blows, first to her knife-wielding hand. The other two broke both of her legs at the thighs.

As Susan screamed, she managed to yell, "White River, find Red Cedar, go!"

The dog came off the grounded attacker, looked at his mistress, and took off down the road. Three shots hit the dirt to the side and behind the running dog. One came close to the left side of her hindquarters, kicking up gravel. White River continued to run on as the snowfall and lowering clouds obscured her escape. She sprinted off the road, taking an animal trail down the mountain.

The larger man staunched the blood on his arms and hands as best he could. Turning to his partner, he said, "Put up the gun before you cause an avalanche, shithead. Let's finish this thing, man. Then we'll go get that fucking dog."

Chapter One: The Aerie
NICK SECHI'S JOURNAL

The winter skies over Aspen were deep gray and loaded with snow. The flight from Ft. Lauderdale to Denver was crowded, but the trip was without incident. Many winter sports enthusiasts were headed to the northwest to take advantage of late February's excellent existing and promised snow conditions.

Since Thanksgiving, Arctic temperatures and heavy precipitation have blanketed the lakes, mountains, and Alpine valleys of the American Rockies. Wave after wave of winter snowstorms moved across the Arctic and down into the western states. Epic snowfalls stalled air and ground travel but increased local tourism on a grand scale.

Kayne Jason Sorenson, Ph.D., and I were monitoring yet another winter snow bomb forecast for the Mountain States on its way to the Central Plains and eventually to the East Coast. The vast system moved like a tortoise, slow and steady. Salt Lake, Park City, Jackson Hole, and Tahoe were wrapped in white, to the delight of even more skiers and snowboarders. Everyone was headed to the slopes and resorts of the American and Canadian Rockies.

We joined the winter migration. What promised to be a much-needed snowbound getaway seemed about to become a reality. The terror of the reign of the Palm Killer in South Florida had left us mentally, emotionally, and physically exhausted. I was on extended leave from the Wilton Manors Police Force, and Kayne had begun a sabbatical year as a professor of criminology at Florida Global University. A renowned psychopathologist, Kayne was an internationally recognized expert on criminals and served as a consultant to law enforcement operations when other experts were baffled.

Kayne was a striking beauty with dual citizenship from his native Australia and the United States. Earlier this year, I was hit by the thunderbolt, as we say in my Italian American family. It happened when Kayne and I first met and began what was meant to be only a professional collaboration.

The meaning of this very traditional metaphor is that you experience an intense jolt of intense love (or firey lust) when first encountering someone. It is love at first sight on steroids. Bam! You get your socks knocked off, and you are in it up to your neck, instantly swamped by crazy romance. It usually happens to me in spring; make that every few weeks (or OK, days, really). It is especially compounded if you are a frisky, overly visual, gay, "bad boy" with the combined lustiness of a vibrant French and Italian ancestry.

Amid the horror of the very well-publicized case in South Florida earlier in January, we had struggled to keep our relationship professional. Not a chance. The attraction was powerfully magnetic and intensely primal. At 35, Kayne was just as energetic as this horned dog at the ripe old age of 26.

So, we struggled, and I mean we *fought*, trying to make sense of what was going on with us. After some enormous difficulties, horrific dangers, and major screw-ups, we gave it a "fair go," as Kayne would say -- took a chance. Lately, we had settled into a very comfortable yet thrilling love affair. Our sexual chemistry was well-matched. In the end, our emotional connections were positive and grew stronger every day.

True, but I still had this very essential question in my head, *Nick Boy, is this love or lust?*

"You play the cards you are dealt, Mate, with honesty, self-awareness, and integrity," Kayne was fond of saying. "So, when this guy comes along, and the missing pieces of your life begin to fall into place, I say, you go with it."

"Ah, *la danza passionale* – the dance of passion! We both had a history of hot men and their sexy ways. Lately, I had screwed up one or two relationships that I thought were the "happily ever after" types. But this one had all the marks of a once-in-a-lifetime connection. Damn, I am becoming such a romantic.

I looked over at his long, black hair, ice-blue eyes, and toned, tall kickboxer physique – yeah, I was in lust big time. Contrastingly, I was a ginger muscle boy, proving that the Northern Italian bloodlines favored the fairer colorings. One of the attendants on the flight asked if we were going to a convention of fitness or underwear models. I thanked her for the ego boost and snuggled into Kayne's shoulder at the back of Business Class. I hate flying, and Xanax is my friend.

Despite my aviophobia, I agreed to board Kayne's Embraer Phenom 300 at the Denver Airport, heading southwest to Aspen. Soaring above first Snowmass, then Buttermilk, and finally Aspen Mountain, the American Alpine valleys scattered between them came into view in the darkening, late afternoon light. Our luggage, skis, and poles secured in the private jet's cargo hold were a hopeful anticipation of some slope time.

"Absolutely rippa of a performance, Nick. One would hardly know you despise being off the surface of the planet," my pilot teased, using one of his best Australian slang expressions. Then with considerably more seriousness, "You doing OK, kiddo? You look a bit green around the gills."

"Great," I said, trying to hide my fight with vertigo. "I am so ready to get snowbound and create enough body friction to melt a glacier, hot man."

"Are you talking right now, or do you think little Nick there can wait till we get to the Aerie?" He indicated my crotch.

"Hey, whaddya talking, 'little'?" I did a package grope to defend my status among the hung. Kayne reached over to gauge my tumescence, but I slapped his hand away.

"Hands on the controls, please, Dr. Sorenson. Arrive alive as they say – then we can sex up like pagans."

He grinned and returned his right hand to the control wheel, "Do they indeed say that? You Americans and your strange yet slutty ways."

As far as we could see to the northwest, a towering wall of steel-gray clouds moved slowly across the landscape. Within the mountains' shadows, one of the vales in the track of the coming storm's path was our destination, a combination ski resort, American quarter horse ranch, and private home. The latter was perched on a high tor at one end of the valley's floor.

I relaxed a bit in the seat next to him and leaned over to kiss his cheek. The calm atmosphere on this side of the storm made for a comfortable flight, and I wasn't white-knuckling it anymore.

Nevertheless, there was the anticipation of nature's power directly off to our right side and spreading like an apocalyptic maelstrom. I pointed to the horizon and said ominously, "Comes the cyclone snow bomb, like the apocalypse. It will be so great to be back on the ground."

He rolled the plane into a bank as we approached an opening in the Elk Mountains. The view now revealed a rolling slope edged by rocky foothills covered with snow-laced conifers and leafless, deciduous trees.

"My brother's place is tucked back against the mountains, there, to the southwest," Kayne pointed. "It provides easy access to a variety of slopes as well as to the Village of Aspen. The hamlet is down through the southwestern pass. Across from the Lodge is the Resort, that huge complex on the opposite side of the Aerie Valley. You can see one of its ski runs ends a few meters from the Resort. The trails connect up and over to the Aspen slopes. "

He banked the plane, returning to where we had entered this Shangri-la, and pointed to the southeast rim. "We'll be touching down there. Eagle Base." He indicated a well-marked, private airstrip at the other end of the valley, rising in the distance as we circled and dropped.

"It won't be long now, Mate. I think you will love this place. Guaranteed to blow you away."

Kayne sent out the radio call to the tower below and aimed the private jet toward the expanse at the head of the runway. He worked the controls and began an expert approach ending in a comfortable landing.

***

"Clear for Eagle One in hangar bay two, Dr. Sorenson. We will unload your gear inside. Welcome to the Aerie."

"Roger that, Earth, and thank you."

Kayne taxied the Phenom 300 to the left of the strip and approached the small hangar as a four-person ground crew in heavy winter kit rolled back the doors of the second bay and waved our plane into the shelter of the building. Bay One contained the identical twin to our aircraft with "Eagle Two" stenciled on its side, just below the cockpit windows. Like

Kayne's plane, a company logo on the tail read. "Aerie Valley Industries, Inc."

Once the jet came to a stop, the ground crew opened the cargo hold and began to remove and pack its contents into the back and onto the roof rack of an idling black SUV parked on the tarmac. As we de-planed, I realized it would not be cool to kneel and kiss the ground. *Butch it up, Sechi!*

Behind me, Kayne bounded down the five steps that sliced off the side of the plane directly behind the cockpit and shook hands with a tall, very stunning, hatless man in western winter gear. His boots and bearing marked him as a consummate horseman.

"Nice to see you again, Dr. Sorenson."

Kayne did a handshake and a one-arm hug up, clapping the man's broad shoulders. "Well, you are looking very fit, Mate. Nick, may I present Joshua Walker. Josh is the Master of Horse here at the Aerie. Josh, Officer Nick Sechi of the Wilton Manors Police Force in Florida."

At the risk of sounding redundant, I have to say that the Master's grip was, in a word, "masterful" -- very confident and a bit primal. From his straight black hair and soft brown coloring to his razor-sharp cheekbones and aquiline nose, it was easy to conclude Josh was a Native American— a knockout in his mid-thirties. He had full lips and dazzlingly mysterious brown/black eyes. He wore his hair long and partially braided with leather thong trim.

I extended my hand. "It is a pleasure, Josh. This is quite a place."

"Nice to make your acquaintance, Officer...."

"Nick."

"Welcome, Nick, a bit different from the Sunshine State in January, I imagine." His smile was broad, but his eyes maintained a sober, piercing gaze.

Walker gestured with a sweep to the panorama of mountains and skies through the open doors of the hangar. To the west, the storm front seemed to swell like a devouring beast, tumbling forward and blotting out all in its path. Like a white and gray magician, the tempest lowered its cloak of invisibility, shrouding the mountains, hills, and valleys as it approached.

"You are about to be grounded here for a bit, I'd wager. This one is going to be bigger than the last."

"Excuse me."

I left them and dashed to the crew, loading the SUV with a huge crate.

"Hey, I'll take him out, guys, and then you can collapse the cage for easy travel."

I opened the large animal carrier, and my "Butterfly" bounded out of his confinement and knocked me to the ground, to the delight of the group.

Covering my face with slobbering dog kisses, I commanded my best friend, *"Chouko, orite suwaru. Ima!"*

As my Akita came to attention, I stood up and wiped his wet greeting from my face. He had behaved very well during the flight from Ft. Lauderdale but was eager to run free.

I pointed to the opening in the hangar doors. *"Chouko, wa hashitte modotte kuru. Hai!"*

Excitedly, wagging his curled tail, he turned in the direction I was pointing. Instantly, the black, brown, and white beauty sprinted out the door, circled part of the runway, marked a few airstrip indicators, and trotted back. He came to commanding attention, sitting beside me with a slightly smug look on his canine features.

I walked him back to Kayne, whom the dog greeted by jumping up and placing his forepaws on my friend's shoulders. Kayne hugged his bud and spoke him down in Japanese.

Josh received a long stare and an in-depth boot sniff from my buddy. Looking at me, Josh said, "OK, so your dog understands ... is that Japanese?"

"Yes. It is Chouko's first language," I joked.

We were joined by an attractive African American woman in flight livery. She warmly shook Kayne's hand and smilingly received the flight manifest.

"And Nick, this is Earth Rae Jordan. Earth is Aerie's Mistress of the Skies, no pun intended," he joked.

"Earth, this is my good friend, Nick Sechi."

The Flight Controller first knelt to dog level and offered her hand, palm up for Chouko's inspection. "You are the most beautiful creature. My goodness."

Standing, she addressed me, extending her hand, "Very nice to meet you, Nick. I hope you will enjoy your stay with us."

"Thank you, Earth. We are looking forward to it. Reports say we are in for some nasty weather. Could be dangerous?"

As if on cue, a gust of wind blew through the closing hangar doors.

Aerie's Flight Controller smiled, "Depends on how you look at it. For the mountain folk, big snow equals big business. But considering the predicted intensity of this one, I'd say you both arrived just in time. We are closing the strip and securing the guest's planes as best we can. This hangar is one of two. Resort guests' and owners' planes are housed separately."

"We are counting on a few days of snowbound conditions." Kayne wrapped an arm around my shoulder and gave her a bad-boy grin.

As we walked to the SUV, he added in a serious tone, "Any word on Jeron?"

Earth paused before answering. "Not since he went missing, Dr. Sorenson. No one seems to know. It's been almost two months. Both the county law enforcement and the tribal police keep coming up with dead ends. I am convinced someone must know something, but I find it hard to stay hopeful. Trying to concentrate on my work here, but it's difficult."

Kayne took her hand as she continued.

"I remember when you got him into Notre Dame. Thank you again for your help with that. He is so proud of his degree in environmental science. After those difficult early years, his life had taken a turn for the better."

"I am going to make some inquiries while I am here and will let you know what I find out, Earth. This is all passing strange."

"Thank you, Dr. Sorenson."

She reviewed the transport situation and said, "Looks like we're loaded up. Josh will drive you to the Lodge, and we will take good care of the Eagle One up here. I will let you know when we will next open the strip, but I am afraid it may be a few days of hunkering down, possibly a week."

Earth rolled her eyes with that last remark, and I could feel a bit of a blush rising from my neck as we scrambled into the back seat of the Range Rover.

"Red, I just love it when you redden," Kayne whispered, pulling me close and tousling my hair.

***

Josh exited the airstrip and drove southwest through the valley.

"We will be passing the Ranch and the Resort on our way up to the Lodge, Nick." He took a turn to the north, crossing the valley before continuing to the southwest.

I could see acres of white rolling fields between the foothills and mountains that surrounded the lower, flatter pasturelands through the falling snow. The acreage was substantial, carpeted with snow, and crisscrossed by pasture fences and roads. Commanding the mid-valley floor up against the northern rim was a complex of three buildings. Josh eased the Rover through the main gates of the ranch and up the main road for a drive-through tour.

"That large building is the Horse Palace – very Kentucky Derby. It can house the entire head of fifty. Behind it is the old barn, and to the right and to the rear are the living quarters for the ranch staff."

The Palace was a steep-roofed, blue and white building with three hexagonal turrets, one in the center of each of the three wings arranged around a quad that opened out to the pastures. The broad expanse of roofs was pierced by windowed gables on the second floor and circular windows for the third attic story.

A pillared portico wrapped the stable's sides that faced the courtyard with large barn doors on the first and second floors of the two wings and a grand entrance in the center. Each horse stall had Dutch doors that were closed against the coming storm. An impressive bronze statue of what must be a champion breed group, stallion, mare, and colt, dominated the courtyard.

"The design is based on the grand equine architecture of Lexington, Kentucky," explained the Master of Horse. "Right now, the crew is bedding the herd and securing the buildings against the coming blizzard. Once it passes, I will be glad to show you around. Nick. Do you ride?"

"Yes, I really love it, although I am a bit rusty. So, you will have to give me a few brush-up lessons."

Kayne elbowed me and softly "harumphed." I just grinned at him.

"I know Dr. Kayne is an accomplished rider." My turn to throw the elbow.

In the bay behind us, Chouko was vocalizing in soft whimpers. To my knowledge, he had never seen a horse before.

"Will this storm be a concern for the safety of the herd?"

"Not really, Doctor. We've gotten them through worse. If they were to be left outside, other measures would need to be taken. Our small herd of cattle is sheltered in the Old Barn during the cold weather, but lately, the Palace has provided better shelter for them. It provides plenty of warmth, and we have provisions for crew and livestock to allow us to be snowbound for a while."

We watched as a small crew of handlers led the last of the horses into the stable and closed the doors against the quickly rising wind. Josh drove us back out the ranch gates, circling back to the main road with windshield wipers blasting snow and ice. The Aerie's Horse Palace was quite a place. I looked forward to a more extended visit.

Behind the ranch, the foothills quickly rose up to the mountains. The winding roads and ski runs were becoming obscured by the descending storm clouds. High mountain passes were already feeling the initial impact of the storm. The way was quickly becoming unpassable.

Josh punched his mobile and contacted the Eagle's Nest. "Earth, secure quarters as soon as possible and make sure the crew is housed safely. Yep, Mr. Sorenson said the Aerie is available. OK. Check ya later."

As we turned south again, the winds picked up. Kayne pointed out a complex high up on the mountain surrounded by ski slopes and steep roads. "That is a US military training facility, Clarion Base, off to the right. You can just make it out. Soldiers from many branches of the Armed Forces train there -- ski warfare and backcountry survival. In the warmer months, the facility is equipped for mountain combat training."

He pointed to a cleft in the ridge, "Directly behind the ranch and up the slope is the border with the Native American lands, the Nu Ci Nation. And off to the south, although you cannot see it from here, are the trails for cross-country skiing, connected to the downhill slopes."

Kayne addressed our driver, "Josh, do we have time to swing by the Preserve?"

"Yes, Sir. It's on the way, just up ahead. I'd arrange a tour, but I want to wait until after this winter monster passes."

The southern slope of the valley was etched by a rolling mountain stream that coursed down and away through a wide rocky pass. Ice sheets covered the flow as it made its way.

Josh pointed as we crossed a sturdy bridge, "This is the Palouse River. It cuts through the reservation's highlands and hits a spectacular gorge north of Eagle Base before coursing through the valley pastures and out through the lower pass."

Tall, green conifers and naked deciduous trees were denser at this end of the valley. The landscape seemed to pull a blanket of pure white snow and fog over itself as we continued our journey.

"This section of the valley has been set off as a private wildlife habitat specializing in raptors and other indigenous birds of prey. But we also have indigenous species of *Canidae, Cervidae, Ursidae,* and *Felidae.*"

22

Kayne said, "Lions and tigers and bears...."

"Oh, my."

Josh ignored our fabulousness and continued, "That building off to the right is a rescue and medical facility. Above the preserve, you can just see the Resort at the west end of the pass. It is constructed to have views of both the Aerie Valley and of the greater Aspen area as well, including Buttermilk, Snowmass, and most of the Richmond Ridge of the Elk Mountains."

Connected to the Valley's hills by three winding roads, the Resort was cloaked in a swirling, descending haze of gray and white. Lights from the lower slopes were coming on to illuminate the beautiful western architecture of the complex. In contrast, amber-colored interior lights winked through the snow mist. The whole structure seemed to be lifting into the whiteness connecting earth and sky.

"It would appear that the guests' very expensive view will be obscured in a bit of a whiteout for a while," remarked Kayne.

Swinging up to cross the southwest rim, we took a steep, winding road to a vast building complex of stone, wood, and glass crowning the mountain wall. Like the Resort, the Western-style villa seemed to lift off the stone pillars that swept up from a flat plateau carved from the living rock. I estimated the mansion to be 400 feet above the valley floor. It appeared to hover weightlessly against the mountains.

The Lodge's first floor stretched forward between its six arched pylons, with an outdoor patio boasting a large, roaring fire pit. The grand entry stairs were flanked by entrances at the ground level, which led to the garages beneath the building.

The main floor, 30 feet above the ground, had glass walls under multi-level peaks and the rafters of broad, rough-hewn wooden beams. The structure was crowned by a third story, which complimented the entire design. As we approached, we could see through the massive window walls elegant staircases sweeping to the upper levels. Enormous stone chimneys pierced the inside floors. They seemed to break through the roofs before rising against the mountain skies with columns of welcoming smoke.

The entire effect was a building that seemed to be soaring and stretching up. One had the impression that it was either about to lift from its mountain perch or was lighting in a descent from the heavens.

Josh pulled the Range Rover through one of the stone arches that served as a very modern *porte-cochère*.

"Welcome to the Aerie Lodge."

"Rather ostentatious, eh Mate?"

Chapter Two: Identical

Josh led the way from the transport up the steps to the entryway. A veranda wrapped around the entire main floor of the Lodge. The next story boasted a series of private balconies. The whole structure radiated an interior light that suggested welcome and style.

We removed our boots and crossed through the thick, wooden, leaded-glass doors etched with rising eagles into a spacious great room. As Kayne and I took off our winter coats, a man, clad only in a white towel, bounded across the enormous living room and greeted us with a broad smile on his face.

"Kayne! So good to see you, Brother."

As he hastened his approach, I knew that he was more than just strikingly familiar. He wrapped his arms around Kayne and lifted him off his feet, kissing him with much enthusiasm.

The excited young man spoke very rapidly. "How was your trip? Did everything work out right? Did the Eagle perform well? You guys made it just in time, don't you think? Storm-wise, I mean. We are going to have a great stay." The handsome muscle boy shot off about ten more rapid-fire questions and statements as he put Kayne back down on his feet. His exuberant chatter was in a language, not English and not Australian slang.

I was bewildered.

Josh Walker, behind us, brought our gear in from the outside and stood attentively, awaiting further instructions. The presence of the nearly naked man seemed to have no effect on the Master of Horse.

I stepped back, my mouth agape, pointed at the two men, and said, "Holy shit, twins!"

Kayne, looking a bit flustered from his brother's bear hug and lack of clothing. The eminent professor caught his breath and introduced us.

"Nick, this is my little brother Tommy." He said his name in a very teasing way.

With an expression of annoyance, which then changed back to an infectious smile, Kayne's brother grabbed me and kissed both my cheeks, saying, "What's up, Nick? Please call me 'Kick.' It's a childhood nickname." Looking back at his brother, he added, "We are such a sporty family."

Kick Sorenson is Kayne's identical twin, or so I thought. As if reading my mind, Kayne said, "No, Officer Sechi, whereas we are identical, we are not twins. So, therefore..."

"Sweet Jesus! Don't tell me you are multiples. Lord, help us. There are more of you. OK, I'll start with the lowest number then." I pointed. "Triplets!"

Kayne nodded, and Kick smiled, saying, "Cheers, Mate. Identical trips, but I am still the best looking of the three." He thumped his chest. "Last one out, too, so that makes me the baby. But no runt." He brimmed over with magnetic charm.

Ignoring his brother's rivalry, Kayne spoke up, "We rarely discuss our other brother. I am afraid he is the black sheep."

"Hold it. All this time, I thought I was the black sheep," argued Kick with a childish pout.

"You can't be everything, Boyo. No, I think you best live up to the appellation of 'One Hot Mess.' Suits you best."

They both laughed and embraced a second time. Kick, in his enthusiasm, almost lost his towel.

"I will say this, Nick; he is the family exhibitionist." Kayne helped him hold it in place, readjusting it around his brother's narrow waist.

"Just coming from the shower, eh Mate, or is it laundry day?"

Kick threw a mock punch at his brother. "As a matter of fact, I was going to hit the hot tub one last time before the storm jobs on us. I crushed it on the slopes this morning and am a bit sore."

He rotated a nicely fashioned left arm.

I turned to look through the glass wall to the deck, watching the snowfall increase and begin to stick to the outdoor furniture. The young blizzard was engulfing a sizeable hot tub, sending clouds of steam into the frigid twilight evening.

"And your robe is...."

"Robe," he said, feigning shock. "And hide all this?" He threw a double bicep shot, which almost resulted in the towel slipping to his feet again. Kayne threw his hands up in playful resignation.

Kick looked at me and said with a smile, "I was definitely standing behind the door when the family modesty genes were passed out. My brother, Kayne, got a double helping."

I smirked, "Naw, your brother is far from Puritanical. I, um, can attest."

Kayne swatted my butt and smiled. "Careful, my love, everything Kick knows, he tells."

Kick called out to his staffer, "Hey, Josh, let's get the luggage up to the guestroom in the wing opposite mine, please." Looking at me, he added, "Kayne and I learned a long time ago the wisdom of some distance between our bedrooms."

He winked as Kayne turned to me with a spread open-hands gesture that said, "Whatevah."

"Look, why don't you both take some time to relax and get comfortable. You're welcome to join me for a soak if you like." He looked over at the grandfather clock that dominated a space next to the bar. "We eat dinner late here at the Aerie, like the Europeans. In the meantime, my home is yours."

It was as I suspected. Along with Kick's supremely over-the-top personality, graciousness ran in the Sorenson family. He was an extraordinary guy.

We were interrupted by a demanding bark at the front door. When we arrived, Chouko had bounded out into the falling snow to frolic a bit and mark some territory. He was amazed at his new environment and entirely invested in securing the parameter. I confess, having been somewhat taken in by the beauty of the Aerie and meeting its master, I had forgotten my best pal.

"Well, I can see I am going to have some stiff competition being the center of attention around here," remarked our surprised host. "Gorgeous males just have a habit of popping up everywhere at the Aerie."

I walked over to let my Butterfly in. Chouko immediately made for the Sorenson brothers but stopped to a dead halt before I could issue a command. He was transfixed by the duplication despite the difference in their clothing or lack thereof.

Picking up on the joke, Kick and Kayne hit a back-to-back, arms crossed, Blues Brothers pose. I surmised it was a standing joke stance. The very confused Chouko let out a bark of frustration, sniffed Kayne for reassurance, and approached Kick cautiously.

Kick offered a palm for the dog to sniff. Once he was assured of no threat, Chouko bounced up on his new friend, raking Kick's towel to the floor. Unabashed, our naked host knelt and offered some snuggle love to his new friend.

In Japanese, I ordered Chouko to sit at attention behind me.

Standing, Kick exclaimed, "Jesus, he understands – what is that?"

Kayne stooped to retrieve his brother's lost towel. With a smirk, he handed it to his delighted brother. Then, straight-faced, he said, "Japanese."

Josh quickly descended the staircase and approached us across the hardwood floor of the enormous expanse of the living room. He was ending a call on his cell.

He said, "I am sorry to interrupt, gentlemen. Will you need anything more, Mr. Sorenson? If not, I'll get back to the stables and ensure that everything is secured with the horses. There is some concern about the power going out in the storm. I believe we are OK with the backup generator, but I want to make sure, Sir."

Kick addressed his employee, "Umm, yes. I want to ask you something before you go back down."

Turning back to us, he said, "Scott has left out some sandwiches for you in the kitchen. He will make sure you are well-fed throughout your stay. And the Aerie's bar is always well-stocked. So, I'll leave you boys to it."

The Master of the Aerie walked over to the front doors to speak to his Master of Horse. Josh nodded and exchanged a few words privately with his boss before exiting into the swirling snow. I noticed that Kick had briefly placed his hand on the chest of the handsome Native American, making an intimate point.

Kick walked over to the sliding doors that lead out onto the veranda adjacent to the hot tub and sprinted to the hot tub, tossing his towel on a nearby rack. He climbed into the bubbling, steaming water. Smokin' sexy "arses" also ran in the family, I observed. *Damn nice.*

Kayne led Chouko and me past a raging fireplace, so immense a tall man would have no problem standing inside of it, to the sweeping stairway rising to the floor above. Our guest room was directly across from a third-floor sitting room that led to the master wing.

The accommodations were sumptuously laid out. A cozy fire burned in the fireplace. Josh had placed our gear in front of the sliding doors that led to a balcony overlooking the deck below. He stowed our skis "below decks" in the Aerie's equipment garage.

Most of the view from our room was concealed by the storm clouds now sitting on the Lodge, the Resort, and the Valley below. The wind howled and spiraled the snow as far as could be seen.

Kayne hugged up, looking frisky. "So, what are you up for, Mate?" He ran his hands over my back and shoulders, accompanied by some kissing. My frisky Aussie felt so good in my arms.

I opened a few buttons of his red and black flannel shirt and said, "I say we grab a bite and then inaugurate this very comfortable-looking queen-size bed. What do you say, sexy man?" To punctuate my answer, I reached around and slapped him on his version of the rock-hard Sorenson butt.

"I agree with your excellent plan. Last one to the kitchen bottoms."

"No fair, you're very familiar with this house. I am not," I said, dashing after him as he darted from the bedroom.

*** *** ***

Kayne was snoozing pleasantly beside me after our lovemaking. He had gotten to the kitchen first. His long hair spilled over part of his face and the pillow. A light sweat still glimmered on his naked torso. I got out of bed, wanting to check on the storm as the evening settled over the valley. Gusts of snow were blowing heavily across the balcony, entirely obscuring the view and piling against the glass doors.

Below our windows, in the spa, I could make out Kick in the arms of a stunningly hot man. The ferocity of their sex play was matched by the intensity of the storm. Because of the mirror resemblance to Kayne, it was very much like one of those porn videos where the dude watches his partner sexing up with another man -- very hot.

A voice from the bed shamed me. "Nick, voyeurism is only appropriate under special circumstances like crime-fighting. And, although my brother enjoys very rough coupling, I do not think we are talking about criminal activity here. Come back to bed, my love."

I turned and said nothing.

"Josh, correct?"

"How did you...." I stopped myself over the obvious answer.

Indicating his superior intelligence, Kayne pointed an index finger to his head in an "I am one smart bloke" gesture, winked, and pulled back the covers.

"Enough stamina for round three, or did I wear you out, my poor lad?"

I dove onto the bed, pulling him underneath me.

30

Chapter Three: Equus
NICK SECHI'S JOURNAL

The winter storm raged around the shelter of the Lodge perched on the mountain's crest. In jeans and a T-shirt, Kick was holding court around the blazing first-floor living room fireplace. Earth had joined us as the road through the pass to the village had become impassable very quickly in the early evening. Two of her crew, Mike Sampson and Carol Blue Water Lawton, had also been invited to spend the night at the Aerie.

"Most highways have been closed, although a few are being kept open. The Governor is about to declare a state of emergency," Kick said as he flipped through his mobile. "Have no fear, Mates. We can last this out. Plenty of food, drink, and warmth."

Kayne, the self-appointed bartender, had finished making and delivering round one. Chouko was snoozing before the fire. Kick raised his glass of Perrier and toasted his guests.

"Josh drove us by the stables, Kick. What kind of horses do you raise?" I asked.

"The Palace is kick arse, right Mate? So amazingly beautiful. So, New-Western Aristocracy."

He added, "We specialize in the American Quarter Horse. Are you familiar with the breed, Nick?"

"Not by very much, to be honest."

"They are bred for racing. Quarter horses are best at short-distance sprints. Our beauties are known to hit almost 90 kilometers per hour. Sorry, 55 miles per hour for you Yanks."

He continued, "They are also excellent ranch horses and excel at the equestrian sports. We will not contract with rodeos. Mitch and I have been appalled by that barbaric animal exploitation for a long time. And let's not even talk about the circus and how they destroy critters."

His passion for the dignity of animals was apparent.

Kayne, aware that his brother loved the spotlight, asked a question to which I was sure he knew the answer. He swept his forelock back from the left side of his forehead. He said in his best college professor voice, "How does a line that descended from the British Colonial occupation of North America, bred for racing and battle, become a cow horse?" Kick eagerly took up the bait, waving his hand in the air like an overperforming honors student.

"Oh, oh, pick me."

Kayne pointed at his brother, who jumped up like an "A" student anxious to impress.

"The horse was introduced to the Americas by the Spanish. Pioneers setting out to the West needed strong horses that could manage livestock. What they found were feral horses on the plains who were descended from the Spanish lines, Mustangs, domesticated by the Native Americans. Well, they crossed their colonial horses with these western horses – and bam, a new breed with a great instinct for working with cattle, a fine ranch horse – the American Quarter Horse."

Kayne teased, "Excellent, 'Lil Tommy. You may be seated."

Kick threw a couch pillow at his brother and continued as he landed back on the sofa. "A few of our racing Quarters have rivaled the Thoroughbred champions both here and abroad. Our entrees have collected some lucrative purses for the organization."

"Do you just have Quarter Horses?" asked Carol.

"No, we do have a few Thoroughbreds – very spirited and bold lines. We use them for racing sometimes but mostly to improve other breeds. Our neighbors, the military, actually love our Thoroughbreds and use them to strengthen their cavalry breed lines."

As Kick continued, Kayne freshened our drinks and sat on the arm of my chair. I reached up and touched his hand on my shoulder. I drifted from the horse talk to my private thoughts.

This man is getting to me. I mean big time.

On the rebound from a terrifying breakup, I was reluctant to throw in with anyone for more than a "no strings" sexual relationship. But, in the weeks that followed, Kayne was feeling oh so good in more than just an erotic way.

As if reading my thoughts, he brought his face down to the top of my forehead and smell-nuzzled me. His long, jet-black hair cascaded over my ginger buzz cut before he sat back up, ran a hand through it, and softly squeezed my hand.

Coming back "online," I heard Kick saying, "We are especially proud of our Appaloosa line. They are from multiple breeds and have a variety of spotted coat patterns."

Kick pointed to the picture above the mantle. "Yep. That is our first 'Palouse' horse, Chief Ouray, named for the famous Ute leader. He shows the leopard-spotted coat pattern. Unfortunately, he suffered from night blindness, which is genetically linked to the coat coloring."

"I thought the Appaloosas were Native American horses," Earth commented.

"They are." Mike Sampson took up the narrative with eyes shining. "My great, great grandfather fought in the Nez Perce War in 1877. His tribe, the Nez Perce people up near Oregon and Idaho, were among those that developed the original breed of Appaloosa way back when – like in the 1700s, I think. I remember him saying that after the war, the tribe lost most of their horses, and the breed almost went out of existence."

Kick said, "Yep. Some dedicated ranchers brought it back from near extinction. Our Aerie line DNA has some Quarter Horse, some Thoroughbred, and even some Arabian. The resulting crosses produced horses suitable for racing, halter competitions, and ranching."

Kayne added, "Native Americans continue to be integral in the industry of producing strong American horse lines. Aerie Ranch's most important breeders have been Indigenous People. My brother has been fortunate to have Josh Walker on staff. The business alliances with our friends on the Alpaska Reservation to the north have resulted in a lucrative partnership and a strong Appaloosa line."

Carol Blue Water asked, "Dr. Sorenson, is Josh Walker a member of the Ute people?"

"Yes, but not your tribe, Carol. Whereas you are of the Timpanogos Tribe from the north, Josh's line comes from the Southern Utes, the Muache band, also known as the Taos Utes. So-called because they traded with the Taos Pueblo people, most likely the source of his tribe's expertise with the horse."

"How did you guess my people were Timpanogos?"

"Delightfully easy. "

I interrupted. "Oh, not a guess. Oh, no."

Kayne ignored my slight mocking of his superior deductive powers.

"When you entered the Lodge, you stopped before my brother's framed photographs of indigenous peoples. You were especially drawn to the picture of Antonga, or Black Hawk, who led a confederation of Native Americans against the Mormons in Utah between 1865 and 1872. You touched the photograph with observable reverence and then touched your heart. Also, the design of your wristband is Timpanogos – northern Ute."

"I am amazed at your deductive powers, Dr. Sorenson. However, Chief Antonga is not referred to as 'Black Hawk' by my people. That is the name that Brigham Young gave to him. It is not a Ute name."

Kayne bowed slightly, "My apologies. It is also interesting that Josh Walker, though southern Ute, was named for the Shoshone chief who fought the Mormons in Utah, Chief Walkara, leader of the Timpanogos. His name in Shoshone means 'Hawk.' Very appropriate."

Kick said, "I am a bit confused. Who are the Ute, and how do the other tribes and bands fit in?"

"Good question, Mr. Sorenson," said Carol. "Ute is like a blanket name for many tribes that share a cultural and linguistic heritage from Mexico to Canada."

Kayne continued, "In the late 1800s, the Tribe's skirmishes of the so-called Black Hawk War spread from the Utah territory to Colorado, Idaho, and Wyoming. During that time, Mormon migration increased at the rate of 3,000 a month while the entire Ute population declined to just 2,400."

Kick interrupted, saying, "Kayne has a wealth of information about just about everything." He raised his glass to his sibling. "Before my esteemed brother's lecture continues, would anyone like a second round?"

I remember thinking what a smart way to retrieve "the mic" and consign his brother back to the role of the evening bartender. *Ah, sibling rivalries.*

Before Kick could return the narrative to the horses of the Aerie, the main door to the Lodge blew in, emitting gusts of freezing wind, ice, and snow and delivering the Master of Horse. The group turned to the totally snow-encrusted man. He stood his snowshoes against the rack and began to remove his protective goggles, gloves, and the rest of his storm gear. Chouko left his place at my feet to greet his new friend, his entire hindquarters wagging.

"Josh! Glad you got through and right on time. All is well?"

"Yes, Sir. I just did a walk-around of the Lodge. Fierce out there. All secure, however. The backup generator is ready to go in the event of another power outage.

The herd is bedded down at the Palace, and the staff is holed up in quarters. It is a mess out there, Sir."

Kick knelt before the semi-frozen man and helped him remove his boots. He murmured a few private words to his Master of Horse. Josh agreed to something, and Kick clapped his leg, smiling. Together, they headed over to the fire.

"Good evening, everyone."

The group greeted the imposing figure of the tall Brave as he stood back to the fire, winding his long black hair into a man bun with a beaded leather thong.

Kayne handed Josh a sizeable glass of Dalmore Scotch.

Keeping a steady gaze, Josh grinned at Kayne as he accepted the glass of amber liquid glistening in the firelight. "Ah, the white man's firewater. Thank you, Doctor. I will suspend my usual abstinence, for I do need this right now." He threw back a quarter of the glass.

"Dinner's ready, folks. We can continue our 'lessons' in equitation and breeding over some excellent Western cooking," Kick joked.

Kayne walked next to me as we brought up the rear of the group and headed for the dining room. We followed behind Josh Walker, who strolled with a sexy masculine grace and athletic gait.

"Behave yourself, Officer," Kayne whispered, pressing his lips next to my ear. "Custody of the eyes, my love. I know that look and can read your mind."

A bit embarrassed, I raised my gaze from the very hot, jeans-clad man's butt and thighs in front of me to meet the one-arched-eyebrow gaze of my lover.

"And you have a filthy mind, Dr. Sorenson, as anyone could attest based on this afternoon's activities."

"I do not recall you being forced into that quite savage display of the carnal arts this afternoon. Some of your shameless moves are absolutely pornographic. Why, I..."

I rib-jabbed him softly.

"Like hell you haven't."

"Anyway, my frisky lad, having a dirty mind makes ordinary conversations much more interesting. Don't you think?" He looped his arm over my shoulder and brought his head next to mine as we walked, whispering a short list of our recent depraved acts.

Kayne looked at my face, and imitating a very familiar Latvian accent from our recent past, he shot his forelock and added with flashing eyes, "Why Niko, you blush again. Is so funny!"

Chapter Four: Boss

Shadowy figures moved in the dark office.

"They won't find the wreck until the spring, Boss."

"You idiots. When I said take care of her, I wanted her contained, restrained, confined – major fuck up. We need her body out of here."

The shorter of the two reporting men continued, "I'm telling you that Jeep bounced almost to the bottom of the cliff and landed behind a pile of heavy rock. It's a bit hard to see in the storm, but I am sure of it. All good." He looked at the menacing figure of his boss' bodyguard, who stood in the shadows.

"And the scene?"

"The way this blizzard is steamrolling through, that area will give up nothing to an investigation."

"Listen very carefully, gentlemen. Our purposes are best served if there is nothing but burnt wreckage. Get your asses back there with some gas cans. And make sure no one can ask the wrong questions. We are fucked if someone gets to that Jeep before you do."

The more massive man moaned in the chair at the back of the room.

"Get him to a doctor, one of ours. Her dog?"

"No way she survived, Sir."

"That had better be the case."

"One more thing, arrange to have our most famous guest moved again. With the arrival of Dr. Kayne Sorenson, I anticipate some unwanted inquiries and want no discoveries. He can make a good deal of trouble for us.

"Once our current guest has been relocated, I want another round of interrogation with results this time."

He slapped the desk.

The Boss added, "I do not understand why you cannot get me what I need."

The speaker turned to face his silent bodyguard and spoke to the other men one last time.

"Leave."

***

Josh sat up in a full-body sweat.

"Hey, you OK?" asked his groggy bed companion. Kick fell back from sleeping across Josh's naked body and rolled to his side of the bed. Kick was a heavy sleeper, but Josh's anxious movements awakened him.

"Do you hear that?"

Kick paused and listened.

"Hey, the storm stopped a bit. Gonna be good boarding in the morning, sexy. Will you go with me? Get some deck under our feet and fly on those hills. Love to get us both up to the cabin. Would be awesome."

"Not the wind. Listen."

After another moment of silence, Kick reached back to the naked, muscular man.

"I'm getting nothing, Josh, but you can make me yell again if you want some real noise."

Josh rolled out of bed and stood. He went to the balcony and slid the glass door to make a small, vertical opening. The rush of icy air was bracing.

"You do *not* hear that howling?"

"No, why? Maybe it was Nick's dog. Or the wind starting back up again."

Rolling back the door, Josh was silent for a minute. Reaching for his jeans, he leaned over and kissed his frisky bedmate, saying, "I need to go, Boss Boy. I'll be back as soon as I can."

Chapter Five: Pillow Talk

Nick Sechi's Journal

In the short time that we had been a couple, early morning hours together in bed were becoming my favorite. Sex, loving, and conversation – it doesn't get any better than that.

"What have you concluded from your observations, Officer Sechi?"

"About your brother?"

"Yes."

"Well, hunkiness definitely runs in your family," I began, stroking his broad back.

Kayne lifted his head from my chest and smiled enigmatically, his black hair cascading across his face and obscuring his steel-blue gaze. I slid my left hand further down his naked torso and caressed his left butt cheek.

"Please use the big head in your scrutiny as opposed to the little head and continue," he said somewhat smugly.

"Well, it's true. You two are crazy hot."

Kayne rolled off me and propped his head on his right hand. He pulled his hair off his face with his left and traced circles on my chest with his index finger. His raised eyebrows indicated that I should proceed with my analysis of his sibling.

"And?"

"Yeah, he is very toned, like you. Athletic training, I conclude, began at an early age."

He smiled, "Easy one, Mate. No credit for that one. We Aussies are a sporty breed."

"Has the ass and thighs of a rugby player. Upper body, too. Slightly bigger shoulders, chest, and arms than you. He moves like a gymnast. He

39

is right-handed and sustained a significant injury in his left hand. His hair falls on the opposite side and is slightly lighter."

"He highlights it. And he occasionally uses mascara. Just whatever."

"Hmm. I would say you are mirror-image twins. But you are triplets, so I don't think that applies unless your other brother is fraternal. And Kick does not have this." I reached over and touched the "Mark of Cain" scar on the left side of his upper forehead.

He took my hand from his forehead and kissed the palm. Looking into my eyes, he said, "My divine curse scar is acquired, not hereditary. "

He added, "Your conclusions are good so far, with one modification. Our sport was Australian Rules Football, footy – the source of Kick's nickname. Although the four of us can handle a good rugby match. What else do you see?"

"The ADHD runs particularly strong in your family, although in Kick, it seems to be a bit more accelerated in his ability to entertain distractions. He is like a cognitive juggler, to be honest. Tends to be a bit confusing when it manifests itself. To an observer. I mean to say that combined with his natural gregariousness, uproarious sense of humor, and very sexy physical presence, he is impossible to ignore and loves being the center of attention."

"Umm hum. Yes, he does."

"And what's with the scars on his back?" I added, breaking off with my dissertation tone.

Kayne's expression got more serious as he said, "Your conclusions?"

"Did he roll his chopper a way back? They are faint but rather extensive."

"My brother has never been on a motorcycle in his life, to tell the truth. He abhors them. Prefers other conveyances. Does the pattern suggest road burn?"

"No. Long and thin, the marks extend to his glutes and the front and backs of his thighs." I thought for a moment and then sat up, back against the pillows.

"Shit, he's whip meat. Rough sexin'."

Kayne rolled onto his back next to me and crossed his arms behind his head, staring at the ceiling. He heaved a deep sigh in this very sexy position.

Typically, he began to deconstruct my observations and conclusions like a true consulting detective, clearing away emotional reactions and analyzing the data. However, I had a sense that the experiences of "growing up Sorenson" were filled with countless landmines of emotion-fraught issues.

"You are correct. My Da raised us on hard work and sport. Our skills at 'footy' easily translated to soccer. We all had scholarships at ND after secondary school, although Eric lost his scholarship in his sophomore year.

"I trained as a halfback, hence a somewhat more balanced upper and lower body, whereas Kick was a forward and designed for speed. He is an extremely agile "gymnast," as you say.

"While we attended Notre Dame, he came under the tutelage of the gymnastics coach. You can imagine that the relationship involved more than sport. Quite scandalous as the man in question was a member of Holy Orders. A substantial donation straight out of Australia made it all go away."

"Sorensons seem to cause trouble a lot. Just sayin'"

Kayne ignored my soft jibe and continued, "Anyway, 'Little Tommy' honed his physical skills as an amateur freerunner, a sometime stuntman, and a top-quality snowboarder. He has more than once competed in the X Games, the Red Bull Competition Art of Motion, and the Freerun Air Wipp Challenge, medaling in all three. Some more than once. Ever heard of *Sasuke*?"

"No, what's that?"

"It's a Japanese competition involving a four-stage obstacle course. Kick won it twice. Does not speak a word of Japanese, by the way. He cannot remember the nuances of most foreign languages. For him, they run together, befuddling his brain."

Shadow of a smile as he continued, "But as I was saying, I was on a case in Tokyo and Kyōto for about a year. Kick came over, trained, and beat out one hundred competitors each time. The US spin-off is called 'American Ninja Warrior.'

In Japan, Thomas Michael Sorenson, the Junior, aka 'Kick,' is known as *Supaidāman*. He is a hell-man at sports of all kinds. And yes, I assure you he *is* a blooming Spider-Man, Nick."

"Nice."

"Kick, Eric, and I are monozygotic or identical triplets with the same DNA. We are, obviously, all three males with the same blood type, hair, and eye color. We do not have the same finger, hand, and footprints. Oh, and I think you will notice soon that we are also cryptophasic."

"Huh?"

"Cryptophasia is a phenomenon of a secret language developed by twins or multiples in early childhood which they only speak with each other."

"Oh, great! And I was having trouble with the Aussie slang, now fuckin' trip speak."

Kayne smiled, "She'll be right, Mate. Two of me is a bit much, I will admit. For that matter, one is pretty much a ripper."

He continued to talk about his brothers, "I forgot one thing in my *apologia pro vita sua*. We are all three gay."

"Sweet. How rare is that?"

"Evidence of the gay gene?' Supposedly. Yes, as ankle-biters — sorry, children, in Australia, we were part of an international study on that despite my Father's initial concerns."

"What do you mean?

"Ace accepted the sexual orientation of all of his sons but did not like attention to be drawn to our family. Anyway, the study, you will not be surprised, was a 'nature/nurture' thing. We ended up part of a more significant research project on the subject.

"The offshoot was we were all outed at an early age. There were some school issues, but the three of us learned to give bullies a real scare -- we being so tough and all. I suppose being raised on a cattle ranch builds the body and character. And then there was Mitch, who made sure no one caused a row if he could help it. It worked most of the time. We scrapped a lot with some haters, but, for the most part, each of us is pretty proud of who we are."

I snuggled down, ran my fingers through his blue-black hair, and kissed him lightly. "Kayne, who is Mitch?"

Brief silence. That Kayne was uncomfortable with childhood memories and sibling relationships became more apparent. He struggled to remain stoic.

"Ace found Mitch on the streets of Perth when my foster brother was two years old. This was about six months before we three were born. He brought him back to the station near Alice Springs and raised him as his own. He was everything one would want in an older brother, athlete, scholar, and all-around excellent bloke. He became a rather noted psychiatrist and business leader here at the Aerie. Came into possession of this valley through the generosity of a deceased admirer. Long story. Mitch was everything one would want in an older brother."

"Was?"

Another pause. Kayne turned and faced me.

"I meant to say 'is,' but you see, there was this accident about a year ago. Mitch was recently married, and ...."

His eyes glistened up, and I pulled him into a hug-up. "I am so sorry."

We did not say anything for what seemed like a long time. Kayne leaned back, attempting to control his emotions, and finally said, "Families – you can't cook 'em, you can't eat 'em."

"How is your sister-in-law doing with it all? Any children?"

Kayne shot me a very sly look. "No, no children and one can conclude that 'she' seems to be taking it exceptionally well, Mate. Cavorting in the hot tub with the Master of Horse is an indication that the Widow Sorenson has moved on."

"Huh?"

"Mitch and Kick were married in Montreal six years ago. "

"Holy incest, Batman!"

For the first time, Kayne genuinely smiled. "Not really. Mitch is not blood. More than a few magistrates in Canada are former Marines, as is Ace. No matter what your corps' nationality, the *Simper Fi* boyos, it seems, are a well-connected community. Military brotherhood is not without its advantages. And in Canada, as in the US, one can marry an adopted sibling."

He pulled back his bed hair and continued, "The Aerie belongs to Mitch and then became one of Kick's assets when they married. My mess of a brother is a wealthy bloke and does not need to work in one respect. The rest of us insisted that he continue with the business of the ranch and the resort and the other interests of Aerie Industries, Inc., however, to support his mental health."

I was intrigued, but Kayne aroused my suspicions. "What's your brother's prognosis? I would presume depression."

Now, Kayne sat up and looked directly at me. "Way more complicated than depression brought on by grief. Kick's condition goes back to his childhood, his early teens. Although Kick has been dancing on the edge of the volcano since he was eight.

"If he continues to take his lithium carbonate, there will be no descent into psychosis or schizophrenia, hopefully. He fights it -- the medication, that is. It takes strong partners or family members to make him stay on the meds. As a lad, his Bipolar Disorder II was not that evidenced. When he hit puberty, the fullness of the mania hit as did its counterpart, depression."

Continuing, Kayne shifted next to me and turned away. He seemed to be speaking to the open space of the large bedroom as he continued to discuss his brother's challenges.

"It fell to Mitch and me to keep him serious about his treatment once we all left Australia for university. His depression takes the form of extreme machoism from time to time. Those whip scars are old and from a series of very dark incidents that occurred after Mitch disappeared when Kick deliberately went off his meds."

He continued, "After we left South Bend, there were episodes of bondage that lasted a long time. He would go missing and then turn up days later, barely alive. These led to hospitalization and electroconvulsive therapy. After a few more episodes, two near-fatal, he made a promise to Ace and me to stick to the pills and lay off the heavy discipline sessions.

"He was doing pretty well for a bit. Mitch stepped in, and the marriage stabilized Kick's life. Then, about six months ago, the accident and his life went off the rails again. To be exact, he decided that Mitch was dead and fell off the wagon of sanity.

"That was a very tough time. Again, it took some pressure from Ace and me. Kick tends to do well when his lovers and partners are dominant men with superior mental strength. Enter Josh Red Cedar Walker."

Now Kayne looked directly at me and continued, "Josh was devoted to Mitch. As Kick descended into madness again, Josh took matters in hand. Josh is good for him, stoic, powerful, and as serious as a heart attack, as you Yanks say. He made Kick see reason better than any of us could. Through patience and sheer strength, he turned 'The Mess' around again.

"So now, Kick has thrown himself into continuing Mitch's legacy here at the Aerie. I find it amazing how he and Josh flip-flop professional roles and intimate behaviors."

"What do you mean?"

"Publicly, Kick calls the shots as the employer. Josh runs the equine industry for Aerie. He is an expert consultant and a guide for the lad. He also serves on the Board of Aerie Industries, Inc., with three other Native Americans.

"He addresses Kick as 'Boss.' Together, they are making some excellent decisions regarding the corporation – profitability, and community leadership are on the rise. Partnerships, especially with the Nu Ci, are excellent. But if you look carefully, Josh calls the shots of their personal relationship, especially in th – shall we say, romance?"

Outside, the speed and fury of the blizzard seemed to have disappeared as the early morning light struggled to break through the last of the wind, snow, and ice.

He continued, "Kick's mania exhibits itself in a rather intense fashion. He is naturally the life of the party, any party. Infectious smile, devastatingly handsome, and I say that in all humility, my love.

"His killer body and overall gregariousness have always been his natural gifts. He is a significant heartbreaker and loves being totally unavailable to desiring women and a huge tease to interested and gay-curious men. He gets hungry as hell when he spies a hot male.

"When he becomes manic, his emotional highs become unbearable. Considering all Kick's personality swings, Mitch referred to him as his 'Hot Mess.' The moniker stuck."

"Kayne, Bipolar Disorder is thought to be genetic."

He sighed, "Correct, I escaped so far with only the Attention Deficit Hyperactivity Disorder. We all have some form of it. I keep my cognition in balance and my moods stable through meditation and sheer force of concentrative will. Kick, unfortunately, has the genetically linked BPD II. My brother Eric is a subject for another discussion if you don't mind."

I reached up and massaged his muscular back and traps. "I am sorry this is all so painful for you, Bud."

He turned again to face me. A veil of emotional detachment descended over his beautiful face.

The intellectual side of Kayne surged to the fore, and he said, "Not at all, Mate." He added as dispassionately as he could muster. "You need to know the crazies with whom we are holed up in this blizzard. But, if you wouldn't mind, let's discuss another topic immediately, please."

Seriously? And I thought my family had cornered the market on selective emotional restraint and I-don't-want-to-talk-about-it avoidance. Responding to the cool Professor Sorenson that had suddenly surfaced, I asked, "And just what is it that you would like to talk about, Doctor?"

He smiled and twisted completely in the bed, pulling me under him. "I thought we might pursue an important topic essential to our relationship. What I like to call 'Nick on the Bottom Again and Begging' as a matter of intensive and deeply probing research. Just how nasty is this man with whom I am snowbound?"

As he began to turn my face down and beneath him, our bedroom door burst open. The interior squall was a gust of beauty, style, and vitality.

"Darlings, have you any idea how hard it is to find this place, especially in a fucking blizzard?"

Chapter Six: Accommodations
NICK SECHI'S JOURNAL

Kayne was exasperated as he slid off me.

"And do you have any idea what absolutely smoking hot, man-on-man sex you have interrupted?"

Rebecca Quinto wagged a finger and batted her sparkling eyes as we struggled into our robes and backed her out to the sitting room.

"*Coitus interruptus.* Isn't that forbidden by the Bible, Darling Kayne? Sex Acts of the Apostles, I believe?" She fiddled with the tented front of his robe like a tempting Delilah.

He slapped her hand away and said, "Genesis, dear girl. The sin of Onanism. In Oz, we say, 'Get off at Redfern.' But the whole man-on-man thingo in the Bible is religiously *verboten* in the minds of the fanatics. So, since when did you get religion and become the gay sexin' police? You broke in on us!"

They exchanged a European triple-cheek kiss.

"Relax, my eternal love. Not anything I haven't seen up close before." She winked at me and added *sutto voce*, "And on occasion participated in. But that, my sweet boys, will be a topic we can pursue over many, many drinks. It is not often that I am in the presence of the two best man asses on the planet."

Once I was, shall we say, under control of myself, I embraced her with my own three-kiss greeting. Then, holding her at arms' length, I said, "Rebecca, what on earth are you doing here?"

"Seems our girl is stalking the two best man arses on the planet," Kayne joked from the sitting room coffee bar. He fixed three mugs and brought them over.

Rebecca accepted the coffee and kissed her best friend again. We three descended to the second-floor living room, where breakfast smells seemed to gather. Through the glass walls, the snowy gloom and the morning light seemed to battle for dominance. The landscape was spectacular. I had that feeling of being suspended over the wild terrain again.

"You should know, my Darling Nicky, that the Fritcher Museum of Fine Art in Lauderdale is working on a fabulous project. It is a joint venture with the Silverman Museum of Native American Art and the Phelan Museum of Fine Arts, both of Aspen, Colorado. We hope for a dual opening in Florida and Colorado next year. So, I am here to discuss with major partners."

"Or to get us all killed. I still can't believe we made it, Rebecca. That is some fucking blizzard you have here, my friends. I think it may kick up again."

The very handsome Mark Gadarn, Rebecca Quinto's latest love interest, entered the living room, trailing snow and ice. The freeze encrusted his bulky winter clothes and bearded, rugged Welsh-American features. He resembled one of the heroic members of the Fellowship of the Ring, as depicted by Peter Jackson's *The Lord of the Ring* epic.

Removing his parka, scarf, and gloves, he tossed them over a hook next to Rebecca's in the entryway. Mark turned and said, "So, who do I have to fuck to get a cup of that hot and steamy brew?" The three of us raised our hands. Mark guffawed.

Pointing to Rebecca, he made his choice, adding, "Sorry lads, perhaps after a few beers. You know what they say ...."

Kayne and I said together, "Anything can happen!"

Mark kissed his ladylove and grabbed me in a warm embrace, "You keeping the black hats at bay, Nicky? Now that you saved South Florida, you out here looking for more trouble?"

The dude has a significantly friendly vibe, is totally self-assured, and is very comfortable with his sexuality. It is easy to see that Mark could be irresistible to women.

"No such, Bud. On complete 'vaycay.' Not even answering emails. Planning to be skiing, eating, drinking, and riding."

Mark glanced at Kayne, who aped innocence. "Horses, I take it," Mark said with a twinkle in his blue-black eyes.

"Well, yeah... OK, horses... yeah." I glanced and smiled lasciviously at Kayne while Rebecca did a spit take. Kayne brought over a steaming mug of Earl Gray from the bar for the magnificent Mark.

"Haroo, my Aussie Mate. You remembered." He hugged Kayne, who remarked, *"Dw i heb dy weld ti ers talwn!"* and, clinking mugs, saluted, *"Llechyd da!"* Mark replied, *"Diolch. Sut ydych chi?"*

Rebecca sank onto a couch and pulled Mark beside her. "OK. Listen up, boys. Rule Number One -- English only. You guys -- no Welsh. Me... no Spanish and Nick is limited to using his Italian to cuss or to make *l'amore.*

She sipped her coffee and quickly added, "Oh, wait. And that Aussie 'Strine mess is out as well. Otherwise, it's gonna be like one big Rosetta Stone here in Downtown Snow Hell."

"I need an exemption for Chouko. Otherwise..."

Looking at Rebecca, Mark sighed and gestured to Kayne as he explained, "Sexy man number one over there said in Welsh, 'long time no see' and 'cheers.' I thanked him and asked how he was doing."

Kayne put his arm around my waist and grinned. He switched to English, obeying the Quinto Rule Number One. "Doing just fine." He clinked mugs with me.

"Yes, I can see that, Mate."

"Close the robe, Big Man," I whispered. Kayne did a one-eighty and tightened his robe while Rebecca and Mark laughed.

"Anyway, I thought I'd tag along and see if I could snoop up a story for the news service. Been a lot of chatter on the international skiing set. Rich and famous bullshit. Rather be back with the troops in the Middle East, but that last assignment in Aleppo threw the network big shots into pretty much of a shutdown. So now it's has become, let's put Gadarn on covering the rich and snobby whose only controversies involve opioid addiction, botched cosmetic surgeries, and illicit liaisons with pilates instructors."

Rebecca added, "CBN lost four reporters in Syria and very nearly five." She hugged Mark affectionately.

"Yeah. So, after I got out of the hospital, I got this powderpuff assignment. Big fucking deal, tweets, diamonds, and martinis on the slopes. Hardly something I can feed my boy, Jake Tapper, at CNN."

CBN was a freelance news reporting service headquartered in Washington, DC. The agency supplied the more prominent news media with cutting-edge reporting. It was noted for taking on the most dangerous and controversial assignments. Furthermore, it was trusted as intelligent and fact-based.

"I had hoped to sneak into Chechnya to report on the human rights abuses of their LGBTQ community, but the execs said I needed to lay off for a while and recharge my batteries. *Cnuch!*"

"Darling, Rule Number One." Rebecca turned to us. "Anyway, that one I know rather well, as a matter of fact. It's Welsh for 'fuck' -- a very useful word."

Mark did an eye roll.

"My warrior journalist," She continued consolingly. "For your reporting, we'll find something hot and sordid or make some of our own trouble, Darling. I am sure the underbelly of this playground has its crimes and scandals. And, I am thinking you look just as hot in ski wear as shirtless and in your camos. Perhaps unzipped down to...."

She traced an index finger from Mark's collarbone to his navel. Mark laughed and gave her a quick kiss, stopping the descent just below his lower abs.

He said, "Holy crap! I totally forgot. We brought you a gift, Kayne. To share, of course."

Right on cue, the stomping of snow-covered boots on the porch brought a fearsome Yeti-like creature through the front door of the Lodge, trailing the remains of the tremendous storm behind him. He was swathed in heavy protective gear, including golden-lensed ski goggles.

The huge man roared, "If this is Hell, Gints has found it! Not Florida paradise, more like Latvian winters of Gints' boyhood. Not a place to hang naked. That for sure."

The muscled bull made for the fire and began to unwrap and disrobe from his icy, wet gear.

"Ski instructor has arrived and will be very demanding. But Gints is not very happy. Please to provide many hugs and alcohol drink for warm-up."

Beaming, Kayne jumped into the arms of his favorite bartender, bodyguard, sometime bed partner, and our faithful friend.

"You sexy bear, how did you manage to get away, Studly? The hot boys of South Florida cannot do without all this." He pummeled Gints' solid pecs.

"They will have to manage, beautiful Kayne. Gints on rebound -- again. So sad. Need very much to clear thoughts and start new, passionate love affair. Come here, Niko. Why you make Gints wait for hugs and kisses? I not steal Kayne from you. Even when he insists. I will fight him off."

I joined the welcoming embrace, sincerely glad to see our good friend. There was plenty of room for more than one in the strong arms of our Slavic, muscled beauty.

"Good to see you, Buddy."

After a bit of friendly loving, Gints held us both away from him with a fake-serious inspecting gaze.

"Oh ho, what is here? In morning robes, the two of you. Do not need to hit Gints over the head with a wooden board, as Americans say. Confess. You two have been doing *jāšanās* and not for first time today."

After a finger-wagging, he grinned and slapped, in turn, the "two best man arses on the planet."

He waved a dismissal. "Do not fear. We do three-way soon. Get very satisfied."

Again, Rebecca almost choked on her morning coffee as she and Mark enjoyed the comic and very shameless interchange.

"Did someone say, "three-way?"

The five of us turned to see Kick, who had entered the Lodge living room from the kitchen wing. He was in jeans, cowboy boots, a tasseled ski hat, and an open, red and black flannel shirt. The muscles of his bare chest were eye-catching. Carrying a snowboard, he was grinning from ear to ear.

Mark jumped up and exclaimed, "Holy shit, there are two of them!"

Rebecca rose and made for the newcomer. "Kick, Darling, you get more handsome every day." She pulled him in for a warm embrace, almost knocking the snowboard to the floor.

As Mark and Gints stared open-mouthed, Kayne just shrugged his shoulders and gave a look reminiscent of a kid with his hand in the cookie jar.

Rebecca said in a stage whisper to me, "I'll bet *you* were surprised. Just think of the possibilities, Nicky. Twins can be so hot."

Kick proclaimed, "Rebecca, you gorgeous woman, the mountains agree with you. And the apparel – very *Givenchy* ski chic – you are so channeling Audrey Hepburn in *Charade*."

She did a twirl.

"If only. Hubert lost the edge, I am afraid, after the 60s, Darling. His sportswear is not to my liking. Although I adore the rest of his current line. This...," she swept a hand over her winter ensemble, "is Bogner."

An astonished Gints pushed his way forward, "Ho, no, no. One minute, please. I am Gints, and you are very hot ski boy, Kayne's brother, yes?"

Kick was amazed at the physical presence of our Latvian beauty and started to speak, but the words would not come at first. He did a dramatic "what-am-I-seeing" eye rub and said, "Super delicious."

Kayne spoke up, "Mark, Gints, please allow me to introduce my brother, Thomas Michael Sorenson, Jr."

Kick winced slightly at the mention of his given name and swung the snowboard as if to swat his brother. In turn, he took the hands of Gints and Mark, saying, "Please call me 'Kick.' Only my father calls me

'Thomas.' When I am in trouble, which is quite often, he refers to me as 'Thomas Michael.'"

He continued in a very cordial manner as Gints embraced him in a hug-up, "Welcome to my home. I hope you will be staying for a while. But how did you guys manage to get through this storm of the century?"

Mark spoke up, "It damn well was not easy. Flying from Florida to Denver was fine since the storm had stalled a bit west of the capital. The rest were canceled flights to Aspen. We have been in a major huge ATV/SUV since midnight. Into the heart of the beast! HOO-RAH!"

"Thought we damaged an axel in the climb up here. Boulder. Hard to make out the road. Gints and I decided we were OK, however. We did another blizzard roadside inspection in your driveway."

Gints agreed, "Yes, Mark, I check it out again. Go all underneath. Seems no damage. But to be sure, Gints recommend mechanic."

Kick stared at the exuberant Mark with an appraising eye. Rebecca injected, "Mark is an expert driver over rough terrains and inexhaustible in extreme conditions. I refused to stay in Denver and insisted we chance it."

The double meaning of her first sentence was lost on no one in the group, and Rebecca realized that she had stirred the pot. "OK, sooo, I am gonna need you boys to back off. This one's all mine," she half-joked.

The woman in the sexy snow boots attached herself to her man hunk.

"Such a brave and beautiful woman," Kick said. Despite Rebecca's warning, he hungrily looked Mark up and down. He added, "And I am thrilled that you folks risked the trip."

In a stage whisper, Kayne said to his ogling brother, "You make undressing someone with your eyes an absolute art form, Baby Brother. Show some subtlety if you can." Mark just smiled.

Kick pulled a face at this sibling and then whipped out his mobile. "Excuse me, just a bit."

He punched in a number and spoke into the phone, "Scott, may I see you, please?"

He turned back, remarking, "The Resort is full, and, with this snow, it will probably stay that way as the winter sports conditions continue to be super good. This Lodge has nine guest bedrooms, and the best view of the three mountains to the west on the third floor is near my brother's suite, if that is OK. Once the storm passes, the view will be awesome."

Mark responded, "Awfully nice of you, Kick. Rebecca's assistant had contacted the Resort for accommodations, but they gave the rooms away due to our travel delay. So, if it is not too much of an imposition, we would love to crash the party. Once traveling becomes somewhat less hazardous, we both will be in and out. That OK with you, Rebecca?"

"Yes, Darling, and so kind of you, Kick Darling." Having recovered from the experience of driving through a monstrous snowstorm, Rebecca had her "Darlings" in full gear. I wondered what she knew about the third copy of these Sorenson Aussie beauties.

I was intrigued. *Let's save Eric Sorenson for another time,* I thought. *And how about Moms Sorenson?* Perhaps it was best to wait on all of this. I suspected a few landmines, and Kick gave every indication that he would be enough of a challenge for us mere mortals to figure out.

"I'll have my staff grab your gear and get you settled in."

He approached Gint's, saying, "Now, you, big studly, well, I am afraid that none of the guest rooms has larger than a queen. Oh, wait, wait...."

Here it comes, I thought.

"There is one king-sized bed. I can show you and let you decide, Muscles. It's the Master, so, ahh...." Gints grinned broadly.

I watched a bit amazed at how Kick commanded the room charmingly and effortlessly. This was the extrovert in full force. I reached over to slip my arm around the more introverted brother.

Kayne murmured, "He puts the moves on faster than an escort trying to fill his weekend calendar."

Scott joined us from the kitchen.

"I am sorry, Mr. Sorenson, but most of the staff is unable to get up the mountain this morning, so there is just me here in the main house.

Your flight crew left earlier to see the airstrip. Not sure if they are coming back. I will find out."

Kick turned to his guests. "This is Scott Iverson. He runs the Lodge, is an awesome cook, and only calls me 'Mr. Sorenson' when we have company."

Turning back to his majordomo, Kick said, "OK, then we will all pitch in. We can put Mark and Rebecca next to my brother and Nick. Gints can bunk in with me for now. We should have a full house if the folks from last night can get back up here." He spun the snowboard on its edge.

A gust of powerful storm winds slammed against the front of the Lodge. It appeared that a second round was decreed by heaven. A banshee-like scream and a pressurized 'whomp' shook the lodge.

"I was out in it, and conditions are amazing. Class A blizzard, children. At some point, I need to get down to check on the horses and Josh and the crew at the ranch. We will gather for breakfast. Say in an hour?" This last remark was directed at Scott.

"Yes, Sir."

"Gints very impressed that you have breed stock business, Kick Sorenson. We go see them together."

Speaking to Gints but looking directly at Kayne, Kick said, "Sexy man, if we are going to share the Main Bedroom for the duration of your stay and it may be a bit crowded in there, just sayin', you can drop the Sorenson."

He looked back to the Latvian, "And we are so going to find out way more about your interest in breeding." He touched Gints' chest seductively.

Kick switched his attention in a flash. "Well, my friends, into the cold for the luggage. Except for you, Older Bro, and your crazy hot police officer. You seem to be dressed for other things." Kayne cocked an eyebrow at his slightly exasperating brother.

Imitating the eminent Dr. Sorenson's lecture style but with an exaggerated fey affect, Kick put one hand on a hip and wagged an index finger. He announced, "Yes, from your appearance this morning, I deduce that you two have had other activities in mind."

He aped a Kayne forehead sweep against his close-cropped head. "Do we have any volunteers in the class to join in the activities?"

Everyone's hand, including Mark's, went up. Rebecca grabbed it, pulled it down, and said, "Oh no, you don't. I don't need any more surprises in this lifetime."

"Merely to watch, gorgeous," Mark grinned in a snuggle-up. "Gay porn is way hot. And anyway, Miss, was your hand up to swat a winter mosquito?"

Laughs all around.

Kayne hugged me close. "Regarding your little pantomime, Kick, my Brother, I think you mean 'induce.' And concerning your salacious suggestion, I will guarantee Nick and I have this covered. Cheers, anyway."

"See you kids around lunchtime," I said as I led Kayne back to our room.

As we left, I heard Mark say to Gints, "*Jāšanās,* Mate. And I will wager very hot *jāšanās*."

Gints nodded solemnly.

Rebecca added, "Count on it."

Chapter Seven: Birds of Prey

NICK SECHI'S JOURNAL

As usual, Rebecca reigned over our gatherings. She was especially gregarious at brunch in the Aerie's kitchen.

"Yes, Darlings, I so needed to get back to work after *Seed Blood*. A triumph, but what a nightmare. Please pass the eggs, Darling."

Scott stood and brought Rebecca the plate of smashed avocado on sourdough topped with poached eggs.

Kayne and I remained silent at the mention of *Seed Blood*. The details would not be appropriate for breakfast conversations.

Kick said, "I want to hear all about your adventures with my brother and Nick in Ft. Lauderdale. I saw the news story, but I need to feast on the gory details. I love a thriller."

"You are a handsome but rather depraved devil, Darling." Rebecca touched Kick's nose. "Over drinks or...." She pantomimed puffing a joint. "A smoke. Legal here, yes?"

"Yes, but they say that the Native tobacco sage or peyote is a better high. But I don't really know. No poisons in this body, including demon drink."

"Is smart of that, Kick Sorenson. Keeps you fit like Gints." The big man thumped his rock-hard chest.

I recalled Kayne's comment regarding Kick's resistance to taking his medication. I looked over at him, but Kayne was staring off through the floor-to-ceiling kitchen windows with a blank expression.

Switching back, Rebecca commented, "The Silverman and the Phelan Museums promised me an educative experience while we are here. They want the project. I am afraid my staff and I are not very familiar with Native American Art."

"I can get Josh's sister-in-law to sit down with you. She is a Native American historian. Lots of tradition, history, and First Nations lore."

"Thank you, Kick Darling."

"Niko, you and Big Doctor too silent for this company. Why? Ah, Gints think you are both having... what you say...?"

Mark jumped in, "Afterglow."

"Yes. So, Gints give you small coin for what you thinking." This was the Latvian's best "penny for your thoughts."

We all laughed. Kayne came back to earth from his reverie and managed a smile. He remained silent and observing.

Kick took up the conversation, "Mark, I keep hearing of the dangers of reporting from the Middle East. Is it as bad as they say?"

"Very much so. I was embedded in Syria until a few months ago. Took a bit of shrapnel, and they sent me home.

"I started out as a young journalist in Kabul about ten years ago. My exit there was due to the high numbers of foreign press who were captured and held for ransom by the Taliban. CBN withdrew me from there. Also, not my choice."

"He was all of twenty-two then. And his wounds of late, we speak, Darlings, were because he dove in to save two soldiers who were in harm's way. Humble, heroic, and sexy as hell."

Gints pointed at Mark with his fork. "Rebecca's Mark also very fit. You will train with Gints."

I observed that seven of us were all very attractive and in good shape. Strange. I have a theory that beautiful people attract each other -- pheromones attracting like to like or some shit like that. We resembled a posse of supermodels.

Even Scott was a cutie. He was small in stature but sporting a gym-toned body. Scott was a Swedish American with striking blonde hair who could not take his eyes off the stunning Gints. In fact, he had wobbled pouring Gints' orange juice. He received a steadying hand to the small of his back that had the opposite effect of unnerving him and almost turning his legs to Jell-O.

"You sound like a man who enjoys the daring and risky, Mate. Do any freerunning?"

Mark answered, "I am a bit familiar with Sébastien Foucan's book. How he formed the discipline from military obstacle course training. They use some of the moves as a means of weapons avoidance and closing the distance to an opponent."

"Right." Kick continued, "I was asked by the military at the base at the northern rim of the Valley to provide training to their trainers. I also consulted on the construction of their parkour assault course."

Kayne interrupted, "From the French, *parcours du combattant* -- obstacle course or assault course. Sorry, Kick."

The gymnast/acrobat continued, "Some of the military are even interested in tricking."

Rebecca jumped in, "Do you mean escort services, Darling?"

Kick laughed heartily, "No, Divine One. But it's not like I haven't tried." Kayne looked at me with an expression that could only be described with the words of the immortal Dorothy Parker, "What fresh hell is this?"

"Tricking in freerunning refers to the acrobatic moves that bring the discipline to the aesthetic level. Here, watch this ...."

Kick's acrobatic demonstration was interrupted by the chirping of his mobile. He excused himself and walked to the window wall of the kitchen.

In the last few hours, the last of the storm had abated slightly so that in some parts of the Valley, the sun was shining over the newly fallen snow -- a lull in the blizzard. It appeared that there had been a substantial accumulation. We could see some of the skiers across the Valley at the Resort who were getting an early jump on the runs.

As Scott passed the last of the hoecakes, sausage, and gravy around, I asked, "If the pass is blocked, will the folks at the Resort be able to get to the slopes on the Aspen side of the mountains?"

Scott smiled brightly and responded, "Oh, yes, Officer. One of the runs ends about 200 yards from the back of the Resort. There is a towline that takes skiers over to the main chairs. It is one of the features of Aerie

Resort. Just steps from your room to the slopes. Once there, they can ski the Aerie side or move to the northwest and hit the Aspen side of the mountain. For my money, the Aerie has the better runs."

He left the table to grab the coffee pot and refresh our mugs. Rebecca caught my attention as he returned. At the same time, Kayne nudged me. It seemed our chef and steward had caught the eye of our very randy Latvian pal. As Scott bent over and poured, never one for propriety, Gints patted the young man's butt.

Attempting a bit of decorum, Scott stopped what he was doing, took the muscled man's hand from his ass, and bent to fill the big man's mug. Whatever was whispered between them brought a grin to Gints and a stoic face from the young man. Nonetheless, one could see that Scott welcomed the attention just a bit.

I was confused. Apparently, Gints had garnered the attention of the Master of the Aerie. Still, he was casting his lustful eye on the young staffer. Kick was oblivious to the subtle cruising of his young employee by the bodybuilder. *This is going to get good*, I thought. The Aerie holiday promised to be an exciting couple of weeks.

Scott addressed the group a second time, "I heard that the pass will be reopened soon, but there is another storm coming right behind the one that is clearing out."

Rebecca poured cream into her coffee and turned to Mark. "That might be good news. I would like to get down to Aspen and meet with my museum counterparts between the snow blasts."

"OK, but please, no shopping, beautiful. This man shudders at the thought of following behind you carrying boxes and shopping bags from the trendiest shops in the American Rockies."

"Mark, Darling, a woman needs her couture." She turned to the rest of us and continued, "We make such a stunning couple, me in my Chanel and Mark in his Levis and Tony Llamas -- adorable rugged male in his rustic cowboy boots."

Kayne teased, "I seem to recall an Alexander McQueen and a Tom Ford tux at your recent stunning Gala."

I agreed, "Seriously, it was like Michele Obama meets Daniel Craig."

Mark slipped an arm around the glowing Rebecca. "Shaken not stirred, eh, Becky?" She pushed him off playfully and nailed him with a croissant as both Kayne and I did a spit take. Rebecca hated any diminutives of her name. Mark was aware but teased anyway.

Kick returned to the table and said, "Something is going on at the Palace that I need to see to right away. Now that the storm has cleared a bit, would you all consider a trip down to the stables?"

"Only if you unleash the Birds of Prey, my brother."

Kick did an excited little jump. "You know I will, brother. You up to flying?"

"Will beat the hell outta you, Mate."

"Care to make it interesting?"

"Loser serves the winner breakfast in bed."

Kick spiced up the wager, "Wearing only an apron."

Kayne pointed at his brother. "You are so on, 'Mess.' Scott, make sure your Boss has a clean apron."

He rolled his ice-blue eyes at his brother, looked him up and down, and grinned. "Size small should cover it."

Kick reminded his teasing brother that they were two of a set of identical triplets.

I jumped into the salacious discussion, "Whoa, whoa, whoa. OK, so If there is a possibility that near-naked men and a scantily clad woman will invade my bedroom, I need to ask a few questions."

"By all means, go ahead, Nick."

"Birds of Prey?"

"Don't tell me you have stealth aircraft at your personal disposal," Mark joked.

Kick ticked them off on his fingers, "*Hawk, Falcon, Osprey,* and *Kite.* My late husband named everything around here. Our Polaris

Snowmobiles, Mate. Some serious ditch bangers. Who's up for some blasting?"

Moving his attention from Scott, Gints spoke up, "Let's go, Kick Sorenson. I drive, and you ride -- now and later." He winked wickedly.

Kick did a butt wiggle, and Scott went back to his coffee maker.

"Grab your ski bunny outfit, my girl. I have been looking to carve some snow country since I left Afghanistan."

Tousling his gold-brown curls, Rebecca stated, "Love a man who wants to dominate any terrain. Especially..."

We all finished her sentence individually, one at a time.

Me: "Mine."

Kayne: "Yeah, mine, we know, we know!"

Kick: "Mine. Yep, frisky 'hets.' They're everywhere."

"Mark, you stay and provide satisfying *jāšanās* for Miss Rebecca. Gints know best in matters of the sexing."

Before Mark could answer, Rebecca waved off Gint's suggestion saying, "Bollocks, Darling." Turning to Mark, she added, "Grab your jock, studly. We're gonna fly."

Chapter Eight: White River

Josh Walker surveyed the damage. The jeep lay on its nose in a narrow crevice against the mountain cliff at the top of a series of steep, low hills that gave way to the Aerie Valley floor. Mountain crews were clearing away the newly fallen snow that surrounded the approach.

Local law enforcement was represented by Sheriff Stefan Connelly and three of his deputies. Two Native American police officers from the Alpaska Reservation stood back. They allowed the recovery crew unobstructed access to the vehicle in their search for bodies.

Stepping forward, Josh tried to calm White River, who stood menacingly between the crushed vehicle and the humans. The dog snarled and barked, protecting territory. From time to time, she set up the mournful howl that had started last night and had echoed throughout the mountain valley.

"White River, come to me. Come to Red Cedar, girl."

Tribal Blood

Chapter Nine: The Horse Palace
NICK SECHI'S JOURNAL

Kick soared into the air and did a complete summersault high above the Polaris, flipping the towline handle from hand to hand. Below him, Gints pointed the snowmobile down the slope in the direction of the Aerie stables with ferocious speed, tightening the line that attached the whooping snowboarder.

Behind them, Kayne and I were neck and neck with Rebecca and Mark as we sped down the slope like winter raptors sending up large wings of snow and ice. The others, like me, were stunned by Kick's athletics as he swerved and spun, lofting at every snowdrift behind the speeding *Hawk*. He flipped the handle of the towline behind his back and lofted backward over the next rise.

I heard exchanged remarks of joy and daring ("Watch this one, children.") through our helmet communication system. I remember thinking, *What a complete wonder and total showboater*, as Kayne raced the *Kite* to keep up with his speeding brother."

Mark, aboard the *Osprey*, hung on with one hand. With the other, he snapped pictures of the flying winter acrobat. I heard him direct Rebecca off to the right of the racing group. She turned the speeding snowmobile.

"We don't want to run over Kick when he takes a tumble, gorgeous. Try to go around them," Mark shouted through the helmet microphone.

"Going for it! Hang on!" Rebecca returned and again swerved the machine down and off to the right. "Darling, I have no idea where we are going."

"There. Keep those turrets in sight." Mark pointed at the snow-covered roof peaks of the stables.

The racers spun through the new powder, blowing back fountains of snow and shooting cascades of white over the windscreens. Kayne concentrated on passing the speeders just ahead when Kick, without a helmet, rode a slope and lofted directly above and over our speeding

Polaris. I looked up to see an expression of unadulterated and exciting joy on the upside-down face of the manic brother.

Kayne cursed.

Gints pulled across our direction, causing Kayne to swerve away to avoid mangling the towline and creating a catastrophe. As we hit the valley floor, we fell back to third place in the race to the Palace. Maintaining a safe distance from his brother, Kayne sprinted the *Kite* to catch the *Osprey* only to gain second place.

Suddenly, within 50 yards of the gates of the stable compound, Kick lost it and wiped out, releasing the towline and flying through the snow, ice, and rock without his snowboard. Gints slowed, and Kayne pulled to a complete stop in a skid that spewed powder to our right side.

Kick jumped up, apparently uninjured, and threw off his goggles in what could only be described as a full-on tantrum. He threw himself into a snowbank and tossed snow in the air, kicking up a fracas and cussing. He sat up and pointed behind us as he let out a howl of anguished frustration. Turning, we saw Mark soar the *Osprey* across the snow and take the stable's gates as Rebecca whooped over the microphone in a victory cheer.

✳✳✳

"You can't compensate for beauty, skill, and speed, Darlings. As I said, Mark is an expert with just about any transport, but I can match his power driving any day."

Pulling off his helmet, Mark wrapped his arms around his adoring ladylove and teased, "I suggest you guys get those four sets of glutes in shape for Rebecca's breakfast in bed. She is the female version of an ass man."

"Such a sexist!" Rebecca took off her helmet and shook her long black hair. She then jostled her embracing beau. "Women have their own favorites regarding the male anatomy, and yes, my second favorite is the man butt, Darlings."

Mark said, "I think we can guess the first, my bad girl." He raised his Canon 5D Mark III from around his neck and photographed the Palace and our group.

Kick laughed lustily while Gints and I smiled. Kayne had his one-cocked-eyebrow look at the prospect of serving breakfast in only an apron. I found myself unconsciously slipping my arm around his back, something I was doing more and more whenever we were next to each other.

"Gints has major muscled glutes, horse-like hindquarters. No brag. Is fact."

Kick moved in behind his driver and palmed the goods, saying, "Anything else on you resembles a horse, big boy?"

"No, Kick Sorenson. You not deserve all this." He threw a double bicep pose to taunt the rascal.

"You are reason we lose bet. Too much show-off. Boy need lesson. Now, I gonna show you."

Gints turned to face the imp. Kick stuck his tongue out at his new buddy and tossed a handful of snow in the giant's face. Gints chased him up the snow-covered drive to the Palace with a roar, catching him in a tackle and rolling into a huge snowbank. They wrestled in the piles of snow with fantastic energy, one massive and powerful, the other agile and wiggly.

Ranch snowplows were easing back the new snow on some of the trails around the Palace. Tractors were tossing bales of hay into cleared paddocks as ranch hands were opening the upper parts of the Dutch doors of the stalls. In each opening was the beautiful head of a horse taking the morning air. Clouds of warm horse breath hit the frosty air.

"Your brother dearly loves his horses," I said to Kayne. "Let's see, Josh Walker, most likely the 'Gints Bull.' Yes, your brother likes building his own stud herd."

As we walked to the tussling polar bears, Rebecca added, "Darling, are all the Sorensons polyamorous? So decadent."

"By that, are you referring to consensual and responsible non-monogamy?" Kayne asked. "If so, I'd say definitely. We are a passionate bunch. That is a fact, my dear. We are the descendants of the criminal classes, to be honest, deported to the British penal colony that was Australia, very hot-blooded." Kayne punctuated his point with a wink in my direction.

"I thought the troops in Syria were a frisky bunch, but you all put the horny armed forces to shame," Mark chided, referring to all his snowbound mates.

As we got closer to the stable, a ranch hand ran out to talk to Kick with much excitement. He dashed up the drive toward us and stopped to turn around and point up to the mountains. As Kick approached, he said, "Let's postpone the tour and ride up into the hills. Josh left word with Luke here that something bad had happened up there on the crest."

I took the binoculars from around the young rancher's neck. "May I?" I aimed them in the direction he was pointing.

"I'd say law enforcement is involved. I see emergency vehicle lights. Let's hit it."

***

We hopped on the Birds of Prey and followed Kick's *Kite* up into the foothills behind the ranch. As we approached the red, blue, and white flashing lights of the police rescue vehicles, we saw a snow-trampled footpath up to a crash site, a Jeep wedged in a cleft of the rocks.

We parked the Birds near the Romanian Ghe-O Rescue Trucks emblazoned with the insignia of the Colorado State Police. Next to these exotic monsters were two emergency Land Rovers carrying the Alpaska Reservation Police Department markings and Josh Walker's SUV. The former road monsters had plowed the way for the other vehicles to get close to the crash.

As we alighted, Mark pointed up, "That is a Draganflyer X4-ES helicopter drone." Kayne said, "Most likely a loner from the military base. State troopers and Native American forces use them for search and rescue operations -- skiers, hikers, hunters, and others who get in trouble in the mountains."

Kick led the way up the trail and into the rocks. The rescue team was carefully beginning to remove a body from the smashed, red Jeep as we hit the site. The First Responders set a stretcher bag as best they could in the tight spaces between the steep rocks and newly fallen snow. Storm winds seemed to have blown most of the snow out of the cleft in the mountainside.

As we arrived, Kayne looked up to the cliffs above and back to the Jeep. He shouted, "Officer, please stop!"

The troopers and police turned to the six interlopers. "You folks need to head back down. This is a police site." Kayne ignored the warning and shifted his focus to the crumpled Jeep.

The trooper in charge started to place a hand on Kick's chest, stopping his forward movement as our expedition leader. I intercepted to make sure the officer kept his hands to himself. We locked eyes.

Before the trooper and I could finish, a tall man stepped from the shadow of the deeper rocks, followed by two Native police officers and a white dog.

Josh Walker spoke with authority, "I would like Dr. Sorenson to examine the body of my sister."

Chapter Ten: White Singing Bird
NICK SECHI'S JOURNAL

Kayne moved over the site, inspecting every detail.

The Jeep landed in a nosedive, crushing the front and causing the entire vehicle to lean forward into the rocks. Kayne hopped up on surrounding rocks to examine the rear of the truck. I moved carefully to the body for an examination inside the Jeep. Kayne also probed the damaged cab as we slowly extracted Susan Walker.

He began to speak, "Let's start there." He pointed to the uppermost end of the wreck.

"Damage to the rear bumper would indicate the vehicle was pushed over the cliff above. Officer Connelly, you can verify my observation by a careful inspection of the snow on the road above. It will present a challenge, but I am sure you can determine the number of cars in the area and possibly get a tread print. Look at the soft earth on the shoulders under the snow. Remove the snow carefully with heat guns or soft brushes."

Kayne continued, "Gentlemen, what you see here is not the site of an unfortunate accident. This is a crime scene. Susan Chipeta Walker was murdered. The impact of the Jeep was enough to finish a debilitating assault that occurred on the terrace above before the crash.

"The anomalies on the body indicate that Ms. Walker was brutally beaten and put into the Jeep before it was pushed over by a vehicle with this shape to the bumper guards."

He traced two ovate shapes divided by horizontal bars in the snow. The height of the bumper marks on the crushed back of the Jeep indicates it was a truck."

"Dr. Sorenson, you mentioned anomalies on the body." The speaker was Matthew Strong Bear, Alpaska Police Medical Examiner. Kayne began to answer, but I interrupted him.

"Officers, please look at this. I believe Dr. Sorenson was referring to this," I motioned them over to the conveyor bag where Mark and I were standing over the extracted shattered corpse.

Kayne moved forward and responded to the question, "See here. There are massive breaks on both thighs and the right wrist. The shape of the impact is the same on all three. Nothing is protruding from the dash or interior that would have caused these breaks."

I carefully folded back the clothing covering the right side of the neck and shoulder and slowly cut back the jacket and jeans of the deceased.

"Please note that the seat belt was not used – none of their typical bruise marks appear. Blood patterns on the interior will further support the trauma to the legs and wrists as pre-crash wounds."

Mark was taking pictures of the body and the site with his Canon. Kick, kneeling to hold and calm White River, spoke softly to his stone-faced Master of Horse. Rebecca had left the wreckage with Gints and returned with a blanket from one of the Reservation's Land Rovers. Mark moved over and snapped a few photos of the dog.

State Trooper Stefan Connelly remarked, "Dr. Sorenson, I am aware of your international reputation as a consultant to law enforcement and national security operations. I have also kept abreast, through the FBI, of the recent case in Ft. Lauderdale in which you were involved with young Officer Sechi here. While I respect the wishes of Tribal Elder Walker, I assure you that we are quite capable of...."

"Officer Connelly, my team and I mean only to assist the investigation, but I must tell you that I have a time-honored, professional respect for an undisturbed crime scene. In this case, relatively unaltered, for you could have done better.

"Officer Sechi has exceptional forensic skills and has examined the body in situ before it was removed. Mr. Gadarn is a war correspondent on hiatus from his work with the United States Marine Corps in the Middle East. We will make his photos available to both departments, yours and that of Officer Strong Bear."

Kayne continued, "Ms. Quinto's credentials include training with the FBI and serving as our liaison with that agency. Our colleague, Mr. Bergovic, is team security.

"Your research will show they were an essential part of the resolution to the recent and much-publicized case in Florida. My brother, Kick, I think you know. He has invested in just about all the Aerie Valley interests. He is an honorable member of the Nu Ci band of the Utes and special consultant to the military over at Clarion Base."

Kick gave a "what's up, dudes?" salute to the police officers.

"Thank you, Dr. Sorenson. We appreciate your family's support of the Aerie and Aspen community. Your brother-in-law gifted us last year with the Ghe-Os. I would like to get with you and your brother while you are here to discuss his case."

Mark interrupted, "Kayne, the dog."

He pointed to White River but looked at the picture on his camera. Kick peered over his shoulder at the image.

Before Kayne could respond, Kick opened a pouch on the dog's tactical service vest and, with two long, gloved fingers, extracted a sealed plastic bag from a pocket. Inside was a small piece of human remains.

"My friends, we may have just discovered the motive," Kayne said, carefully taking the artifact and dramatically holding it in the air.

Rebecca moved forward and said, "Gentleman, let's remember we have a person before us on that litter. Can we not finish this in a more appropriate place?"

She carefully, almost lovingly, placed the Native American blanket bearing the image of Buffalo Calf Woman over the body of the White Singing Bird as she lay on the ground.

Sitting next to Josh, White River let out a long and mournful howl.

***

"Dr. Sorenson, we have some deep tire tracks in the snow here against the retaining divider and some partial tire prints from the ground where we removed the snow with heat. The frozen ground did not yield much, I am afraid."

Kayne examined the tracks and said, "Officer Connelly, you are looking for a 2015 Chevrolet Silverado Duramax. The treads and the wear are distinctive. The front wheels are slightly out of alignment. A specialized push bumper was added to the chassis."

Kayne looked over the lookout terrace, which was by now a mish-mash of footprints and tire tracks. We both knew the discovery of additional forensic evidence was useless at this point. Mark moved around, carefully taking pictures of the scene.

Moving to the low retaining wall, Kayne indicated that the snow on the middle section was much more reduced than that on the sides. He brushed away snow near one spot on the wall and revealed a gap. Broken blocks marked the spot where Susan's truck rammed the retaining bunker. He peered over the rim to the crushed Jeep below. Brushing the snow from the front of the broken stone, he revealed deep gouges.

"Mark, can you get this, please?" Kayne turned to Stefan Connelly and said, "The red gouges are the Jeep, but look at the black marks on the blocks to the side of the opening. I'd say they were fresh, and the truck that pushed her over skidded a good bit, backed up a few times, and swerved to the side. They had some trouble upending the Jeep over the cliff. The wall presented a challenge."

I further inspected the marks on the retaining wall, carefully brushing off the cover of snow. "Seems to have caught some colored paint here. Orange and green. Trim or insignia?"

Officer Strong Bear squatted next to me and remarked, "I'd say corporate markings, Officer. Unusual to trim a truck in those colors. Nice find."

I stood up and couldn't help appraising the reservation cop. Tall and fit, with high cheekbones and sparkling dark eyes. The Officer was hatless and styled his long black hair to reflect his ethnicity. An eagle feather hung down from one braid, plaited with a leather, beaded thong. A shock of white hair crested over the left side of his forehead.

Officer Matthew Strong Bear continued to pick at the scraped stone as I stepped back to view his legs and ass. Kayne moved up next to me and shot his own forelock, whispering, "Nice work regarding your analysis of the scrapes on the wall, my love. Please consider leaving something on that young police officer. He'll catch a cold."

I felt one of my deep flushes of embarrassment rise from my snow boots to my hairline and grinned at the teasing Kayne. The light snow gusts around us landed some flakes on his long lashes, and his frosty breath created an image of incredible beauty, complete with his sparkling Siberian Husky ice blues, which seemed to deepen in the cold.

"Got it, back to police work, Professor. Sorry." I did a mock salute, lightly touched him, and said softly, "Just because I am on a diet doesn't mean I can't look at the menu."

"Forensics, please, Officer."

Mark continued to record the investigative team's findings as police officers and troopers held off damaging snowplows on the adjacent road. They created a bypass for the small amount of traffic that started to move up and down the road.

Matthew Strong Bear stood up, responding to a mobile call. He said to Officer Connelly and the three members of Team Sorenson on the cliff, "The sun will be setting soon, so our research up here should end and reopen at first light. We will secure the site. They have removed the body of the White Singing Bird to the Reservation Mortuary. Josh is requesting our presence."

✻✻✻

"Mr. Sorenson said he would be with you as soon as possible. He is still meeting with Mr. Walker at the reservation but insists that you begin without him." Luke set the last of the big platters on the table where Rebecca, Mark, Gints, and I were seated.

Kayne was filling drink orders from the bar. We were surrounded by the trophies and other honors in the Horse Palace's kitchen and tack room. The space was equipped with audio-visual and wireless internet. Mark pulled up his photos of the crime scenes and Susan Chipeta Walker's body on the wall-mounted monitor.

'Kayne, look there."

Mark had created a side-by-side image of a wound in the deceased's chest and the ragged edges of the severed finger.

"I am willing to bet those cuts were made by a bayonet tactical survival knife. Its fingerprint is unmistakable regarding the serrations, puncture signature, and teeth imprints. I saw them in Afghanistan and Pakistan many times."

Kayne placed a Guinness next to Mark's keyboard and peered up at the screen. Mark split the bottom of the dual images and pulled up a black and silver knife picture.

"This is a Bayonet HK56142B-Tactical/Survival Knife. Supplied to our military by Schlachtross, private military contractors. If I had my laptop, I could superimpose the blade and the cuts, but I think you can see that there is most likely a match."

"Same company thrown out of Latvia for arming Russian-backed mercenaries two years ago. Also, some trouble with them in the Crimea," Gints offered. "It was a bad political issue. Unstabilized the Latvian government, almost. That company is a very shady business. Also, they play very dirty when questions are asked. Big Doctor, you use Gints to keep those *Jauni vīrieši* away. Gints keep everyone safe."

"Thank you, my friend. Your *Latviešu* mountain fighting back home is something I have come to rely on." Kayne placed a hand on the boulder-like shoulders of our friend.

Rebecca asked, "Anything else on the body, Darling? How about the severed finger?"

"Not much else on the deceased," I offered. "Susan was beaten and placed into her Jeep and sent over the precipice. The cause of death was most likely a forceful impact on the brain and internal organs on the interior roof of the Jeep. The airbags deployed, but the force of the impact was too great to spare the body."

Kayne indicated the image of the finger and said, "I asked that authorities collect data on the small amount of debris in the bag and on the finger. Skin fragments indicate it is most likely from a darkly pigmented individual, although post-mortem darkening may figure for that. The police are tracing the fingerprint of what is indeed a proximal phalange joined to a metacarpal of the fifth digit, the little finger."

He paused. "Law enforcement has so far found nothing by way of a body associated with this amputation."

Kayne continued, "Please note that the marks on the bone suggest it was severed and not gnawed off. This would suggest that the victim was tortured. I suggest the dismemberment was, in fact, *pre-mortem*."

Kayne stopped, seemingly trying to collect himself.

"Kayne, there is something else, isn't there? You have never had a poker face, Darling. What is it?"

As all eyes were on him, Kayne looked around to make sure Luke had left the Tack Room.

"I would like this to remain with us until our evidence is conclusive. When she received no satisfaction from regular law enforcement, Susan Chipeta Walker, a seasoned bounty hunter, was hired by Earth Rae Jordan to find her son, Jeron. Jeron Adobo Jordan was the environmental officer for the Nu Ci, and he disappeared over a month ago."

He took a deep breath and pointed to the image of the severed finger.

"I believe we may be closer to finding him."

Chapter Eleven: Night Flares

The snow had begun to fly again, but initially without the furious winds of yesterday's storm. In the darkness, the whiteout condition made traveling slow on the mountain road. The danger was compounded by its many switchbacks. Kick climbed the ridge from the Reservation, crested the hill, and headed down to the valley turnoff close to the cut-off for the Resort. From there, the road across the Aerie Valley floor would take him to the foothill climb to the Lodge on the other rim. Josh would only let him return if he took his SUV, a guarantee of a safe trip to the Aerie Lodge.

Since discovering the body, Josh remained relatively silent, rigidly controlling his emotions. He presided over the preparations for his sister's burial in an almost mechanical way.

After a thorough examination, Susan Walker's body was released to the family. The women of the Tribe purified the corpse. They dressed it in traditional garb, including jewelry and moccasins, for her trip to the next world. Susan's life partner, Joletta Golden Tree, seemed to be working out her grief by calmly participating in the preparation customs. With dry eyes and attention to the details of the prayers, songs, and sacred markings, Joletta observed the traditional rites that would shepherd her beloved forward in the endless cycle of birth, life, and death.

The body would be wrapped in a shroud – no coffin or embalming fluids and placed on a mound of ice and snow with a campfire burning nearby. Members of the Tribe, primarily women, would attend Susan through the night. Prayers, songs, and simple ceremonies focusing on respect for the earth would continue through the watches of the night. The body would be returned to the sacred ground on the reservation burial site following the funeral.

Kick was torn between staying over with Josh to offer comfort or returning to the Aerie and spending the night with his guests. Tribal leadership had closed around the Master of Horse. Although Kick had been granted honorary tribal membership, he understood he was an outsider in times like these. He would allow his adored Josh Red Cedar Walker the space needed to grieve with his people's traditions and customs. The obsequies enabled the Tribe to pass through the suffering of losing a member in such a violent manner. He would return for the funeral with members of the Aerie Valley staff, his brother, and his new friends in two days.

Kick pondered the last four hours on the reservation with Josh while driving through the snow. He knew of the history of tears of the Reservation's people – the variety of types of stress and suffering. The 1940s saw a massive conflict with state contractors who manipulated a land steal to create a reservoir from the Tribe's prime farmland. The result was decades of poverty for the Nu Ci clan on the Alpaska Reservation.

In the last half of the 20th Century, the residents were also challenged by a lack of access to public health resources. High unemployment and a preponderance of below-poverty-line incomes added to a 75% rate of alcoholism on the reservation. There were indicators of the rapid decline of the Nu Ci clan on the Alpaska lands. Life expectancy on the Reservation was the third lowest in the Western Hemisphere, surpassed only by another reservation in South Dakota and Haiti.

In 2008, when Mitch was appointed to the Board of Red Eagle Energies, he was the only white man supervising the Tribe's potential economic boom, which accompanied the discovery of oil and natural gas on the Reservation. As wells were drilled, fractured, or fracked, the oil and gas began to flow in vast amounts. Red Eagle Industries contracted with a Non-Native company, Kriegston Gathering LLC, to handle the extraction and transport of their natural resources.

The wipers of the SUV scattered the blowing snow as the truck carefully took the twists and turns of the mountain road. He thought how the snail's pace of the vehicle made him impatient. He loved the speed and daring of soaring through the winter landscape on his snowboard or on one of the Birds. The plodding of the truck took him back to the trip with Mitch last year and the storm that caused the wreck.

He remembered very little of the journey through the mountains northwest of Vale -- the intensity of the wind and rain and then the impact. He had languished unconscious for three days in the hospital only to awaken and be told that they had not yet recovered the body of his husband. The treacherousness of the gorge and the raging stream at the bottom slowed the search and rescue, which became an unsuccessful search and recovery.

In the end, the case was left as "missing presumed dead." Kayne had come from Florida, and his father from Australia. He had never seen Ace in such grief. The loss of his first son cut deeply into his soul. He wanted Kick to come and stay at the station in Alice Springs. However, Kick wished to forgo the trip back to Australia and remain at the Aerie with the reminders of Mitch and the things he so greatly loved.

He'd convinced everyone he was going to be fine. However, he soon experienced a delayed descent into madness with brutal sex partners. Enter Brother Kayne and some real "Come to Jesus Moments" after his third hospitalization. New meds, *yuk!* And a changed attitude about the next steps in his life.

As he drove through the heavy snow, Kick reflected on Josh Walker's importance in his life. The man had been a great comfort to him, handling the affairs of the ranch and serving as a liaison to the Native Americans of Alpaska. Josh's close friendship with Mitch had transferred to a solid personal relationship with the new Master of Aerie. The Master of Horse was honest and direct. Early on, Josh made it clear that Kick needed to reign in his crazy-assed behavior. The sexual relationship just seemed to happen, a bit of a surprise for both of them.

Typically, his mind jumped from one set of thoughts to another. The loneliness of the drive was broken up by the need to pay attention to the twists, rises, and falls of the pitch-dark road. On the stretch that rose behind the Horse Palace, he squinted but saw no lights below through the dark and blowing snow.

Kick's thoughts returned to his buddy and the scene he had just left. He thought of Josh standing near the shrouded body of his sister and the way the man glared at the white strangers who had intruded on the preparatory rites for the slain Susan Chipeta Walker. There were three in the company of the Tribal Leader, Jake Gray Wolf Mingan. He was accompanied by Albert C. Renault, CEO of Kriegston Gathering. Kick knew him from the Red Eagle Board meetings. The third dude looked like some kind of security asshole.

Josh had spoken to Gray Wolf in words he could not hear. The Leader seemed pissed as he left the gathering with the strangers in tow. As Kick walked to Josh's truck, Matthew Strong Bear came up behind him. He nodded to Kick but said nothing, waiting for the Tribal Leader and his entourage to pass them on their way to the parking area.

"Mr. Sorenson, will you need any assistance returning to the Aerie?"

Kick turned to the handsome police officer. "Matthew, are we back to 'Mr. Sorenson?' I keep thinking you are speaking to my father. It's "Kick," Buddy. Especially considering our mutual closeness to Tribal Elder Walker. Otherwise, I need to call you Officer Strong Bear." Kick smiled at the young man.

Matt had a troubled look but tried to hide it as he said, "Sorry, Sir. I mean, Kick. Are you concerned about this snow starting up again? Might be a rough trip back to the Lodge."

They broke into a side-by-side walk to the trucks. The men from Kriegston lingered near their Ram Power Wagon, Renault speaking into his cell phone. Strong Bear eyed them suspiciously.

"Naw, I will be fine. Josh lent me his SUV."

"Red Cedar hates the sight of those guys. He is making a case with the Council to get rid of them. Josh calls them a pack of swindlers. More whites are screwing Indians, if you ask me. I think he just told them this part was for Natives only to get them to leave."

He paused and added with embarrassment, "Oh sorry, Kick, it's just that...."

Kick slid a hand up the officer's back to his shoulder in an intimate gesture. "Matthew, I am aware of the sins of my race. Look at how the British colonists massacred the Aboriginal Australians in my homeland."

Matt said nothing. Again, a troubled look crossed his face at the touch of his rival.

Kick opened the door to the SUV and added, "Go take care of our bud, Mate. He is shut up in a well of silence, as they say. His grief is intense, as is the rest of his personality. He needs some understanding...."

84

He tapped the young officer's chest. "And some loving."

Matthew looked at the ground and said, "Yeah, thanks, I will. Hey, can I ask you another question?"

"Sure."

"What's the situation with Officer Sechi?"

"Ah, the Nicky Boy. Umm humm. He is on hiatus from the Wilton Manors Police Force in Florida. Quite a hotshot. Spunky as they come, Bud."

Matthew said nothing.

"Ah, I see, Buddy." Kick raised the man's chin, looked him in the eyes, and joked. "Bad medicine when an officer of the law is too horny to keep his mind on the job, Mate. Well, I am afraid my brother has taken quite a fancy to that ginger boy. But together, they just might...." He rolled his eyes wickedly.

Matthew was embarrassed by Kick's overt sexuality and stammered as he said, "No, that's quite alright. I'm not that good at sharing, as you well know. Just think the guy is cool." Kick understood his reference to their grieving mutual friend.

He smiled and pulled the young Brave into a hug up. He thought they needed to clear the air about Josh at some point, but that time was not now.

They said their goodbyes as Kick mounted the truck and took off down the road, rising over the mountains. He began the journey to the Aerie through the blowing snow.

✳✳✳

As he approached the last ridge before the turn-off, Kick looked across the dark expanse and saw the tiny glint of light that was the Lodge. He would enjoy spending time with his guests and looked forward to some hot tub time. Boarding, wrestling, and climbing had made for an exhausting day.

Need me some of that Gints studly, tonight.

His snowboard was on the back seat of the vehicle. The confinement of riding in the SUV caused him to squirm a bit as he descended to the turn-off.

Up ahead, about 300 yards from the intersection, Kick saw the hazard lights of a black truck on the side of the road. Blazing ground flares were mounted fore and aft. Two men were attending to the open hood with flashlights while a third was talking on a cell and waving him over. Kick brought the SUV over to the shoulder behind the truck and stepped out.

"You guys overheat? What seems to be the problem? Call Triple-A for a tow?"

The man with the cell phone said, "Man, hard time getting a signal in this storm. Not sure what's the trouble. Think you could take a look?"

As he approached the two men at the truck's front, one turned the light directly into Kick's face. Blinded by the beam, Kick blinked and shaded his eyes. The man behind him wrapped him in a bear hug while the third man ran to him and covered his mouth with a chemical-soaked cloth.

The hyperactive athlete and Master of the Aerie collapsed to the ground.

Chapter Twelve: Soak

NICK SECHI'S JOURNAL

I pulled off an intensely romantic kiss and said to the wet, hard-bodied man in my arms, "Kayne, what's going on with the Nu Ci? Strange doings all around."

Kayne pulled away from me with a frown, the bubbling water from the hot tub splashing over and around our entwined bodies. "Nick, my love, timing is everything, and yours is a bit off tonight. I know this has been a long day, but I was about to make some of the moves for which I am extremely well known on this continent and others on your hot, wet, and very sexy body. And you choose this moment to discuss crime-fighting? Even superheroes take time for romance, Red."

I reached for our drinks and said, "Sorry, handsome, but the Susan Walker case has triggered some automatic responses. Yeah, I know. Supposed to be on holiday. However, my mind keeps racing. In the case of this murder, there is a huge amount of intrigue surrounding all this."

"Nick, even with my ADHD, I can't satisfy both our intellectual yearnings and our savage instincts at the same time. So, how about we shag like we invented it and then get back to intellectual pursuits?" He hauled me over through the frothing hot water and settled me on his lap, facing him in a colossal hot tub make-out. My arms pull his head and neck into my eager lips, his hands and arms claiming his man.

"Is this a private porn session, or can anyone join, Darlings?" Rebecca pranced across the snow-covered deck and dropped her fluffy robe on the rack holding our towels. Her white bikini went transparent as she slipped beneath the bubbles and foam. Rebecca did not wait for an answer to her question.

"Tell me, Ms. Quinto, are you determined to interrupt every carnal moment I may have on this expedition? And why are you solo at this time of night? Please don't tell me your fine Welsh-American studly is lying exhausted in your bed, never to walk again."

I settled back next to Kayne as Mark, right on cue, bounded through the patio doors in a towel carrying a beer and Rebecca's signature cocktail, Marie Laveau.

"Relax, Darling, I brought my own distraction so you boys can just carry on with your lusty business."

Kayne harrumphed, and Mark dropped his towel after handing Rebecca her drink. Almost comically and very stereotypically, Kayne and I sat up to appraise the naked body of the very fit, straight man standing on the snowy deck.

"Darling, I told you at least briefs. These randy gay boys will jump all that hotness before I can pull them off you."

Yeah, Mark was in excellent shape. His military assignments and regular fitness training had resulted in the superb body of a field warrior. A scar on his right deltoid and pectoral gave him a tough mercenary look.

Loving the attention, he did a slow, naked twirl and said, "Everyone says I have a nice ass. What do you think, guys?" Kayne guffawed, and I gulped, noting that the cold did not have much of a shrinkage effect on Mark's... um... enthusiasm... yeah, enthusiasm

My thoughts were interrupted by, "Darling, stop waving a red flag in the face of these sex-crazed boys and get that spectacular butt and everything else in this hot tub. We have important matters to discuss."

Mark slowly slipped in behind Rebecca so that she was sitting on his thighs. He fiddled with her bikini and dropped both parts over the side. "Equality is a bitch, my girl." She showed no discomfort whatsoever, but feeling behind her said, "Just stay calm with that, big boy."

"So easily said, my girl."

The large, eight-person hot tub brought comfort to sore muscles and soothed our racing minds as we clicked plastic glasses to our friendship. Careful not to overdo our alcohol consumption, we resolved that one drink in the hot waters of the sauna would be the safest choice.

Mark said, "Kayne, have you been in contact with Earth regarding the possibility that the bone we found might possibly lead to the whereabouts of her son, Jeron?"

"No, Mate. Best to wait until the evidence is conclusive. I fear the DNA analysis will take a bit of time up here in the mountains. I will meet with Earth once we know."

"That's best. I'd like to help with that, Darling. She seems like a wonderful person. Sometimes men can be so... well, you know."

Snow fell like soft confetti around us but melted in the rising steam of the tub. A few ice crystals managed to make it through and laced Kayne's black hair and long lashes. I pulled him closer and said, "Professor Sorenson, you can do a one-eighty as fast as your brother Kick."

"Huh?"

"You were just telling me to take my mind off work so you could get frisky, and now...."

Kayne did about five things with his face, which could be summarized as, *So, I'm fickle. What can you do?*

I gave him a brief kiss and continued, "You have most of your team assembled, Doctor. What's the investigative plan?"

Before he could answer, the sliding doors again opened to admit four new interlopers to the snowy and steaming patio. The first revealed through the mist and snow was a naked giant, towel over his shoulder, who said in a booming masculine, "So much *jāšanās* in this place, inside and out. Gints is appalling."

"I think you mean appalled, Big Bro," I corrected.

"Whatever is. I am here to bring more décor and ...."

"Décor, decorum, you bring both, sexy Darling. Get in here."

"But see, Gints brings the American snacks." He raised a muscled arm like a prize caresser on "The Price is Right," and Scott walked into view carrying a platter of heavy hors-d'oeuvres. He snapped small trays on the edge of the tub for convenience.

Kayne eyed the young staffer in his towel and joked, "Bloody oath! I'd say you brought along a special snack of your own, ya hot bastard. Thanks, Scott." He picked up a slider saying, "Bog in, Mates."

Tired and a bit "cocktailed," Kayne's Australian slang had ramped up and peppered his usually exact and coherent speech. Mark was amused, Rebecca, Gints, and Scott perplexed, and I continued to be charmed by this adorable Aussie beauty.

Referring to his young companion, Gints said, "I tell Boy Scott is not to bother being so formal. He is what you call 'off cock.'"

"Off the clock, Big Man," Scott exclaimed.

"Either way is same." The Latvian shrugged his massive shoulders.

Gints lowered himself into the sauna, causing the water level to rise considerably. Scott stripped and joined him in a cuddle. Their growing intimacy, apparent to everyone, triggered at least three sets of exchanged glances. Gints was very frisky and rocked a body that was hard to resist. Also, he was a stalwart – reliable and brave.

I yelped as I received a slurpy dog kiss over the edge of the hot tub. Chouko announced his presence and love for his best buddy. His curved tail and brown and white hindquarters were in excited motion. He yearned to be the center of attention.

I acknowledged the dog love, gave him a wet petting, and spoke, "Chouko, *Yoko ni naru. Yoi otokonoko!*"

My Beautiful Butterfly obeyed the command, hopping onto one of the cushioned, teak chaises to keep watch on his wayward humans. A forlorn-looking White River padded over slowly and sat on the deck next to him, looking through the balustrade into the dark, snowy valley.

Mark said quietly, "She waits."

"Yes, a dog's faithfulness sometimes knows no bounds. I am glad Josh sent her back to the Aerie," I said. "My Butterfly is good company." From his place on the lounge, Chouko sniffed the snowy air around his new, sad buddy.

"I had a chance to speak to Josh privately after the examination. Righteous bloke, that." Kayne said. "Speaking on behalf of the Tribe, he wants us to take on the investigation of his sister's murder in support of the local authorities. Let's start with Joletta Golden Tree. Rebecca and

Mark, will you please find out what she can add to our knowledge of Susan Chipeta Walker's activities?"

"Absolutely, Darling. We have an appointment tomorrow in Aspen regarding the possible museum collaboration. I believe Ms. Golden Tree's shop is on our way." Mark nodded agreeably, saying, "I understand they lived on the Reservation and had been together for many years."

Kayne responded, "Yes. Ms. Golden Tree is the Tribe Historian and a member of the Nu Ci Council. Same-sex relationships are not always seen in a negative light by Native Americans. Among the indigenous peoples of North America, attitudes vary from acceptance to homophobic.

"The appellation 'Two-Spirit' is an umbrella term that refers to certain individuals who fulfill a traditional third-gender role in their community. Two-Spirit must be understood from its context in a First Nations culture."

White River interrupted Kayne's lecture with a sudden barrage of barking and growling. It seemed like her frantic attention was focused on the landscape across the dark and snowy valley below. As I slipped out of the tub and knelt beside her, I found she would not be comforted. Chouko eased down next to her and seemed to be trying to determine the far-off cause of her excitement. He dashed around the deck in search of a way down the mountain.

"It's OK, girl," I soothed. I called Chouko back from his exciting run.

My five companions looked in the direction of the valley, but little could be seen through the snowy gloom below.

"Perhaps a coyote. We have a den of them just below the Lodge. They hunt at night, I believe."

White River set up a howl.

"Not likely, Scott. *Canis latrans* would usually hunt at dusk when prey would be plentiful. No, I suspect it is something else. However, exactly what is disturbing our friend at this hour is unknown to me. Perhaps something has recalled the memory of her mistress in the poor beast."

As suddenly as she had begun the alarm, White River settled into an alert but quiet sitting position, still gazing into the dark. Chouko came back from patrolling the perimeter and gave me a good-natured slurp. I leaned over and patted the bed of the lounge chair, and he jumped up and settled in the cushions.

Rebecca said, "So, let's get back to the lesbians, Darling. Two-Spirit is not so much about whom one is sexually interested in or how one personally identifies?"

"Correct," Kayne responded as I slipped back into the hot waters. "Two-Spirit is a sacred, spiritual, and ceremonial role that is recognized and confirmed by the Elders of the community.

"Third and fourth genders usually embodied by Two-Spirit people include performing work and wearing clothing associated with both men and women. They are traditionally honored during ceremonies. Not all Indigenous Nations have rigid gender roles."

Mark spoke up, "So, to put a point on it, their sexual orientation or gender identity is secondary to their ethnic identity. One's primary orientation is an awareness of being part of a Native American community."

I added, "I once read of a Native American confronting the hypocrisy of American Christian leaders. It went something like, 'You stand on our soil and claim gay marriage has never occurred here. More than 130 tribes in every region of North America performed millions of same-sex marriages for hundreds of years.'"

Kayne beamed at my "Teacher's Pet." He was standing in the center of the bubbling, steaming bath up to his chiseled upper abs.

"Right, Nick, the homophobic statements of the right-wing are, as usual, both hateful and ignorant. While religious fundamentalists consider the homosexual an abomination, many Native Americans believe us to be traditional Two-Spirit individuals and recognized as sacred by the elders of the tribe."

The other two couples were a bit awed by the impromptu lecture of Professor Sorenson and his exchange with his protégé.

"So, these women you mention, they well respected by Tribe and part of ruling class."

"Gints Darling, you are so right, but the terminology nuances it a bit. A Council of Elders governs the Nu Ci clan of the Ute Tribe. Pretty Democratic. The CEO, the Tribal Leader, is elected."

She continued, "Did you know most Native American tribals are set up like that of the United States federal government. Their administration has three branches that allow for a separation of powers, the council of elders, a tribal leader, and a judicial body – the tribal court."

"Impressive, my girl," Kayne said, raising his glass. "Yes, the Council is the legal authority of the Nu Ci at Alpaska Reservation. They are a branch of the Ute, a tribe rich in history and with some of the worst travails."

He tipped his glass to his beloved friend, saying, "Fine shelia, that."

Mark patted Rebecca's head in a gesture that was part condescension and part admiration. Rebecca turned her head to smooch the man behind her and remarked. "You see, beautiful and intelligent, Darling. I did my homework before coming to Colorado." She saluted and sipped her cocktail.

"Please see what Ms. Golden Tree can tell you regarding Susan's investigations as a bounty hunter."

Kayne turned his attention to Gints, saying, "Gints, please go with Nick and have a Captain Cook at what forensics can be found regarding Jeron Adobo Jordan. Josh told me that White River is a tracker and may be helpful. I will call Earth to ask for an article of Jeron's clothing, which you can pick up at Eagle Base for the dog to scent."

"You got it, Big Doctor. Niko and Gints on it. But who is Captain Cook? Is he police officer?"

I jumped in, "Big Doctor means 'have a look.' It's an Aussie rhyming slang expression. Studied up on my 'Strine, folks and will be happy to serve as a translator of the Professor's cryptic speech."

I pulled Kayne closer to me and wiped back his dripping hair. He grinned with his ice-blues twinkling. Gints nodded, gave the thumbs up, and continued to nuzzle his new boy crush with affection.

"What can I do, Dr. Sorenson?" Scott asked.

Kayne shot his wet forelock that had stubbornly drooped across his left forehead.

"We are going to need to be fed and hydrated, Scott. As Chief Steward here at the Aerie, your job will be to provide and pack up the provisions for our fieldwork, Mate. We can round up here at about six pm tomorrow evening to compare notes over dinner.

"I hope that my brother will join us and update us on how Josh and the family are doing. His last text was that he was at Alpaska, and the Tribe was beginning the funeral preparation rites. He is spending the evening with Josh, I surmise."

I found my man deliciously attractive in his teaching mode, whether dashingly attired or buck-assed naked and wet. My mind drifted back to my first criminology class with him in Ft. Lauderdale. The connection was very sudden and hyperintense, but not without some serious challenges in the following weeks.

"Any questions or items I may have bungled?"

"Kayne, let me handle the press on this. I can collaborate with Josh Walker and the Tribe's communications office to let them know I am available to help out."

"Thanks, Mark. Good catch. I am sure there will be media on this. I suspect there will be a swarm of interest, especially if this case reveals troubles within the Nu Ci people. I also think they will appreciate your assistance, given your impressive credentials. However, it may take a bit to earn their trust. There are many landmines, I fear."

"Kayne, allow me to be the liaison between local, state, and Native American law enforcement."

"Excellent, Nick. Rebecca can help with the FBI should they become involved."

"Darlings, as a graduate of the FBI's Citizen's Academy and an intimate friend of Special Agent Mary Chaffee, I accept the assignment. You can count on this woman."

"Thank you, my dear."

Gints yawned and stretched. "Past your Gints' bedtime, friends. We gonna say good night."

He climbed out of the water and, standing on the deck, helped Scott from the tub into his arms. Grabbing a towel and the robe, they dashed through the snow back into the Lodge. Scott turned in the doorway to say, "Please just leave everything. I will get it in the morning."

Through the steam and snow, I thought I saw the two naked men dashing up the curving stairs to the floor above. A light went on in Scott's bedroom in the staff wing.

In her best Gints imitation, Rebecca said, "I say it once again, so much *jāšanās* in this place."

"I would not mind some of that myself," Mark said.

"With them or me, Darling?"

Mark made as to dunk Rebecca in the swirling waters. She pushed back.

"No? Have to prove it, my sexy boy," she challenged.

Mark slid out from behind her and pushed himself up and onto the edge of the hot tub to deftly drop to the deck. He wrapped his towel around his waist and picked up Rebecca's robe before leaping back onto the rim. Holding it like a royal attendant before his lady love, he shielded her modesty in an almost comic way.

"Darling, I assure you I am far from shy in front of my gays." Nevertheless, she stepped up on the underwater seat, turned, and donned the robe held by her champion. She deliberately slipped out one naked shoulder as Mark assisted her down to the deck -- so 1960's sex kitten.

He stopped to retrieve the two pieces of her bikini and bowed in mock obedience. "Lead the way, my Goddess."

Turning to us, the Divinity said, "Oh, one more thing, Darlings...."

She never finished. Mark let out a barbarically virile roar and caught her at the waist with his shoulder. Standing upright with her laughing over his back, he yelled, *"Mae'n rhaid i mi gael y wraig hon nawr!"*

He abducted her into the Lodge and up to the second floor as she faked protestations all the way.

"I think I know, but what did he say?"

"The Welsh equivalent of 'boy's gotta have it.' In this case, it loses nothing in the translation, Mate. That one's a rippa journo, my love. His blood's worth bottling, as we say."

I pulled him into my arms and resumed where we had started with a passionate kiss. My Aussie Prince felt so good in my arms, and we both were responding with ardor.

After a while, I said, "Let's take this inside, Sexy Man. I need to clear your mind of the view of Journalist Gadarn's rockin' arse. Shall I throw you over one shoulder, or do you prefer a fireman's carry?"

"Have a go, yer mug, but I believe it is my turn to have a naughty as the top bloke during our upcoming shag."

"Your method of keeping score is way inaccurate, bro."

He pulled away, dunked me under the hot water, and vaulted over the top of the tub to the deck. I surfaced to spout water like a figure on an Italian Renaissance fountain, only to be hit in the head with my towel.

"You are so gonna pay for that," I shouted.

"Chouko, nakanihairu," Kayne commanded, and my dog bounded through the patio doors as he opened them, dashing up to the second floor.

I stepped out of the sauna and patted the forlorn-looking White River, who continued to stare into the blowing snow and darkness into the valley beyond the Lodge.

"Come on, girl. Time to go."

***

"What is it?" I asked softly.

Kayne had left the bed and sat in his meditative position in front of our bedroom's floor-to-ceiling windows. His naked silhouette faced the panes softly lit from the deck below. The window framed crystals of swirling snow.

Our lovemaking had been passionate and exhausting, with a previously untapped ferocity on both our parts. My passion responded in sync with Kayne's lustful intensity. Typical male, I drifted off soon after. He apparently was unable to sleep.

"Something. I don't know. Sorry, my love. It's just a feeling... there is something out there...." He seemed to focus on the darkness outside. I remember a somewhat similar condition with the staring White River earlier in the evening.

I left the bed and stepped over the sleeping dogs. I sat beside Kayne and took his hand.

"Tell me."

Kayne lowered his head. Then, taking a deep breath, he faced me, struggling to put words to his thoughts. Finally, he said, "Since the events that brought us together in Ft. Lauderdale, more and more, I have this growing feeling that we are encountering a powerful and dreadful evil, lurking just beyond our intellectual reach and connected to much that is malicious and deadly. I feel the presence of a criminal mind that seeks to profit from great destruction and death, no matter the cost to the earth or its inhabitants."

He peered into the darkness around us before continuing.

"There was something unresolved in the horrors of our case in Florida. I was sure of it then but unable to approach it intelligently. Everyone involved, including me, seemed willing to close the books – case solved. But, Nick, I feel it again, and it's...."

His face was that of a man staring into the abyss. He was unable to continue.

I hugged him and brushed the hair from his face. In the dim light, his returning classic beauty slipped in and out between light and shadow. I ran my hands over his naked back and shoulders.

"We got this, my man. We're an incredible team, you and me, the unstoppable power of two. It will all come about for good. Let's sleep on it. We have a lot to do tomorrow."

"Nick, one more thing." He paused, looked into my eyes, and placed his hands on my shoulders. The blue of his eyes seemed to deepen in the dark while glowing slightly in the incidental light from outside and the dying embers of the bedroom fireplace.

"Lately, I have been obsessed with one thought. I feel like I am bringing you from one horror onto the precipice of another. There is much danger in all of this, my love."

Kayne pressed closer into my arms, placing his cheek against mine so that his lips were next to my ear. His chest heaved against me as he said, "You mean so much to me, Nick. I am not sure that... If anything should ever...."

His conflict was deep-seated, and he hesitated with a frustration that came from his soul. I did nothing, nor did I say anything for a long time remaining in his embrace. As usual, I also struggled with feelings and the words to express them. Slowly, I pulled slightly back and brought one finger to his lips, a gesture he used on me many times.

"Kayne..." I stammered but, with a deep sigh, gathered the rest of my thoughts together. "OK, you see... well...."

Shit! Deep breath, Nick Boy.

"Please believe me when I say I'm falling in love with you. Um, yeah... and...."

A sudden moment of clarity.

"And in this time and in this place, there is no one I'd rather be with or no place I'd rather be than with you, here with you."

His eyes glistened, and one tear broke loose over a lower lid to slide down a classic profile.

He said, "And that is not likely to change for any reason?"

Grinning broadly, I said, "Afraid not, big man. Happens when you get hit by the thunderbolt, Beauty."

His lips formed a smile beneath my barrier index finger. He took my hand, kissed it, led the way to the bed, and pulled me on top of him as I yanked the comforter over both of us.

Eventually, we slept.

Chapter Thirteen: Search
NICK SECHI'S JOURNAL

Kayne roused me from a deep sleep. I was steeped in a troubling dream and coming out of it. His gentle shakes and soothing voice were disorienting but welcome.

"Let's go, Nick. New developments."

I sat up and rubbed my eyes. "Good morning. What's with all that light? Ow!" I stretched.

"Nick, Kick is missing. He did not stay at Alpaska last night. Josh sent him home in his truck. He never got here."

"Holy shit!" I stared wide-eyed at a fully dressed and ready Kayne. I figured he had very little sleep even before the bad news about his brother. I hit the floor and dashed into the bathroom to relieve myself, calling over my shoulder as he pulled my wardrobe together, tossing clothing on the bed.

"How did you find out?"

"Officer Stefan Connelly. They found Josh's SUV on the mountain road near the Wild Life Preserve, just across the valley. It was parked on the side of the mountain road empty."

"Damn, just once, I like us to find an undisturbed crime scene."

"Hey, I am gonna head to the kitchen and get us some transport. Meet you there. Please hurry."

Although he was rushing around, he came up quickly behind me and turned me to him for a kiss.

"We'll find him, Kayne. Guaranteed."

"Gotta be fast, Mate." He opened his hand to show me a prescription bottle.

Thomas M. Sorenson -- Lithium Carbonate.

***

"So, please see what you can find on Kriegston Gathering. Please broaden your research to include any energy scandals involving Native American lands."

I arrived at the kitchen to see Kayne and Gints gathered with Scott over his laptop. Rebecca and Mark were quaffing morning brews. Both were in business dress for their meeting with the leadership of the Aspen museums.

Kayne was saying, "Gints, we'll postpone the forensic search on the road. Hold down the fort here, Mate. We need the Aerie secured."

"Count on Gints and Scott, Big Doctor. This we got."

Mark handed me our provisions backpack, so expertly prepared by Scott, complete with a thermos of fresh coffee.

"Thanks, Buddy. Ready when you are, Boss."

"Great, Nick, let's roll."

"Let us know what you find out, Darling. I am sure you will find him. Please contact us if you need our help."

Kayne grabbed up the keys to Kick's Ford F-450 Limited, and the two of us raced for the stairs to the garage below. I tapped my SmartWatch – 15 minutes, bed to front door -- awesome.

***

"The SUV was running, keys in the dash and door ajar, just about out of gas. Josh tells us it was half full when Kick drove out of Alpaska last night around ten-thirty pm. We calculate that the vehicle was parked here at about eleven pm. No sign of your brother, Dr. Sorenson. He seems to have wandered off. Disoriented and snowblind, most likely."

Officer Stefan Connelly and his Deputy, Jack Barberi, met us at the turn off the mountain road near the Aerie Valley Wild Life Preserve. The Black SUV sat on the shoulder, snow accumulated on the windshield and body, Kick's snowboard on the back seat.

"Interesting conclusion, Officer. Very interesting. And my brothers' tracks would be... where?"

Connelly seemed to be caught off guard.

"Well, with all the snow...."

Kayne dismissed the Trooper and surveyed the site. He muttered loudly to me, "My brother has never been disoriented in his life. If anything, he is hyper-aware of every situation he is in. If I understand you correctly, you conclude that my brother had the clearness of thought to drive six miles through the valley on icy, winding roads only to park his vehicle along the road a half-mile from his destination, leave the truck running, lose control of his mind and stagger off into the mountains, walking on top of the snow."

The policeman withered. He said, "Huh?"

Matthew Strong Bear walked up from searching the shoulder and the scrub that ascended into the surrounding cliffs. I nodded and motioned for him to join me in scanning the area ahead and behind the abandoned truck.

Kayne pointed to the field of snow adjacent to the shoulder of the road. He continued to use his correction voice to say, "The blanket of newly fallen powder would have covered any footprints. That is true. However, in these conditions, we would see indentations – more like skid marks, where packed ice and snow lay under the new fall. That would suggest a trudging motion of someone in crisis moving across the landscape in that storm. Nothing like that near the vehicle."

He stepped closer to Connelly, trying to contain his frustration.

"A disoriented and snowblind man stumbles and falls. My brother is a sizeable man, exactly my proportions. There are no imprints of a trashing body anywhere near us. Those bushes and trees have not been hit by a stumbling human. Considering the incline, he would have rolled back down here."

Kayne had wasted the guy.

"In short, Sir, your conclusions are absurd."

"Mr. Sorenson's phone and wallet were in the console," Matthew continued. "I happen to remember him tossing them in just as he left Alpaska last night."

I asked, "You were with him when he left the Reservation? Any idea what was on his mind? What did you guys talk about?" I looked back to see Kayne scrupulously inspecting the interior of the vehicle.

Matthew dropped his gaze and then looked off to the valley. "Um, nothing of importance, really. Mostly, he was concerned for Josh. But, ah, he did say that he felt like an outsider while the preliminary funeral rites were getting underway."

"Really? But I thought he was an honorary member of the Tribe."

"You don't know my people, Officer...."

"Nick."

What was going on with this dude? He seemed super uncomfortable.

"Right, Nick. Anyway, the Nu Ci closes ranks when big shit happens. It's how we deal with stress, controversy, and suffering. The memory of White atrocities against First Nationers runs deep."

"Got it. So, Kick borrowed Josh's truck to...."

"Said he was returning to his brother and guests at the Aerie Lodge. It was snowing a bit when he left, but the big stuff and wind came later in the night. We both thought he would have no trouble getting through."

I dropped to a squat approximately where the roadbed met the shoulder a few feet from the front of the SUV. The actual demarcation was hard to determine in the snow.

"Matthew, take a look at this."

The snow had dipped significantly, forming a rounded depression about six inches across, which sunk almost to the roadbed. A dark center suggested something unusual. With my gloves, I carefully brushed the ice back to expose a circular scorch mark on the asphalt and the stub of the casing of an emergency flare.

Stepping back on the road, Matthew carefully searched the shoulder further ahead.

"Here."

A second impression revealed an identical indentation in the snow where an additional flare had burned to the extinguishing point.

I looked at the Reservation Officer and said, "He was offering roadside assistance."

Kayne joined us. When he saw our discoveries, he said, "Please keep everyone back from this area." He dashed to the opposite road bank and, removing a jackknife from his parka, cut two branches from a spruce tree. Shaking the snow from the small boughs, he returned, handed me one, and carefully began to brush the snow off the area between the flare stubs.

"Dr. Sorenson, our forensics team can...."

Kayne dropped to his knees and continued brushing the terrain like a field archeologist with his pine branch. I followed his example off to his left.

Without looking up, Kayne responded to the Trooper, "We do not have much time, Officer. You will kindly indulge me."

Our efforts produced the faint images of tire tracks in the frozen mud of the shoulder and a few distinct footprints, more like the impressions of a scuffle. It was as if the road gave up secret markings in the frosty layer beneath the concealing white powder. Its secrets revealed in patterns of gray ice, crusted gravel, and frozen mud.

"The temperature had actually remained above freezing last night before the storm powered up. Right now, we have below-freezing temperatures. The results are this record of frozen imprints."

Officer Connelly snapped pictures of the marks with his cell phone.

We were careful not to disturb the area between the front and back flare impressions. Kayne and I brushed more of the shoulder free of covering. Suddenly, the consulting detective let out a cry of discovery and, with two fingers, lifted what appeared to be a frozen washcloth.

Chapter Fourteen: Golden Tree

MARK GADARN'S NOTES

Rebecca and I gazed at our unique host.

"OK, you ready? Because I have a lot to say. A mess of shit going on around here if you ask me. And those murderers got her, and anyone else who pushed back is now missing, afraid, or dead."

Joletta Golden Tree Collins was a slight woman in her late fifties. Her mix of Native American and African American blood created an exotic beauty with long, gray, and black hair. She had features that blended American Aboriginal nobility with African royalty. She carried herself in a distinguished manner and dressed in American contemporary with jewelry and accents of her Tribe.

With sad but flashing dark eyes, she had received our introductions and our expressions of sympathy for the loss of her partner, Susan Walker. She told us that she remembered Dr. Kayne Sorenson and was sad to hear that they were looking for Mr. Kick Sorenson, whom she described as a valuable friend to the Nu Ci.

"But first, as I understand it, you are here in Aspen to meet with museum officials regarding a possible collaboration with your Museum in Ft. Lauderdale. Native American exhibit?

"How did you know?"

"Word gets around. I volunteer to give presentations at the Silverman from time to time. A pretty good outfit. No bull shit."

Rebecca nodded. "We are proposing an exhibit of eastern and western Native American art. Specifically the Ute and the indigenous tribes of Florida."

"Rich history, the First Floridians. Let's see…." The cultural expert counted off, "The Miccosukee, the Seminoles, the Calusa, the Tequesta. First Nationers have been there going back to 12,000 BCE.

"I hope your program will represent our culture with accuracy and dignity. My people are tired of being a tourist attraction."

Joletta moved around the Golden Tree Trading Post and directed us to couches and chairs while putting on the teakettle. Around us, we could see the most fantastic collection of one-of-a-kind art, furniture, and collectibles from local and international sources.

On one wall, a large map of North and South America showed the tribes that populated the two continents. Dates accompanied the locations and names of the Nations. The prehistoric timeline showed thousands of years before the birth of Christ when North America was still inhabited by prehistoric beasts. Small tribes of primitive hunters crossed the frozen wastelands of the Bering Sea. Over countless generations, they migrated southward and eastward to the southernmost tip of South America.

Joletta saw my interest. She said, "My race arrived in the Americas between 16,000 and 20,000 years ago. There is some scientific evidence that the migration may even have gone back 40,000 years. They could not imagine the impact of the arrival of people from Europe in the 15th Century, 600 years ago. That was a fuckin' game-changer."

We had driven down through the plowed mountain pass to Aspen below the Aerie Valley. The Trading Post was easy to find, with its logo of a blazing aspen tree. I hopped out of the jeep and snapped pictures of the shop, its sign, and the street. Ms. Golden Tree had met us as she opened the Post and agreed to talk to us.

"Excuse me. Are you doing your email, young man?"

"No, Ma'am," I answered. "If it is OK, I want to take notes for Dr. Sorenson's investigation into the death of your partner."

"What, those goof-offs in the State Troopers not getting any traction on this? Not surprised. Gonna find a lot of closed mouths and scared folks on this one. My money is on Sorenson. He has an international reputation for solving the tough ones. And his brother is very respectable. A bit high-energy but a friend to our Nation, like his husband was."

Rebecca said with respect, "Ms. Golden Tree, please tell us about Susan."

"Well, I guess it's all over but the telling. My White Singing Bird, an elder of our tribe, lies in state up there at Alpaska. My people are preparing her body for the final journey of her spirit. In many ways, she represents much of our history.

"Been together twenty years next month. Hard to put in words today about how much Susan meant to me. Our shared life has been one that has been filled with much grief, some dangers, and many tears. Many struggles but much happiness if truth be told."

She looked off for a bit, eyes glistening and then back to us. She spoke in a sad voice, saying, "The only reason I opened the shop this morning is that I need to get away for a bit to clear my head."

She looked directly at us and said, "I am sure that the troubles at the Reservation led to her murder."

She visibly shuddered, rising in the silence that followed to pour the tea. It seemed the task composed her a bit. Joletta settled on the couch next to Rebecca.

I asked, "Let's start with the challenges faced by the Nu Ci."

"Mascots and casinos, Mr. Gadarn?"

"I beg your pardon."

"That is how most Non-Natives conceive of my people. But the legacy of Native People reveals many atrocities worse than you can imagine. Our history has been one of resettlement, discrimination, and extermination by the white settlers and the federal forces. Come to Alpaska, and you will see the upside-down American Flag, a signal of dire distress in instances of extreme danger to life or property, on many of our homes. You will also see the poverty and desolation."

Joletta took a colorful shield from an adjacent table onto her lap. As she spoke, the ethnic, sing-song lilt of her speech patterns increased.

"Almost 600 Native communities have been recognized throughout the United States, and that includes more than 200 First Nations of Alaska and Hawaii. Each sovereign entity establishes its own relations with the United States through the Federal Bureau of Indian Affairs. Our rights were affirmed by the United Nations more than ten years ago. Each of our nations has its own culture, history, and language."

She lovingly turned the shield in her hands as she continued.

"Today, we live in great poverty and with extremely high levels of unemployment. On some reservations, the poverty rate is three times the rate of the rest of the US. Unemployment rates of some First Nations are sometimes more than 60 percent."

"I had no idea," Rebecca said.

I was highly interested in more information, thinking of a possible exposé for CBN.

"You should know. Everyone should know. Whites either demonize or romanticize First Nation people. Sure, we contribute to our own plight in many ways. Most oppressed people do. We need the education that will help us to think critically and arrive at viable solutions for improvement," Joletta continued with conviction.

"The challenges that Indigenous People face sometimes seem insurmountable. Polling places are at long distances from the reservations. Financial institutions are reluctant to invest in Native businesses. This results in stagnant economic growth in our communities. Many of us have no banks.

"Our healthcare situation is horrible. One in three of us is uninsured. We have high rates of diabetes, obesity, substance abuse, HIV, and other sexually transmitted diseases.

"Native Americans are still living with the fact that we have been deposed of our land throughout most of our history. Add to this the exploitation of our natural resources on our remaining national soil. Alpaska's current turn to drilling, hydraulic fracturing, and fracking for the oil and gas is fraught with environmental issues."

She paused and thought for a moment.

"That young man, Jeron Jordan, was hired to guide the Tribe with our oil business. What the hell did we know about oil and natural gas? I believe he was working on a major report of importance when he disappeared. Our Council has been embroiled in a mess of regulation issues.

"We own the wells, but we gave the extraction rights to Kriegston. That's when it all went to shit. Along comes Chief Mingan – in this mess up to his ears, let me tell you.

"We just rushed into it, is all -- eager to exploit the opportunity soon after the discovery of the oil."

She held the shield before her in a very reverent way and continued.

"I am not afraid to say this, although many are. There is corruption there, Ms. Quinto, Mr. Gadarn. You will find it for sure, and it is a terrible horror. I can feel it."

Joletta looked up before continuing as if trying to shake off a ghost or two.

"The Council had earmarked the profits from Red Eagle Energies for a medical center to be built on tribal lands. We have been talking with local higher education institutions to educate our people as medical professionals and eventually staff such a facility. Except, we have seen a minimal return on investment from Red Eagle Energies."

"How is that possible?" I said. "I thought the oil and gas deposits were massive under Alpaska."

"At this time, the boom has brought us many problems and few benefits," she said. "The Council has much work to do if we are to operate our oil company and subsidiaries from our basic belief that our land is sacred and must be respected. You can anticipate a real clash of ideologies there. Furthermore, the Tribe needs to investigate the finances responsibly and keep profits out of others' hands."

I said, "You mean Kriegston."

"I mean Kriegston and those among our people who facilitate their underhandedness. Some of us have suspected corruption for a long time, but the Council has been slow to respond to our concerns."

"Ms. Golden Tree, what is the significance of the design on your shield?"

Joletta Golden Tree said nothing for a long time. Then, tears coursed down her noble visage, and she made no attempt to hide them. When she finally continued, her voice was full of clarity and determination.

"Mr. Gadarn, this is the medicine shield of Susan Chipeta Walker, the White Singing Bird. I will bring it back for her when I leave the trading post today. I wanted to keep it with me today.

"She and her brother were taught by their grandfather, the great Chief Arapeen, to be trackers on our Mother, the Sacred Earth. Susan was a bounty hunter for the State as well as the Tribe. Occasionally, criminals roam these mountains, the river valleys, and the mesas of the south --the wilderness around us, you see? Her record of hunting and turning over criminals was exceptional.

"Recently, she was seeking the whereabouts of the Tribal Environmental Officer I mentioned, Jeron Adobo Jordan. He disappeared about six months ago. I will send over to the Aerie her work files for Dr. Sorenson. She kept many notes of her cases on her computer."

Rebecca said, "Thank you. That would be very helpful, Darling."

Upon hearing Rebecca's favorite appellation, Joletta Golden Tree smiled for the first time since we met her.

"I like you. Both of you. Please call me Joletta, and I will call you Rebecca and Mark, OK?"

"Sounds good, Joletta," I said. "Please tell us more about Susan's shield."

"Oh yes," she said, handing the art piece to us. "It is not a war shield but a medicine shield. It protects the one who carries it. Spiritually rather than physically. The designs represent the spiritual strength of the White Singing Bird, her namesake, the second wife of Chief Ouray of the Uncompahgre Ute Tribe, who led the Nation after he died in 1880.

"Chipeta was a champion for Native rights, a determined advocate, and a diplomat for peace with the Whites. In Washington, DC, she met with the members of a Congressional Commission and counseled President William Howard Taft. In the 80s, Chipeta was named to the Colorado Women's Hall of Fame. Like my Susan, she stood for peace and led with courage and integrity."

She gently replaced the Spirit shield and said, "Rebecca, Mark, any help my people or I can provide to avenge the blood of Susan Chipeta... you can count on us. Our lives will never be safe, and the spirit of my people will never rest until justice is served."

Tribal Blood

Chapter Fifteen: Alpaska

NICK SECHI'S JOURNAL

Kayne spoke with his usual authority when advising law enforcement on a case.

"Correct. Please have the cloth analyzed for the presence of chemicals. Depending on the vapor pressure at freezing, certain volatile substances will have evaporated, but you may find something."

Kayne paused on his mobile to listen to Officer Connelly. I drove the Ford Super Duty up the mountain road to the Alpaska Reservation.

"I know. Yes, fingerprints are a moot point considering this is glove weather, but Connelly, go for DNA."

Pause.

"No. My brother's. Right. Yes. On the cloth. I will text the Aerie, and our man there, Scott Iverson, will turn over Kick's hairbrush."

Pause.

"He's on meds, Sir. This is a life-threatening situation. No, not a case of wandering off, as you previously concluded, Officer. My brother was abducted."

He took a deep breath and listened to the Trooper.

"No, that is absurd. We have been over this. The likelihood of my brother wandering off due to an interruption of his medication is not supported by the facts. You saw the tracks of the other truck in the snow, Officer Connelly. There was a stopped vehicle in front of his."

Kayne hit "Mute," swore, and then unmuted.

Connelly continued to argue, and Kayne interrupted, "Precisely, the cloth will connect the two vehicles in a case of what was clearly a very forceful abduction. Correct. Get an analysis of other fibers trapped in that cloth, also."

More talk on the other end.

"Alpaska. We are almost there. I want to talk to the Tribal Leader. Joshua Walker has obtained a meeting. Right. I will keep you posted." He ended the call.

"Bollocks!" He shouted. "Something's not right with that man. He refuses to accept scientific evidence. His behavior suggests something rather sinister."

"Kayne," I said, "How much time do we have?"

He calmed a little and answered, "Hard to say, Nick. Knowing my brother and his relationship with Josh, I'd say he has been faithfully on his meds. But, with his history, it is hard to say for sure. If they have him holed up somewhere without his lithium, it could be just a matter of a few days."

He looked into the frozen hills.

"So, time is of the essence."

***

The green and white sign on the northwest turnoff of the mountain road announced, *Entering Nu Ci Nation, Alpaska Lands.*

Continuing north for another 10 miles would have brought us to the entrance to Clarion Military Base. As we approached, I looked down into the valley and saw the airstrip on the far side below us.

A plaque on a stone tower contained a carved map of the sacred lands under the title, *Entering Alpaska Reservation, U.S. Department of Interior.* The Palouse River, flowing to the northeast, cut into the top left side of the map. The main road etched across the territory is outlined on the sign with the only other markings labeled *Visitors Center.*

Josh Walker, dressed in somber black and astride his black horse, met us at the Center. His long hair was plaited with one black feather, which hung down from the left side of his head.

"I want to say again how sorry I am for your loss, Josh. Susan's passing will be mourned by many, both among the Native American Communities and the Non-Natives as well."

"Thank you, Dr. Sorenson and Officer Sechi. The Tribe has experienced a tremendous loss. My family also thanks you for your expressions of sympathy."

"Josh, Kayne and I want to restate our dedication to bringing Susan's murders to justice. But we need to locate Kick as soon as possible."

"Let's talk in my office. It is through those trees in the Executive Administration Center."

We followed the plowed driveway up to the large building and parked. In front of the doors to the Center were tall poles hung topped with black feathers, ribbons, and strips of black leather. On one side of the entrance was a large, painted medallion embossed with "Nu Ci Tribal Administration" around the clan's crest. Its twin, on the other side, said, "Nu Ci Tribal Court."

Josh tied up his horse and met us in front of the Center. The strikingly handsome Brave looked gaunt and despondent. "This way, gentlemen."

Officer Matthew Strong Bear broke into a trot to intercept us as we walked across the Nu Ci Police building parking lot. "Nick. Dr. Sorenson, any news?"

Matt shook hands with us, and I brought him close for a manly shoulder bump. "Let's talk inside, Bud."

We entered Josh's office and took our places around a small conference table as Josh asked his assistant to bring coffee and water. Josh's office was decorated with Indigenous American art.

One framed poster showed a vintage picture of Braves standing in front of a tipi announced, "Homeland Security: Fighting Terrorism Since 1492." Another was a portrait of a chief with the script, "The biggest genocide in human history occurred not in Nazi Germany but on North and South American Soil. One hundred million Native Americans were slaughtered and lost their homelands."

Fearing that neither Josh nor Kayne had eaten anything lately, I opened Scott Iverson's provisions. I tossed four sandwiches on the table, one to each.

"Here is what we know from our end," Josh said. He then reiterated what Matthew had told us, namely that Kick had left Alpaska last night in Josh's truck at about ten-thirty p.m. with the expressed intention of returning to the Aerie. In addition to doing a forensic follow-up of the alleged abduction site, Trooper Connelly had four members of State law enforcement in the field.

Matthew said, "To that, we've added five members of our police force. These guys are the best Native trackers we have. Still, with so many stomping around the site and the surrounding wilderness, I must tell you that they have a very challenging job to do. But, if anyone can find your brother, they can.

"We are following up on the tire tread prints at the site. I just found out we have an anomaly on one of the tire prints, a plug, so we have a leg up on evidence that will lead us to the truck."

"Winter sports in the immediate vicinity have ramped up due to the abundant snowfall," I said. "This can work to our advantage in that someone may have seen something."

Matt said, "Officer Connelly said that he was following up on traffic in the vicinity. I suggested questioning Resort folks, but I got some pushback. I still can send one of my officers over there, regardless."

I responded, "Connelly's resistance is unacceptable. Aerie Industries, Inc. has staff there that will assist. Kayne, let me take care of this. Matt, I will connect them to your investigation."

They agreed.

Kayne shot his forelock and referred to his cell phone, saying, "Rebecca has just texted me that she has communicated with her contacts in the FBI. They are aware of the disappearance of my brother. They are coordinating with their local office and Officer Connelly's command center."

Josh ignored his sandwich and said, "There is no doubt Kick has been abducted. Right now, I can't understand why."

"Could be ransom," said Kayne. "My family's investment in the Valley continues to be substantial, but to ignore the connection with the disappearance of his husband, Mitch, six months ago as pure

118

coincidence would be illogical and a critical mistake. The crimes are indeed part of a conspiracy."

Matthew offered, "Mr. Sorenson is not without enemies, I know. There was a group of land investors that have been, since Mitch's time, interested in portions of the Aerie Valley for purposes of tourism and commercial development."

"What kind of commercial development?" I asked.

Josh answered, "Recreational facilities and natural resources. This valley holds substantial mineral, gas, and oil deposits. Same prospects as the reservation, although we are higher up. Maybe even richer."

"And you say these developers showed some animosity toward my brothers?"

"Definitely, Dr. Sorenson," said Matthew. "They had a few aggressive altercations with both your brothers, so I understand. Josh knows more about it than I do."

"They were pretty hostile to Mitch when he showed no interest in developing the Valley. Mitch stood up to them as only he could. My man was strong and assertive, and the land boys got a bit nasty." Josh added.

"Is," Kayne affirmed."

"Beg, pardon?" Josh said.

"My brother Mitch *is* strong and assertive. Always has been and still is. His body has not yet been recovered after six months. It helps to talk about him in the present tense. I know they are both out there somewhere, gentlemen."

"And we'll find them," I said.

Josh continued. "It wasn't too long since Mitch vanished that they made some moves on Kick. Greedy bastards. But he turned them away. I saw their last interaction. They got very belligerent. It should come as no surprise that Kick gets very excited and determined when he encounters bullshit. We threw them off the land."

"Do you have some contact information on this development group?"

Josh stood and went to his desk, and returned, handing Kayne a business card.

"Hawthorn Development. Are they in any way connected to the Red Eagle's subcontractors?"

"Not that I am aware of, Kayne. Their primary interest is tourism. They are just branching into the mining and extraction business. Different from Kriegston Gathering. Then there is the trouble with the horses."

"Please continue, Josh."

"Aerie Stables has been bringing in awards statewide and nationally with our champions. Two months ago, Kick went international with some breeding offers in Hungary and Poland. There was a bit of a nasty hoopla about Aerie being an interloper in an industry that was pretty much sewn up by their respective national breeders.

"I was with Kick in Warsaw a month ago. He went a bit far bragging about our breeds, which turned the Europeans off – they saw it as American swagger in a proud national industry that had been going on for millennia. At one point, Kick lost his temper and was extremely frustrated. The result was some threats that got physical. We left pretty much in a hurry."

"Josh, was he taking his medication at the time?" Kayne asked.

"Yes. I insisted that Kick stays on the Lithium. If you'll excuse my saying so, meds or no meds, your brother is still a firecracker, as you know. Not a really good ambassador for the business at times."

Josh looked down at his hands and continued, "Something else. Kayne knows this part. When Mitch went missing and after Kayne returned to Florida, Kick went into a downward spiral, and it got extreme with the violent sex and all. He was hooking up with some nasty guys – extremely rough. That's when I moved in, so to speak."

I noticed that Josh avoided Matthew's gaze. The younger man was both silent and distracted, looking away towards the window – *some tension here.*

"I was close to your older brother and felt I owed it to him to see that Kick remained under control. It started with me having to run off those nasty fuckers who were using your brother like their whore. Sorry to be so crude, but it was all of that and more."

"Nothing I haven't heard before concerning my brother's mania. I saw the scars."

"In the hospital, I laid it on the line with him. Either he quit with those guys and got back on the meds again, or I was history, and Aerie would fail miserably. We got close to almost losing him, but he promised to change. I fear this may be at the heart of his disappearance."

Matthew stood up and went to get coffee. It was easy to see that the conversation was not going well, considering the man's emotional turmoil.

Josh continued, "Lately, I found out some intel about the guys he was hooking up with. They were not from the area. Interlopers. It appeared that they were part of a coordinated effort bent on his destruction. I'll send you what I have on them, but soon after, they are nowhere to be found."

"Josh, can I also get the information of the horse breeders in Europe that Kick crossed? I want to follow up on that."

"Sure thing, but that information is down at the Horse Palace. I'll have Luke send it."

"Great, please copy that to Scott at the Lodge. I also want to talk to the administrators at the Resort about the land development conversations."

"Nathan and Monica Clifton. You know them, right?"

"Yes."

Realizing that we needed to get this moving quickly, I said, "Kayne, I will get them to meet with us. Rebecca and Mark have a meeting there. Sending a text...."

Matthew Strong Bear returned to the Office.

"Josh, Gray Wolf asked if he could see you guys now."

121

The tall, handsome Brave did not attempt to rise to the summons. "Thanks, Matthew. Have a seat. We will finish this conversation."

He continued, "For a long time, Mr. Mingan's leadership has concerned the Council. The Tribe recently re-elected him by a very narrow margin."

He looked at the young police officer. "Matthew here has been party to my thoughts on this, so..." He drifted a bit. It seemed his recent stress was becoming more physically apparent.

"Anyway, his passion has been the oil and gas project in which he is personally invested. Massive conflict of interest if you ask Joletta, a few others, and me. Many are afraid to speak out. We are not. Neither was my late sister.

"Mingan seems to have surrounded himself with some gruesome characters from the gathering company and now sports a personal bodyguard, a Non-Native bruiser named Sebastian Moran. Mingan has a lot to answer for to the Council. This is the truth."

* * *

"Dr. Sorenson, welcome to Alpaska. The Nation is pleased that you are visiting us, but let me say how sorry I am to hear that your brother has wandered off." The Tribal Leader extended his hand.

This line indicates a rehearsed cover-up. With whom do they think they are dealing?

"No, Chief Gray Wolf. You are mistaken. My brother is hard-wired for an extraordinary awareness of his surroundings. As I continue to explain, disorientation is not the case here by any means. Kick has been kidnapped in the very shadows of the Reservation. Of that, I am sure. Consequently, I want absolute assurance from you that it has nothing to do with any Tribal issues the Nu Ci Nation is currently facing, most notably with the oil and gas extraction industry.

The Tribal leader was extremely abashed by Kayne's candor and refusal to shake his hand. He took it as a personal insult.

"Mr. Moran, please leave us."

A gigantic white man in a business suit nodded and left Gray Wolf's office. I figured the brutish bodyguard would remain close, however.

"Please, gentlemen, have a seat, and let's get to the heart of the matter. Frankly, Officer Sechi, Dr. Sorenson, I am very taken aback by your insinuation."

I thought it was interesting that he knew who I was without any introduction. The Wolf has connections.

Kayne addressed the Tribal leader with barely controlled passion, "I do not regret my truthfulness at all, Chief. My brother's safety is paramount, and time is against us."

We remained standing, but the Chief sat back behind his desk.

"Officer Strong Bear, I'd like to take this meeting in private. You are dismissed."

"No, he stays," Josh said. "This is a police matter."

Mingan punched his office phone, and his assistant came on the line. "Cynthia, get Steve Mallory on the phone for me. I believe he is traveling. Use his cell number."

Looking up, he said, "If I am under suspicion, I want my lawyer in on this conversation."

"I would say right now, Chief Gray Wolf, you are indeed a person of interest. Both my brothers, Mitch and Kick, were challenging what they considered the regulation practices of Red Eagle Energies both from an economic and environmental standpoint. It is a matter of record. Each of them was an honorary member of the Tribe and had testified before the Council, Mitch, more than a year ago and Kick only a few weeks ago. My brothers are noted for asking the hard questions, Sir.

"Furthermore, your Environmental Officer and his report on the industry to the Council have conveniently gone missing. Tribal Council Woman Susan Walker, in her attempt to locate Jeron Adobo Jordan, now lies on her burial pyre as we speak. Murdered."

Josh shifted visibly.

"Steve here, Jake, what's going on?"

"Need you in on this, Steve. Some accusations were coming my way regarding the so-called abduction of Kick Sorenson just last night. Also, Susan Walker...."

"Wait a minute, Thomas Michael Sorenson, the owner of Aerie Valley and its subsidiaries? Holy Shit."

"That's the one, Steve. His brother and a police officer from Florida are in my office right now and are making some outlandish accusations."

Kayne ignored the legal counsel and continued to get in the face of the Tribal Leader. "I demand full access to the files for Red Eagle Energies and access to Jeron Jordan's office. I also want all communications regarding the Tribe's dealings with Kriegston Gathering. I will take up the matter of their records with them later today.

The lawyer on the phone said, "Ever hear of a search warrant or a court order, friend?"

"Truthfully, he only needs permission from the Tribal Council. Dr. Sorenson, I will poll the members with your request for an immediate vote." Josh said.

"Thank you, Councilman Walker."

"What about my authority here? I will not be countermanded," Gray Wolf sputtered.

"According to your Nation's constitution, your powers begin and end with your responsibility to convene the Tribal Council. Whether or not you have remained within that boundary, perhaps the Council should investigate along with some issues about conflict of interest. How are the profits coming in, Jake?"

The Tribal leader sputtered, "Under my administration, the Nu Ci have experienced great community and economic development. We have an initiative for student success with an expanded library and a program with the Boys and Girls Clubs of America. I am working on a tourism initiative that includes a Native learning center and museum, an RV resort, and a historic Native village.

"Admittedly, the oil and gas profits are falling a bit short, but this industry takes time to turn a reasonable profit. There are start-up and overhead costs to consider. Next quarter will...."

Kayne held up his hand, "It's been four years now, Sir. The oil and gas have been flowing copiously with no sign of letting up. Do you presume your people have little or no understanding of business?"

Josh stiffened perceptibly.

I jumped in with, "Chief Gray Wolf, we are not here to evaluate your performance and or even your political acumen. We need information related to the activities of Susan Walker, Jeron Jordan, and Kick Sorenson. Kick was last seen leaving the ceremonies here on the Reservation last night. His location and destination were known to only a few, and all were here in Alpaska."

Kayne ran a hand through his hair and used his left forefinger to tap Mingan's desk in emphasis. "This entire business smells of corruption, and we will uncover it, I assure you."

Gray Wolf jumped up and shouted for his bodyguard, who came through the door like a bear.

"Mr. Moran, these gentlemen are leaving the Reservation. Please escort them." The hired muscle moved behind Kayne and slapped a hand on the back of his shoulder.

"Let's go, friend."

I jumped to stop the assault by grabbing the offending wrist, putting Moran in a hammerlock, and stomping on the back of his calves. I reached into his jacket as he hit the floor and removed his gun from his shoulder holster. I tossed it to Matt.

Josh placed himself between Gray Wolf and me. He addressed the Tribal Leader, saying, "Dr. Sorenson and Officer Sechi are my guests. They are also here to pay their respects to my family. They remain on our National Lands at my family's invitation. They are assisting the tribal police in the investigation. You would be smart not to interfere."

Jake Gray Wolf was astounded by the shut-down of his bodyguard with such speed and indignity. Moran rose, angry and mortified. With nothing more to say, the four of us left the office of the blustering Tribal Leader.

***

"We have known for many years that Susan's profession was one filled with danger. She brought many to justice over the years. Like our Queen Chipeta, she was courageous and prudent. Still, her passing is a great sorrow for our nation. "

Elizabeth Rising Lark Walker was small and in her mid-60s. Her face was careworn, and her long gray hair was neatly styled. She had the bearing of tribal nobility, but the death of her firstborn had taken its toll. Sorrow and grief filled her delicate features. She stood with a small group of women offering prayers and songs before the body of Susan Chipeta Walker.

"Arapeen was my father, a great Chief, wise and strong. He brought this nation through tough times. Sickness and death were everywhere then. It was he who stood up to the White Fathers when they wanted more of our farmlands and mountain strongholds for profit. He defended our sacred land against those who would defile the earth."

Elizabeth Walker tapped the chest of her youngest boy. "My father taught my children respect for the old ways and the importance of contributing to the progress of our people. In many ways, the Spirit of Arapeen is still with us in this one. In many ways, he is wise and fearless."

Josh looked off to the horizon, slipping a gentle arm of comfort around his mother.

"But I worry about this Brave," She continued as she studied his face. "Red Cedar is *too* silent and intense. His work at Aerie has brought forth many of his gifts and strong medicine." She looked at Kayne and continued. "He has been very close to your family. That is a kind and loving thing."

The smoke from the fire rose above the preparation site as Elizabeth joined Kayne and me. We moved forward to offer our respects before the shrouded body of the Tribal Elder. I instinctively made the sign of the cross and said a short, silent prayer. Kayne ran a hand up onto my shoulder, obviously touched by my somewhat shy display of piety. It was a family thing and pretty much automatic at wakes and funerals. The Nu Ci women were murmuring behind us.

"She will be buried tomorrow on our land in a mixed service -- Christian and Ute. My sisters saw your Christian prayer sign and were impressed. Also, they rarely have seen a red-haired, white man. They believe you have a strong and brave spirit like the red mountain lion. As does this one with his eyes the color of a frozen sky," Josh's mother said.

"But you must go and find Dr. Sorenson's brother. He is known among us by his Tribal name, 'He who flies to the Sun.'

"Do not the Christian Scriptures say, 'Leave the dead to bury the dead?' Get going, both of you, but thank you so much for coming."

Kayne excused himself and headed over to Josh and Matthew to make our goodbyes. Elizabeth Walker stopped me.

"Officer Sechi, please forgive my boldness, but I speak on behalf of one who will not speak."

I turned back to the Elder.

"You are Two-Spirit, yes?"

"Yes, Ma'am, I am."

"And proud to be who you are. That is a good thing."

"Thank you. I have worked at it. Can't be any other way."

"Then you must help that one." Rising Lark nodded in the direction that Josh had gone."

"Your son is an authentic and well-integrated man, Ms. Walker. I have not known him long, but there is no struggle with his identity there as far as I can see."

She took my hand.

"No, Officer. I was not speaking of Red Cedar. My son has never questioned who he is. His father taught him the importance of standing proud and fearless."

She looked me in the face with an expression of grave concern.

"It is Strong Bear who struggles with self-hatred and longing in his empty nights. He must find peace in his soul, whether with my son or with another. If not, I assure you his spirit will die. What will remain will be a husk of a man, bitter, angry, and filled with shame. I have seen it before."

She pressed my hand forcefully.

"Help the Strong Bear to find the courage he seeks. My people need powerful men who are wise, brave, and loving. Men who fear no one, leastwise their own spirit. Strong Bear has much potential."

"I will do my best, Ms. Walker. You can count on me." Adding a farewell, I headed over to join Kayne.

Chapter Sixteen: The Resort
MARK GADARN'S NOTES

On the way back up from Aspen, we stopped at a scenic overlook. We made a picnic of Scott's provisions, reviewing our meeting with Joletta Golden Tree in the back seat of the Jeep. The museum project partners changed our meet-up to the Resort at the last minute. The storm had snarled traffic in the city, and since the Resort had done a quick and complete cleanup, it promised to be a better place for our meeting.

Rebecca and I enjoyed a short time together, eating and enjoying the winter views of the mountains before continuing the work of the day. I reviewed my notes and messages.

"I was copied on some local press inquiries into Kick's disappearance. He and his husband are huge in this community, statewide also. They serve on a slew of boards and state commissions. Aerie Industries, Inc. is one of the most profitable privately held corporations in the west."

Rebecca said, "Astonishing, considering the highly charged personal dynamics of Sorenson and Sons. Kayne keeps much of his private life to himself. I knew he had family in the US and Australia. I had met Kick and the father, but Kayne never mentioned the other brother or many of the details of his foster brother. He plays those cards close to the chest.

"I came across mention of the family when I was researching Colorado's art scene. Sorenson money is an essential resource here, Darling. It comes as no surprise that their father in Australia supports his sons' philanthropic interests."

I said, "Apparently so. I feel that the elder Sorenson must also be a real character. Anyway, I want to run interference with the media. They will want to talk to Kayne, but I can get him to issue a statement. He doesn't need this distraction right now. The main thing is to find Kick."

"Darling, I am feeling somewhat guilty. "

"Why?"

"I think we should be helping Kayne find his brother more directly."

"Talking boots on the ground? Tracking and evidence recovery, that sort of thing?"

"Possibly. This museum collaboration project can wait. Kick's life is most likely in danger, Mark."

I pulled her into my arms. "Listen, Rebecca. We must give Kayne and Nick the space to do that for which they are best skilled. Both are fantastic investigators. Kayne has assisted INTERPOL, for shit's sake.

"There are so many in on this, including professionals, friends, and community members. And now, the FBI. The issue is to keep from tripping over each other and delaying the finding of Kick. Kayne has set out the plan for the case. Our assignment is vital, and the information we got from Joletta is astoundingly essential. I emailed my notes to Kayne, by the way. He appreciated what we found.

"Let's keep our eyes and ears open and report to the good Doctor anything that may be helpful. If we stick to Kayne's plan, it will help him keep the investigation in proper focus. Media and community management, my girl. We have our assignments. Right?"

Rebecca responded, "I did get a text from Nick asking if we can get some intel while at the Resort about any hostiles."

She thought for a moment and then continued, "OK, so I thought I was the brains of this outfit, and you were the beauty, Darling. Such a hot man—when the gays keep checking you out, you've hit another level of babe."

"Yeah, Kick has few boundaries regarding hitting on the men, gay or straight. You know, if I were an experimenting man...."

She playfully swatted me and then moved closer for some smooching. Still, I resisted a bit, saying, "I am amazed by the extraordinarily revved libidos of you and your friends, beautiful. It's a hell of a lot of fun. But full-on, twenty-four-seven?"

"S' matter, big boy, am I wearing you out?"

I made a significant make-out move on my beautiful woman. To my frustration, she rebuffed my friskiness before we made what I would call "progress."

Rebecca sat back and said, "Perhaps you are right, Darling. To be continued. We do not want to be late for our appointment at the Resort."

Damn!

***

The exterior of the Aerie Valley Resort followed the same architectural design as the Lodge, heavily influenced by Frank Lloyd Wright's Arizona studio, Taliesin West. The modern landmark was perched high on a mountain bluff on the opposite side of the valley. Cantilevered main floors rose three stories on stone pillars. Above the central module, another ten stories thrust glass, wood, and stone in a beautiful design of cantilevered wings, balconies, terraces, and sweeping roofs swathed in snow and ice. The massive structure commanded a grand vista of both the Aerie Valley to the northeast and the village of Aspen below, with its three mountains to the southwest.

The ski runs snaked down from the mountains and ended at a grand stone patio at the rear of the building. The Resort had the appearance of being full up, and revelers were enjoying the amenities both indoors and out.

The grand entrance opened into a four-story atrium. A massive bronze sculpture group of a Native American man and a woman on horseback releasing eagles into the air above dominated the lobby's center. The title of the work was "Aerie," and the artist was from the Nu Ci Nation.

A Resort staff member led Rebecca and me to a third-floor private conference room. One can easily find that every space at the Aerie has an astonishing view of the earth, sky, and mountains. Pamela Tabbano from the Phelan Museum of Fine Arts and Adam White Fox Ryan from the Silverman Museum of Native American Art introduced themselves.

"Thank you for agreeing to switch this meeting to the Resort, Ms. Quinto. Our facility has been all but buried by last night's storm, but these media pieces will show you the highlights of our collections at the Silverman. Many of the historical works here at the Aerie Resort are on loan. As you may know, Mr. Sorenson serves on our Board of Trustees."

Adam Ryan opened the discussion for the Aspen contingency of the project.

We had decided not to mention recent developments regarding the Sorensons at this meeting.

Rebecca smiled as we exchanged greetings. "Mark and I haven't had the chance to see much of the Resort, but I have a message from the Director who promises to show us around after our meeting. I am eager to see the artwork here."

Pamela distributed a specially prepared portfolio and said, "I think you will find with these materials, in addition to the collection hosted here at the Resort quite compelling for a case for collaboration. But we should arrange a site visit to both the Silverman and the Phelan."

Rebecca provided our hosts with a set of DVDs made especially for the proposed project, showcasing the Fritcher Museum of Art collections in Ft. Lauderdale. Her materials also included a pictorial background of Native Americans in Florida and a compilation of possible local and national sponsors.

"So, we are here to talk about this project from the 500-foot level. By that, I mean, as Director and Chief Curator at the Fritcher, I represent my Board's interest in your respective collections. We feel that the Silverman and the Phelan are recognized for high standards of quality and have a reputation deserving of the public trust."

"Both of our organizations are very interested in working with Ft. Lauderdale to create new insights into heritage collections," Adam said, taking up a portfolio from the Fritcher. Pamela nodded in assent.

"Before we agree on a process for laying the groundwork for the exhibits and creating a tactical plan, let me put a few items on the table. In a project such as this, partners share what we collect to reach new communities, but there is another goal for us."

Rebecca used her tablet to summarize her spoken points. "We strongly feel that our engagement with your museum collections will provide a focus for American Aboriginal people to explore their unique history. We want to create an experience that supports scholarship and enhances group identity. So, we are committed to a collaboration in which Indigenous people will have a leadership role as curators with images, objects, and field materials that celebrate their history."

Man alive, can she cook, or can she cook?

I sat back in admiration as Rebecca did that which made her famous as a Chief Executive Officer -- organizing the community around a vision for celebrating arts and culture. After a bit, I resumed my note-taking, hoping that tracking the project would provide information for a press packet for the new exhibits.

Sensing that they were leaving me out of the conversation, Rebecca turned to me and said, "What do you think, Mark, Darling?"

"Well, I just got back from Syria, where regimes and forces from all sides are exterminating a people with a rich culture who may soon be wiped off the map. Not many worldwide know that or care to know what is going on in places like Falluja, Aleppo, and Daraya."

Looking at Adam and Pamela, I continued, "I know that Native Americans have suffered a similar genocide, forced removals, and atrocities. If you shed some light through the education component of your project on the near extermination and, in some cases, the total annihilation of native tribes and cultures, it will have a pan-cultural effect of raising awareness for these killings which existed in the past and continue today."

Adam White Fox said, "Your perspective on this project has much in common with the vision and mission of the Silverman Museum of Native American Art. Our initiatives include addressing racism, discrimination, and injustice through education, including the exposing of a biased reporting of history."

"The Phalen Museum also has a strongly interactive and educational component that seeks to support student and family learning. We have a history of programs directed at defeating prejudice, bigotry, and intolerance," Pamela said. "So, a multi-museum collaboration that highlights the history of dehumanizing the Indigenous People of North America and the injustices that are a part of their history...."

"And contemporary situations," Adam added. "I think we are on the same page with this one, and it sounds exciting."

"Well, we are off to a good start. We seem to have alignment from the big-picture level, so what remains is to hammer out a preliminary plan for approval by our respective boards," Rebecca said. "A bit like dating, don't you think, Mark?"

"Yes, it looks like you have the opportunity for some good partners, my dear, but the devil, as they say, is in the details."

"Of that, Darling, I am well aware."

She addressed our hosts, "Let's arrange for a visit to your galleries for next week. Currently, a few other issues have come to light that demand our attention. And you both must promise me that you will take refuge from all of this... this winter stuff, with a trip to paradise and a visit to the Fritcher."

"Definitely. I hear that your new exhibit is off the charts, already making history... *Seed Blood*."

***

"What are you drinking? Ms. Quinto, Mr. Gadarn?"

"Please, Darling, I am Rebecca. He's Mark, and the Aerie Resort is absolutely stunning."

Nathan Clifton was an affable man in his early forties. One could tell he enjoyed his job as the General Director of the Aerie Resort. His wife, Monica, Director of Operations, was also very welcoming and jovial.

We sat at the bar of Kestrel, a five-star restaurant here at the Resort. The bar was jumping with cocktail hour revelers waiting for a table. The venue opened on the spacious back patio of the Aerie Resort. Its lofty two-story windows looked out to a Blue Diamond ski run that ended only yards from the low patio wall.

Turning to the bartender, Rebecca said, "Darling, can you make a Marie Laveau?"

The handsome mixologist smiled, but before he could respond, Nathan interrupted. "You folks need to try our signature cocktail. Danny, four Yum Kaax."

"You got it, Sir."

"Sounds great, Nathan, but I need to drive us back to the Lodge. Please make mine a Guinness. Damn, can you excuse me, please? I have to take this."

I stepped into the lobby, searching for a private spot. We succeeded in directing the media to me on the Sorenson disappearance. Local news broadcasting groups were sending crews to the Lodge, but I told my contacts to switch the press conference to the Resort. I texted Kayne to let him know and headed back to the bar.

"Mark, I was just saying how the Native art loaned to the Resort is astounding, Darling. I need to talk to their Board of Directors requesting some loans for the planned exhibit."

"That should not be a problem," said Monica. We have many backup pieces available from the Silverman and from the Alpaska Reservation itself. Mr. Kick Sorenson has taken Mitch's place on the Resort Board and will surely support your museum's request for anything."

"Anything? Hmmm." Rebecca's eyes could not hide her thoughts.

Our drinks arrived. Rebecca inspected what appeared to be a variation of a margarita. She examined the rim but was surprised.

"Are those...

"Ants. Yes. Delicious," remarked Monica as she sipped her Yum Kaax.

Rebecca took the dare and delicately tasted her cocktail. She sat back, saying, "Actually, not bad."

Nathan turned state's evidence on the strange concoction, "We have a friend in Cancun who is the owner of a hot new bar and eatery named *Hormigas*—'Ants.' He named this drink after a Mayan god. Made with mezcal, corn juice, and lime. In Mexico, the glass' rim is salted and rolled in ants. We make the Aerie's ants from chocolate -- the hot kind, laced with chili."

I stole a sip and nodded my approval. "Truthfully, eating real insects is quite a delicacy."

Nathan said, "Hey, just before we met with you, we caught a brief news clip that Mr. Sorenson has had a road accident. What's happened? Is he OK?

I spoke up. "Kick has been declared by the local authorities as missing since the car he was driving was found by the side of the road last night. There is a full-scale investigation that will include the FBI. His brother, the criminologist Kayne Sorenson, put together an unofficial investigative team to consult the authorities. That call was from a local TV station. They are on their way here with cameras. I am serving as a spokesperson for the family."

Rebecca asked, "Nathan, Monica, you worked closely with Mitch and with Kick. Any leads for us regarding troublemakers?"

The Cliftons exchanged glances. Monica drew close. "Mitch was outraged from the start at the opening of the Landrose ICE Processing Center on government land on the north rim of the valley up by the Uncompahgre Gorge. He fought hard to stop it. Landrose is a for-profit detention center for immigrants. It is part of a program of the U.S. Department of Homeland Security. Opened about a year ago."

Nathan added, "Feds pay big dollars in the business of immigrant incarceration. Supposedly, Landrose provides humane environments under national standards, but there has been some talk, right, Mon?"

"What have you heard," I asked.

Nathan continued, "We had a few folks on our staff enter a training program at Landrose. We ended up rehiring them a few months later. They did not like what they saw. Their guard program hired Danny here."

Rebecca raised her glass, and the young barman came over.

"Another round?"

"Not yet, Darling. The Yum Kaax is divine, by the way. But how about a little information?"

Looking at the four of us, Danny responded, "How can I help?"

"What's going on up at Landrose, Dan?" I asked.

Visibly uncomfortable, the bartender responded, "Well, Sir. I dropped out of the guard program. But I signed an agreement stating that I would not talk about what I saw."

Monica said, "Danny, you can trust these folks. They are the good guys."

"Yes, Darling. We are looking for someone, and that place appears to be a good start." Rebecca put a reassuring hand on the young man.

Danny looked around. Other bartenders and barbacks were handling the crowd, so he found time to talk under the guise of filling an order for another round of the exotic cocktail.

"Well, OK. It's not right what Landrose is doing to those people, anyway. They are mistreating them big time. I will admit I got into it because of the cash, and I thought it would be a minimum-security thing, not like a prison or anything. Man, was I wrong. They are punishing those folks, not just holding them. Talking some extreme abuse."

Nathan added, "There have been some rumors of folks dying up there while in custody. I also hear that they are neglecting the medical needs of the residents."

"Aren't they being monitored by the government?" asked Rebecca.

"See, that's just it, Miss. There is this other part of the facility that is off-limits, back inside the mountain. They hide the troublemakers back in there when the inspectors come. I stumbled on it once and got into a bit of trouble. That's when I decided it was time for ole Danny Boy to check out. Mr. Clifton was good enough to take me back."

"Had no choice. No one makes a Yum Kaax like this guy," Nathan said.

"They also make the inmates cook and clean at the facility. I think they are saving a lot of money that way."

"No doubt adding to their profit margin," I offered.

Nathan nodded. "Mitch and Kick Sorenson were huge critics of Landrose and went public on a few occasions. Mitch had some folks from Congress come here and meet with the Center's administrators, who attempted to defend the facility over reports of abuse. The backlash was an accusation that Sorenson interests were trying to get Landrose out and acquire the property. Pretty much a joke. Landrose is on property leased from Clarion Military Base."

Monica stated, "It's interesting. Traditionally, Immigration and Customs Enforcement has put its jails in border states close to where most refugees were caught. However, a more aggressive demand for detention center contracts under the present administration has increased their presence in central states like Colorado. And ramping up the arrests of illegals is profitable for private companies --big windfalls for the outfit's bottom line."

My journalism genes were on fire. I took notes like a madman.

Danny went back to serving customers. I got the feeling that he felt the less he heard about his former employer, the better.

"Bring this around to Kick, Darling. I assume he was just as vocal as his husband was. Any recent altercations with the Landrose folks?"

"Yes. Kick had been getting some anonymous threats, and then, two weeks ago, there was an unscheduled meeting here in Kick's office. The Director of the facility and some of his goons just barged in. Things got very aggressive. Nathan and I were concerned.

"Turns out, Kick was working with surveyors and county engineers. The Palouse River is on two stretches of land, the Nu Ci's and Aerie's. To put it simply, Kick and the Aerie Trustees were in the process of turning off the water at Landrose."

"Water is a huge resource in Colorado," I said.

"Right," Nathan responded. "It's gold. Kick told me the Landrose folks were super pissed off about his planned interference with the water interests at the north end of the valley. The Landrose parent company was in talks to build a hydroelectric plant at the gorge with government funds – cheap energy for their business. Aerie Industries Inc. went to court to obstruct the project. Those bastards were actually going to reroute the river."

Danny cruised by and placed another beer in front of me. He took my hand to shake it, saying, "My shift's ending, and I just wanted to say it was nice meeting you folks." I took my hand back to find he had pressed a note into it.

"Danny Darling, your ants are spectacular. We'll be back."

I glanced at the message. *Investigate the dumping.*

"Folks, I need to get press-ready here. Gotta have a few minutes to get some copy together. Monica, Nathan, you all are about to be invaded."

"Monica, have you seen Jess? Is he in his office today?"

"Yes, I saw him when we left our offices. Jess Harper is our marketing and media person. You all might want to round up."

"Sounds good."

As we left the bar and thanked the Cliftons, we passed the lobby's center sculpture group again.

"I want that," Rebecca said.

"A bit big for your condo, my girl."

"No, Darling, I am just going to take them up on their offer. This beautiful work will be the centerpiece of my new exhibit at the Fritcher, *Tribal Blood.*"

Chapter Seventeen: NEO

"Scott Boy, how you know this stuff?"

"Long story, Gints. Can you keep a secret?"

"Gints is closed box, boy. All is secure." He made a key-in-the-lock motion at the center of his lips and then tapped the side of his head with an index finger. The muscular Latvian sat close to his new buddy and watched as Scott flew through page after page on his laptop, typing and saving files.

"I think you mean 'closed book,' Big Guy."

Both smiled.

"So, I got into some trouble in my college days, to tell the truth. I was doing some illegal hacking to pay off my college expenses. I was pretty close to going to jail when Mr. Sorenson stepped in on my behalf. Paid my legal fees and got me off with a slap on the wrist. Came to work here as his chef and head of the Lodge hospitality. Every so often, I helped him with technology for Aerie Industries, Inc.

"Kick is good man and hot boy. Like Big Doctor brother."

Scott put a hand on his crush. "Easy there, studly. I was talking about Mr. Mitch — also a looker. I know he is not Sorenson blood, but Jesus, those men from Oz are magnificent stud animals. You should see the father. Total silver fox -- muscled DILF for days."

"Means, sexy what you said. "

"Oh, yeah. DILF means, "Dad, I'd Love to...."

Scott's phone chirped, interrupting his explanation.

He hit Speaker. "Hey."

"Scott, what have you and Gints found?"

"Hey, Dr. Kayne. So, yeah, we got some research stuff. Also, we received the Susan Walker files from Joletta Golden Tree and the files on the Alpaska Oil business. I am putting it into an encrypted report, but I can summarize our findings if you want. You OK to talk on this line?"

"Should be fine. Nick and I are heading to the Resort. There is a gathering of the media there. The press is looking for the story on Kick's disappearance. Mark has prepared a statement from the family, which I reviewed and approved. What do you have?"

"On the companies, we researched a total of 73 sites so far, and I want to dig further because there is deep shit on this. Oh, sorry."

"Go ahead, Scott."

"Kriegston seems to be linked to a Native American oil and natural gas scandal in South Dakota. There were disappearances and accusations of murder for hire. Not known as Kriegston there, but some of the same people involved. Looks like corporation names were changed along with some firings and identity changes. People just dropped off the face of the earth. But it's these guys, for sure. The report gives more detail than I am expressing. You get a meeting with them?"

"No, we went to their offices, but Renault was not there. His blokes would not say where he was or when he would return."

"Dr. S, there is something else. There is a connection between Kriegston and the NEO Group."

"Who are they?"

Gints reached across and pulled up Scott's notes as Scott handled the call.

"NEO is a multi-national based in Serbia with their fingers in a lot of pies. Talking prisons in many countries of all three security levels, immigration confinement centers, minimum-security detention centers, and mental health and residential treatment facilities, all under national contracts. The immigration wave hitting Europe is big business, Sir.

"Also, lotsa lawsuits against these guys, kickbacks, bribery, you name it. The NEO boys run Landrose up on the northern ridge of the valley."

"Is very dirty, Big Doctor. NEO is very shady. Many dumb goons working for them. They have security division -- looks like club of criminals."

Nick's voice came through with, "Gints, anything else suspicious about NEO?"

"Oh, hell yes, Niko. Boy Scott find more crap. Is evidence you need. I let him tell it."

"So, and this took some time to uncover through quite a few backdoors, NEO has a subsidiary that provides security services, aka arms, to militias and armed forces across the globe. I was able to get a connection to a group that works in the Middle East, Schlachtross. Mark may know of them."

"I am sure he does, Mate. Good going, both of you.

"I have some other folks and companies I want you to investigate and include on your abstract for us. We came across some groups who were unhappy with my brothers. I will send you the list. Please review them and let me know what you think.

"We are coming up to the Resort, so...."

"Wait, Dr. S, I need to ask you something important."

"Yes, Scott, what is it?"

"I can get us deep intel, but not legally. I want to hack NEO and its subsidiaries. I can cover my tracks, but I'll bet there is stuff there that may lead us to Kick."

"Do it, Lad."

"Yes!"

Scott did an air fist pump and a fist bump with his research bestie, Gints.

"A few more items, and then we have to go. The FBI is meeting us at the Resort. They will want to impound Kick's computer and phone-- the phone he had with him and his computers there at the Lodge. That is fine, but we need to keep your laptop and these research files out of their hands."

"Got it. Yes, let's keep these files for your eyes only."

"Right, I can let them know what we have turned up without them seeing your actual trail or fingerprints. Am I clear, Mate?"

"Crystal, Sir."

"So, send the report using encryption and secure the laptop."

"Got it, I know just the place."

"Last thing. My father arrives tomorrow morning at Aspen–Pitkin County Airport from Sydney at 9:30 AM. Please arrange for him to be picked up and to have his usual suite at the Lodge."

"Will do, Sir. Aspen Airport – got it."

Nick came on. "Hey Buds, how's chances of some dinner there tonight? Possible? I gotta get this man to eat something."

"All is arranged, Niko. Trust Gints and Scott. He has big catered meal in preparation."

"Yeah, just let me know how many and consider it on. Crimefighters need fuel, right?" added Scott.

"Definitely."

"And most especially, *jāšanās*," said Gints as he nuzzled the young hacker. "You can bring laptop, hot boy."

"Go back to work, guys."

Despite themselves, Kayne and Nick ended the call, chuckling.

Chapter Eighteen: The Fourth Estate

NICK SECHI'S JOURNAL

The security officer greeted us as I rolled down the window.

"Do me a favor and wait until I can get an escort for you guys. Stay in your vehicle, please."

The Resort was ablaze with spotlights that swathed the enormous and sprawling building. The approach and circular drive, the mountain background, and the ski slopes leading to the rear and west sides of the hotel glowed in the winter evening. Overhead, snow clouds threatened yet another storm, beginning its approach over the western pass into the Aerie Valley.

Media vans filled the drive to the Resort, many with their satellite feed discs extended for breaking news reports. I noticed local and national broadcast logos, a BBC affiliate, and Mark's company, CBN. Skiers and guests had spilled out of the Resort. They gathered under the extensive front portico as temperatures began to drop in the early evening.

"Seems Kick is a very popular man in these parts," I said.

Kayne responded in a level tone while staring at the sizeable crowd. "The whole family is notorious on three continents, my love. And there is much more to come in that regard."

He turned to look at me, not smiling but with ice-blues flashing.

"This way, Doctor Sorenson and Officer Sechi. Leave the truck here. We will get you through this crowd." I had rolled the driver's side window down at the approach of Matthew Strong Bear.

We stepped out of the truck, and the entourage of Native American police officers closed ranks around us. They set up a formation that resembled a "flying wedge" football play that pushed our way through the mob of news personnel and onlookers. I gripped Kayne's hand, but he seemed to be very steady as we approached the growing turmoil on the steps to the Aerie Resort. It was then I realized that he was scanning the crowd for suspects.

"Kick, when did you turn up?" shouted a microphone-wielding reporter who had apparently not done her homework.

She pushed her mic between police officers into Kayne's face. I reached into my parka pocket, removed a pair of Ray-Bans, and handed them to Kayne. He put them on. Other press members turned cameras and light bars in our direction, shouting questions as we made our way toward a podium marked with the Resort logo.

As we mounted the steps to the landing in front of the entrance, the crowd pushed against our bodyguards. I fell against Matthew Strong Bear, who had taken the point of our offensive play, losing Kayne's hand. Matthew turned and went down on one knee to help me back into the formation. We continued to push toward a space near a motioning Rebecca.

Mark, flanked by Rebecca, Stefan Connelly, and the Aspen police representative, was in the process of reading the statement from the Sorenson family to the sea of microphones and cameras. Monica and Nathan Clifton greeted Kayne. He introduced me to them and Resort's Media Director, Jess Harper. Next to Monica was a handsome young man in Resort livery. He nodded in a silent man-to-man greeting. Mark did not attempt to introduce Kayne to the noisy crowd.

State Trooper Connelly had previously updated the press on the progress of the investigation into Kick's accident. He fielded a question about the connection of the missing Mitch to his husband's disappearance.

"We believe they are related, and the Mitch Sorenson investigation is ongoing at this time. Recent developments have cast a new light on that case."

"Officer, any connection with the recent murder of Susan Walker of the Nu Ci?"

Stefan shot back, "At this time, we have not determined a connection other than the Sorenson family's support of the Native American Community here at the Aerie."

A reporter with the logo of a notoriously conservative broadcast company on his microphone yelled, "So, given that the three victims were homosexual, is this a religious act to protest a deviant lifestyle? And are we talking hate crimes here?"

I bristled visibly and started toward the reporter, but Kayne put a hand on my shoulder and said, "Easy, Red."

Something was happening in the driveway to the Resort that got the attention of those of us near the podium. A group of protestors had begun to form up, restrained by police at the far side of the driveway.

"Holy fuck, Westboro Baptist. Those assholes move fast." Rebecca looked at the Cliftons.

Monica said, "I got an idea. Come with me. You too, Danny. The three of them elbowed their way into the lobby.

Stefan put off the reporter with a statement that the murder of Susan Walker was not yet considered a hate crime. Neither was that classification applied to the disappearances of the Sorensons.

Mark was about to call on another reporter when a Native American woman stepped forward, spoke softly to Mark, and stepped in front of the podium mics.

"I am Joletta Golden Tree, Elder of the Nu Ci Nation and partner of the late Susan Chipeta Walker. The White Singing Bird's blood was shed on sacred land, and it is on our soil that we will bury her tomorrow.

"Speaking for my people and with the authority of Officer Matthew Strong Bear, Chief of Police, I assure you of the cooperation of our people with the local and state police. My Nation has released a statement to the press on the extraordinary contributions of Ms. Walker to the community and her support of law enforcement."

The protestors across the drive had organized and began to raise their "God Hates Fags" signs. A few placards stated that the Sorensons and Susan Walker were in hell. I thought, *Holy shit!*

Elder Golden Tree continued loudly, "As to Dr. Mitch and Mr. Kick, the Nu Ci have had the privilege of welcoming these two remarkable men as honorary members of the Nation. Their support for my people has been generous, compassionate, and a confirmation that we are all equal partners on the sacred earth here in the Aerie Valley."

As shouts from Westboro Baptist began to ring out, three semi-tractor trailers roared up the drive led by an Aerie Resort security vehicle with flashing lights. All attention turned to the clamor of the arriving caravan rolling up in the driveway. The massive semis entirely blocked the phalanx of homophobes from the Kansas church protesting on the opposite side of the drive. They revved engines to drown out the hate-filled shouting.

Monica Clifton stepped from the passenger side of the security cruiser to the podium. She announced loudly to the crowd, "Sorry folks, our supplies have to get in. We have guests to serve." The expression on her face was that of the proverbial cat who swallowed the canary.

The young staffer, Danny, stepped from the first semi and walked to the cab of the second truck. The driver had come around and helped the dazzling passenger to the asphalt. He kissed the hand of a radiant Rebecca Quinto, who gave him a quick cheek kiss. She waved to the cameras and reporters who flashed and recorded the diva's unconventional arrival. The two other drivers also received chaste smooches from the exuberant woman. She twirled for the cameras, one hand in the air, and took Danny's arm. He escorted her to the podium, where a glowing Mark Gadarn engulfed her.

Reporters were murmuring, "Who is she? Let's get this on tape."

I looked at Kayne to find him roaring with laughter. He caught his woman bestie in a hug-up and a triple-cheek kiss.

Chapter Nineteen: Caged

His first thoughts upon regaining consciousness were confused and sluggish, making little sense. The surroundings flipped in and out of focus.

This cell is like where they held my ancestors when they transported them to Botany Bay from Britain. Was it 250 years ago?

His father used to tell stories to his young boys about their criminal heritage. In the hazy awakening, he fought with old memories.

Wow. Where did that come from?

Kick sat up on the bunk and rubbed his head. He had a headache and was dizzy, drowsy, and had trouble concentrating. His shoulder hurt.

Fuckers shot me up with something.

He looked over his cell. Stone blocks, one window high up, and a metal door with a small opening at the floor and another at eye level. Both were closed. Squinting into the dark above him, he could see pipes running across the ceiling. He lay back, arms behind his head, and rested a bit more.

Kinda cool in a "Count of Monte Cristo" way. Just have to wait for the guy in the next cell to die, and... Jesus! Making no sense, Dude. Try to focus.

He stood up slowly and felt the malaise begin to subside. The place was cool but not cold. His parka, hoodie, gloves, and boots were gone, so only his T-shirt, heavy socks, and jeans remained. He slipped a hand down the waistband of his jeans and into the pouch of his jock. Satisfied, he withdrew his hand.

Turning around, he saw the camera where the ceiling met the wall that held the door. Opposite, in an interior corner, stood a sink and a toilet.

These guys must be fucking kidding me. This place is gonna be a bleeding piece of cake.

I need some fucking attention, Mates. Come to Baby.

Kick sat back on the bunk and pulled off his socks. Next, he stood up and quickly tossed the mattress to the floor. Upending the cot, he leaned it against the wall under the security camera, scrambled up, and slipped one of the socks over the camera.

He quickly put the bed back with the blankets rolled up to resemble a sleeping body. *How many times back home did we pull this stunt to fool the 'govies?'* Kick then raced to the corner. Using his incredibly strong finger power and well-coordinated body, Kick crawled up the wall using the chinks between the stones for his ascent. Defying gravity with the smallest of finger holds, he moved up the vertical surface to hang on the pipes above the door, looping his legs and arms into the framework to take the weight off his arms. Kick dangled, attached spider-like, and awaited his flies.

***

The inmate's leg throbbed. The rod, plate, and screws in his right femur ached when the barometric pressure dropped, and the winter storms that swept through the valley were setting off days of pain. The internal structures held the bones in place. The enormous cast kept the leg immobilized. After a few setbacks, including infections in the wound and incisions, he was on the mend, a fact that he made every attempt to disguise.

As he healed over the last six months, he was aware that he had lost weight – the food wheeled into the cell was almost unpalatable. At first, he was fed intravenously until his head injuries improved. Lack of exercise had left him feeling weak and exhausted most of the time.

The hospital cell was shabby, and he rarely saw medical staff after regaining consciousness after the accident. He woke to find himself in what he believed to be a prison hospital room with his leg set and in traction, his head bandaged, scrapes and cuts treated with stitches, dressings, and bindings.

In the first three months of his incarceration, his interrogators were fewer. The pain medications obscured his thinking. He resisted the strong lights and intense questioning whenever they moved him into the almost featureless cell. Now that he could no longer fake confusion and amnesia, the number of sessions increased, and the elements of torture doubled, leaving him barely conscious and bathed in sweat each time.

***

"Where are the socks?"

Silence. Then, "Mate, I am amazed by your persistence. We have been at this for weeks. My answer is still the same. Sod fucking off."

Darkness completely shrouded the inquisitor, who sat in the shadows beyond the circle of the spotlight. He had never revealed himself. Three assistants in scrubs and masks managed the details, bringing him in on a gurney, removing his hospital gown, attaching the electrodes, and turning the current on and off.

One of the assistants pulled the prisoner's head back by the forehead and, with the other hand, forced down his lower jaw. The second subordinate jammed the thick rubber bit into his mouth, depressing his tongue and keeping his teeth apart. Even with the mouthguard, he was able to scream. It was a combination of a pain-filled roar and a garbled, anguished shriek. Later, the darkness came.

The third flipped on the current, and Mitch's body arched and came off the gurney.

Chapter Twenty: "I Accuse"

NICK SECHI'S JOURNAL

Kayne shook his head. "No, this is one case. I am sure of it. Only one."

He stood at the inside balcony end of the third-floor sitting room, overlooking the Great Room below. Kayne spoke to those who followed him up for after-dinner drinks in the cozy, more informal parlor, complete with a blazing fireplace.

He had his back to us, staring across the open area below and through the glass walls that fronted the second and third floors of the Aerie Lodge. Dinner companions and staff were lingering by the fire on the second floor or mounting the stairway to join us. The entire backdrop was a glistening cascade of falling snow caught in the building's exterior lights as another storm rolled into the valley– forecast to reach ultimate intensity after midnight.

Scott had catered the dinner from the kitchens at the Resort. He served as the host for the moderately large gathering and added staff to cover the event. Gints happily worked the bar. In addition to Dr. Sorenson's private investigative team members, Kayne had invited the Cliftons, Danny Grant, and Jess Harper from the Resort. Officers Connelly and Strong Bear, with Captain Robert Pauley from Clarion Base and Joletta Golden Tree also joined us at the Lodge.

Kayne ate little, excusing himself to scroll through his phone, reading Scott's report.

At the evening's start, Rebecca and Stefan Connelly had introduced FBI Special Agents Kristin Kura and William Ras. "I reached out to Stefan, Darling, after I contacted our friend Special Agent Mary Chaffee, who sent us these two wonderful 'Feds' to assist our investigation."

"I had to make a formal request," Stefan explained. "In a missing person case, as a matter of cooperation, the Bureau will, at the request of a state law enforcement agency, make available their Identification Division and the FBI Laboratory. These will be most helpful. We have evidence samples for which we need DNA analysis in this case – the bone fragment found on Susan Walker and the cloth found where Mr. Kick Sorenson disappeared."

Kayne used the evening gathering to update the FBI on his brother's suspected kidnapping, with State Trooper Connelly and Native Police Officer Matthew Strong Bear in attendance. I remember watching Connelly's body language and thinking, *This dude is not happy we brought in the Feds. Interesting.*

I walked over to Kayne with a snifter of brandy. He declined, but wordlessly, I insisted that he partake in the relaxing quaff, golden and swirling in the transparent orb. I stood next to him as he turned to the group and elaborated.

"Four victims, one nefarious plan to cover up instances of high corruption and gross abuse of power." In a loud and rather dramatic voice, Kayne added, "I accuse Kriegston Gathering of misrepresenting their financial statements made to Red Eagle Energies. They did this to cover their embezzlement and misappropriation of funds.

"Kriegston is guilty of direct commercial bribery of public officials and money laundering. Also, I accuse them of the murder of Susan Chipeta Walker, the disappearance of Jeron Adobo Jordan, and the kidnapping of my brothers, Thomas Michael Sorenson and...."

Kayne paused theatrically before continuing. He gulped the brandy and said to the astonished guests, "... Dr. Mitchell Andrew Sorenson."

"Dr. Sorenson, are you saying that Mitch is alive?" Nathan Clifton spoke over the murmuring of the assemblage. I looked at Kayne in disbelief. We had rehearsed his speech during the trip from the Resort to the Lodge, but his revelation about Mitch was not part of it.

On returning from the Resort, I advised caution over his insistence that we make some trouble. He had argued, "Nick, we have no time with this. Kick's sanity hangs in the balance — perhaps even his life. This Kriegston business has many tentacles. I want to do an Émile Zola on this and make my series of accusations public, hoping to scare the criminals out into the open and delay endless hours of investigation."

His reference to Zola referred to the great writer's public accusation of the French Government in the Dreyfus Affair in his 1898 open letter,

"*J'accuse...!*" He was forcing the issue in a public setting to flush out the "Big Bads."

"After tonight, I plan to have Mark release a statement to the press and stoke the firestorm.

"We are moving from inductive reasoning here to deductive methods. Rather than build a case from evidence to theory, or in other words, hypothesis expanding analysis, we will begin with the accusation and compile the evidence to support the argument."

"Kayne, what if you are wrong?"

He raked back his forelock while sitting in the passenger's seat next to me and said, "Highly improbable, Mate. You know my methods." He had turned to face me as we rolled up the steep driveway to the Lodge.

"In the unlikely event that I have erred, we will have had the opportunity to practice our martial arts against some very belligerent blokes. Would love to go a couple of rounds with that Moran chav. I can guarantee there will be no legal accusations of slander."

At the Lodge that evening, Stefan Connelly insisted Kayne reign in his bravado of allegations against Renault, Gray Wolf, and Kriegston.

"I want to remind you, Dr. Sorenson, we need evidence, not theory. And to that effect, I have the report on the hand cloth found near the abandoned SUV that Kick was driving -- small traces of chloroform. But honestly, this is a pretty weak connection to Kriegston."

"Just as I suspected. Please note, my friends, chloroform is not suitable for overpowering a victim. It is used to make transportation or other manipulation of an overpowered victim easier."

Kayne continued, "Kick would have struggled. Often, a victim is put into a sleeper hold to keep him unconscious during the transport from the kidnapping site. Given my brother's excellent physical health, strength, and training, we must conclude that Kick was injected with an anesthetizing drug like ketamine or thiopental sodium. Therefore, it is logical to say that the abductors were at least three in number, one to distract Kick and at least two others to render him incapacitated."

Rebecca said in a serious tone, "Kayne, you are sure Kick is alive."

He spread his hands in a revealing gesture, "Yes, my dear. Kick and Mitch are alive but not well, I assure you. Two cases of abduction."

I wondered if his remark was more hopeful than factual. I said nothing.

Kayne continued. He moved around the group who were either standing or seated. His audience was wholly fascinated with the inductive reasoning of the renowned criminologist and his charismatic presentation style.

"So, abduction and not murder is the only logical scenario. My brothers are alive but restrained. So, I ask what would cause a corrupt corporate entity and its leaders to strike out at community members. What is the cause of such incarceration with impunity? Rather, one should ask, what is it that the villains most fear?"

"Discovery."

"Correct, Ms. Golden Tree. Fear that someone will reveal their crimes in a way that involves hard evidence of their illegal activities, not just rumor or hearsay. The violence we see addressed at the four victims under consideration – extreme in at least one case, suggests someone has discovered a record of their illegal operations.

"But the murder of both my brothers would point the finger directly. So, we have a series of unfortunate accidents --an icy mountain road in Vale, an individual known for his erratic behavior lost in a snowstorm near Aspen.

"From eye-witness accounts and reports, we have the following: Mitch and Kick were outspoken regarding the suspected misappropriation of funds from the Nu Ci oil business. It was Mitch who began to ask for greater accountability from the Tribal Leader regarding the financial arrangements between Red Eagle Energies and Kriegston Gathering. Cause for making a hit list? Most likely.

"But they are botching it—two kidnappings, two deaths."

He held up four accusing fingers.

"To quote Chaucer, 'Murder will out.' Secrets of misdeeds will eventually be disclosed. I believe the killing of your partner, Susan, was unintentional – very, very sloppy. Homicide is messy."

As Nick, the "Law Enforcement Guy," I thought, *He is forcing a confrontation to crush Kriegston and find his brothers.* Somebody in this room will quickly bring Kayne's aggressive message back to the bad guys.

Kayne was flushed with excitement but retained the calm demeanor of a professional consulting detective.

"Elder Golden Tree, I want to say how much we appreciate your being here this evening. The obsequies for Susan continue at Alpaska tonight, and her burial is the day after tomorrow. Speaking for my family...." Kayne placed a hand on my back and continued, "I want to thank you for your help in attempting to locate my brothers."

"Dr. Sorenson, Susan's council files add fuel to the case against Kriegston. She was troubled by their refusal to be honest about the company funds. Susan reported her fears that they knew more about Jeron than they were willing to admit."

The room was silent.

I clenched my fists and thought, *We are going to get those mother fuckers.*

Kayne continued, "We also know that my brothers were opposed to the Landrose incarceration project. They called out all initiatives seeking to exploit the Aerie Valley for recreational and industrial development. Like the Nu Ci Nation, Aerie Industries, Inc. is committed to preserving the land. This very outspoken position created enemies with the Landrose group, Kriegston, and the development companies. Much animosity resulted in hostile confrontations."

I spoke up, "Kayne, they have something."

Kayne turned to me, as did everyone else. He said, "Please elaborate, Nick."

"Mitch came into possession of the hard evidence that Kriegston is swindling the Nu Ci. Guaranteed. The company wants to suppress that evidence, but he and Kick refused to turn it over – bingo, the motive for a double kidnapping. Additionally, the Big Bads remove significant opposition to Landrose and the snarky environmental issues related to the development of the Valley. Mitch and Kick are nowhere to be found, but if they kill them, they fear that the incrimination evidence your brothers have gathered will be made public.."

"Then we need to get our hands on those financial records," Stefan Connelly stated.

I noticed some interesting things going on in the group. Mark took notes on his phone and prepared Kayne's next statement for the press. Scott was amazingly uncomfortable. I thought it had to do with Gints and the young bartender from the Resort, Danny Grant, cozying up at the bar.

Kayne had no more to add, it seemed, but Stefan said to him,

"Dr. Sorenson, I would like to assign some of my men to keep you safe. If this is the pattern we think it is, you could be the next Sorenson in their sites."

"Thank you, Officer Connelly, but that will not be necessary and may actually impede my progress."

The Colorado State Trooper grimaced, about to insist.

Kayne continued with a smile, "Officer, do you see that man behind the bar? The one who stands 6'6". Yes, that's the one. He bench presses 315# as a warm-up. Mr. Bergovic trained in the Latvian army as a hand-to-hand combat expert. He will not allow anything to happen to me, I can assure you."

Gints looked up, shot a bicep pose, and grunted. The Trooper was impressed.

Kayne put his hand on my shoulder and continued, "Besides, I have my own police officer whose temperament is as feisty as his hair color. No worries.

"But I'll tell you who could use police protection if you are so inclined. My father is arriving from Australia tomorrow morning. I am sure he would be a far more critical Sorenson to protect."

Way to distract the useless police, Kayne, I thought.

Officer Connelly next addressed the gathering.

"Folks, I want to ask your complete confidentiality on the facts of this briefing. Leave the strategies to law enforcement."

Nodding to the FBI Agents, he added, "We have the resources to get the job done. Leaking our plans will only impede our progress to locate the missing and bring their captors to justice."

Knowing well the snail's pace in which enforcement sometimes works, I thought, *Yes, but we do not have the luxury of time, officers.*

***

"I need to talk to you, Dr. Kayne." Scott pulled Kayne and me aside as the other members of the dinner gathering broke into small conversational groups.

"I was securing my laptop as you suggested and came across this." He handed Kayne a small, wooden, rectangular box. It had a glass top and fit in the palm of one's hand. The bottom of the box had a picture of a baseball diamond.

"It was in a very secure place. Where Mr. Mitch kept his most confidential files. Very unusual."

Kayne turned the item in his hand and handed it to me.

"It's a toy. The object is to get the tiny silver balls in the holes over the bases. Why would Mitch have something like this? What do you make of it, Nick?"

I thought for a moment. Then looked up at Kayne, taking the strange item.

"Wait a minute. I've seen this before."

I turned the toy in my hand, trying to remember.

"Dana Andrews, the detective who was struck by the lightning bolt – in love with the beautiful Gene Tierney – "Laura," 1944. He played with one of these."

The fans were amazed by my knowledge of classic films.

Kayne snapped his fingers, "Of course, Nick. Mitch left this as a clue --the clock."

Moments later, Kayne returned to the third floor, concealing a small rectangular device and motioning us to the Aerie Lodge's office just off the living room. After seeing the three of us leave the gathering, Rebecca asked Mark to join her in crashing our little huddle.

"Exactly like Clifton Webb's secret compartment. The hidden latch in the back of the clock and 'pop' — literally, the smoking gun. Excellent, Nick." He handed the external drive to Scott.

"Dr. Sorenson, as part of my duties here at the Aerie, I serve as Mr. Kick's clerical assistant. He has no patience for technology or filing, so I do that. I also manage the records for the ranching business down at the Horse Palace. I know where all the files are kept. This is something new. Dr. Mitch used to do all his own record keeping, but when he died... sorry, disappeared, Mr. Kick asked me to step in."

He turned the drive over in his hand.

"This is Dr. Mitch's, I am sure."

Scott moved to the desk and powered up Kick's computer. He attached the external hard drive. Mark said softly, "Yeah, the dingus that will put them all behind bars. Anyone want to bet?"

Looking over Scott's shoulder as the computer accessed the drive, I cussed, "Fuck."

The screen displayed a flashing warning, "Caution, these files are encrypted. Please enter your password. The files contained herein will be deleted after ten minutes of unsuccessful attempts to log in." A counter ran down the seconds and the minutes.

Kayne sighed and stared at the flashing screen.

"Darlings, we are so fucked. I could be anything." Turning to Kayne, Rebecca continued, "So, your brother, Mitch, encrypts these files, right? And the failed attempts safeguard was created to prevent the bad guys from accessing the hard drive."

Mark picked up the narrative, "Right, so couldn't there be another copy on the odd chance that this drive eats the files when the criminals can't open it?" He ended up looking at Scott.

"No, Sir. If there are, I am at a loss as to where to find them. I am afraid this is all we have to work with."

"Not good," I said. I watched the countdown. "Kayne, Scott, do you have any idea?"

Kayne said nothing.

Scott said, "If this were Mr. Kick's drive, it would be easy. Everything he has operates on the same password -- his name and the six digits of his date of birth. Disastrous! Dr. Mitch's security is more high level."

Kayne stood and walked to the window wall and stared into the snowy night. The counter on the screen flew through the digits. As restless as we all were, no one said a word.

After what appeared to be a long silence, Kayne turned from his meditation and addressed us.

"My foster brother was in love with my brother when Kick was six years old and Mitch was eight. He was the only one of us who could keep Kick in line and prevent him from going off the deep end. Even our father was at sixes and sevens trying to keep his namesake from his very destructive and erratic behavior. Teachers, tutors, and coaches all deferred to Mitch when Kick's manias would drive us all crazy. Mitch was... is... a magnificent older brother, despite Kick's often obstinate resistance to letting anyone make decisions for him or control him."

He walked as he spoke and stood next to the computer, which was rapidly going into a failsafe mode with the encrypted files. The timer said 17 seconds remained.

Looking at Scott, Kayne continued his monologue, "Yes, Kick is a glorious disaster. No one knew this or lived that more than Mitch. Regardless, Kick remains the absolute love of his life."

He turned to the keyboard and said the letters as he typed them.

"H O T M E S S"

Kayne pressed Enter.

The file opened.

Chapter Twenty-One: Sweat

Pacing the floor, the very frustrated guard turned and addressed his supervisor.

"He's a fucking acrobat or some such shit, Mr. Carson. Hanging down from the damn ceiling like a bat. Dropped down and wiped out two security guys. They went in because the cell camera had been compromised."

"How far did he get, Thompson?"

"After he knocked out the guards, he took their guns and managed to get as far as the interrogation rooms two floors above. We went into a major lockdown, but he managed to get around all our maneuvers. Seems he was headed to the roof of the main facility. He was shooting out security cams on the floors and in the stairwells."

"Interesting. One would have thought the boy would have tried to exit from ground level. How was he stopped?"

"The bastard turned back and tried to get to the other inmate. Something must have tipped him off about the whereabouts of our special guest. Three guys with tasers finally dropped him after he tried to physically take them out."

"Where is he now?"

"Solitary – smaller, only enough room to lie down. Must be taken out to piss and shit. According to our intel, that boy will go psychotic soon without his meds. If we are going to pry some information out of him, it should be soon while he can still think."

"I want him used in such a way that makes the bigger one crack. I honestly think that our Batboy doesn't have a clue. Why would anyone entrust him with important information? His behavior is too erratic, and that detracts from his trustworthiness."

Director Carson continued, "For fuck sake, keep him secured. For our next round of interrogation, Dr. Sorenson may change his mind after watching as we... shall we say, annoy his crazy gay buddy? I want it intense and prolonged."

Thompson leered at his boss. "Gonna fry us another faggot."

***

"This is our place of purification and rebirth. Our Braves have prepared themselves for battle since time immemorial in lodges such as this. Here are the strengths and powers of earth, water, fire, and air. We do not come here to talk about God. We come here to talk to God."

Josh Red Cedar Walker and Matthew Strong Bear dismounted from their horses. They met the speaker standing before two concentric earth mounds topped by a blazing bonfire. The outer one, partially encircling the site, represented the moon, and the inner one, with the fire at its center, the sun. Joseph Brave Horse, the spiritual leader of his people, was joined by six Braves of the Nu Ci Nation, all in Native dress. The group moved close to the bonfire to prepare Red Cedar and Strong Bear for the ceremony.

Two of Josh's brothers helped the newcomers disrobe and don simple loincloths painted and beaded with tribal symbols. Josh's had his totem of the cougar, symbolizing leadership and courage. Matthew's cloth was decorated with a bear, representing power and adaptability. The medicine of the totemic animals, aka spiritual energy, is evoked to help each Brave connect to the Great Spirit.

The pair were instructed to sit on stumps near the fire. The Braves opened pots of paint and striped the face and body of Matthew Strong Bear. They trimmed his hair with leather strips and feathers. A red, split feather indicated that the police officer had been wounded several times for his people.

One of the members unbraided Josh's shoulder-length hair and, with a hunting knife, soap, and water, sheared his straight, black locks so that only a center strip of his long hair remained. They then plaited leather strips, beads, strips of rabbit fur, and feathers into his warrior cut. His single red feather signified that he also had been wounded in combat for the Tribe. They painted his handsome face and muscular body in the cold evening illuminated by the bonfire. Others painted the two horses.

Behind the ministering Braves, the approach to a round building not far from the fire had been cleared of snow. It was carpeted with dried sage, sweetgrass, and brahmi, all healing plants. As the Braves were prepared and invited to walk to the lodge beyond the fire, the Shaman, Brave Horse, sang:

Guided by the Cougar and Bear, search for purity of spirit, will, and body within yourself.

Do not let others make your path for you.

It is your road and yours alone.

Others may walk it with you, but no one can walk it for you.

Draw the Spirit of Fire deep into your grief to purify the body and gain power.

My brothers, believe that you will depart here with the strength of spirit and body to do what needs to be done.

Brave Horse handed Josh the sacred ceremonial pipe brought from the fire. Josh drew the smoke and passed the instrument to Matthew, who did the same.

At the end of the path was the dome constructed of 16 pine trunks placed in a circle and covered with hides so that no light penetrated. The sweat lodge represented the womb of the universe from which souls are created anew.

The Braves entered the enclosure, and four warriors brought seven Grandfather Stones from the fire to the center fireplace inside the lodge. Brave Horse came last and took his place beneath a pair of eagle talons.

The brothers sat in a circle on sacred sage within the lodge, passed the pipe, and then the door was closed. The men sat close, Josh and Matthew touching shoulders with no space between them. Soon, their bodies dripped sweat in an atmosphere hotter than a sauna. The last of the fresh air faded as the entrance was closed, and all light was extinguished.

It was hot and pitch-black as Brave Horse's voice broke the silence of the Lodge, telling stories of the grief of the Nu Ci people. He called upon the earth and sky. He sang of the east, where the Sun brings light to all creation. Someone began to beat a drum in the lodge as the Shaman chanted of the thunder spirits of the west who represent death and choose when it's a person's time to leave the earth.

More than once, a participant poured water on the Grandfather Stones, and searing steam filled the space. After the first hour, one Brave threw open the door. He would do that three more times throughout the ceremony for a total of four, representing the ages of humanity described by tradition. Each time, the heat was reprieved by the fresh, cold night air. Subsequently, more stones would be brought in to intensify the heat and start the next round.

During the final hour of the ceremony, Josh started to speak and sing in the old language. He invoked the spirit of his sister for whom he suffered and what he was required to do to ensure her safe passage to the spirit world. He sang of the purity of his intentions and the obligation of tribal blood.

Matthew's head spun in the smoke and heat. In the intense heat, he felt his mind and body descend to a trance-like dream state. He became choked with emotion for the Brave who was next to him. He felt Josh's searing hotness as their sweat mingled in the dark space. Tears ran down Matt's face, and he was glad no one could see.

As Josh concluded his song, he slipped his arm around Matthew. Matt felt the sobs that shook his brother Brave. Pulling his face to his, the Tribal Elder kissed the young Native officer in the dark heat. They both felt the physical and emotional exhaustion of the ceremony as one spirit.

After several hours, the fourth and final time of the lodge's opening allowed the men to step into the night air. Their bodies glistened with sweat emerging from darkness into the light of the fire. All impurity was left behind in the lodge. They helped each other pour jars of ice-cold water over their heads, cascading to the ground, removing dirt, grime, and heat. Animal skins were used to dry wet bodies.

Josh and Matthew dressed and approached the Shaman with thanks. Brave Horse blessed them in prayer as they departed the sacred space. Neither spoke.

As they approached the cut-off on the trail that would take Josh to his home, both men pulled up and turned to face each other in the moonlight. Josh Red Cedar dismounted and stood next to the horse of

Matthew Strong Bear, saying nothing but looking up into the face of the young Brave.

Receiving the silent answer he sought for the unspoken question, Red Cedar reached up and took the reins of his buddy's horse. Turning, he walked both horses up the trail to his house.

* * *

Not much remained of the last watch of the night. The sky brightened with morning light on the day the Tribe would bury Susan Walker. Matthew Strong Bear arose from the bed and looked at the body of the naked warrior who slept soundly next to him. They had helped each other remove the paint and the headdressings during their passionate lovemaking. They made love as strong Braves, drawing power from each other and exchanging affection.

He remembered the savage look of his man as they came together in liberating and shameless desire. There was a fury in Josh that was perceptible as they coupled. He made love like a man possessed. When they finished, Matthew fell asleep on the chest of his warrior and friend.

* * *

"No."

"You are awake?"

"Yes." Josh reached up to his bedmate and pulled Matt to him. "Stay a bit. Don't leave."

Oddly, Matthew, for an instant, thought of Kick. *Does Josh conjure him when we are together like this?* He tried fruitlessly to put those images out of his mind as he returned to Josh's bed.

After, they dressed for the funeral and plaited the Native trimmings back into their hair. Josh applied black, red, and yellow ceremonial paint to his face and his partner's.

Tribal Blood

Chapter Twenty-Two: Energy
NICK SECHI'S JOURNAL

"This is anything but just a second set of books," I said. "Although these reports show some accounting stuff that looks hokey and reveals a good deal of theft, the real shocker is this other set of files about the environmental issues. It seems like the author was preparing a very detailed report that is horrific and incredibly incriminating.

"What do we have, Nick?" Kayne asked.

"These are the reports of Jeron Jordan, Director of Environmental Affairs for Red Eagle Energies. It begins with an incident report wherein Chief Gray Wolf requests that the Environmental Officer remove oil socks from his personal property at Alpaska.

"Until about a month ago, Kriegston was dumping hazardous waste on Nu Ci sacred lands. Jeron reports that in a conversation with Chief Gray Wolf, the Tribal Leader asked Jeron to do him a favor and remove the discarded oil socks from his property before the arrival of the EPA Inspectors. He also instructed that the dumpsites were to be kept secret."

Kayne explained, "Oil filter socks are used to strain liquids during the oil extraction process."

"It looks like Jeron kept notes connected with the incident. They concern his interactions with Gray Wolf." I read aloud, "I was called into the Chief's office, and he said to dispose of the socks as a personal favor to him and be quiet about it. He also repeated a request that Jeron remain loyal to him in all his dealings."

Rebecca said, "I wonder why he did not speak up about it then and there. To the Council, I mean."

I scrolled through files, trying to piece together information.

"Here, wait. So, OK. These documents show Jeron was an avid defender of the reservation's land, air, and waters. Looks like he considered the regulations of the Environmental Protection Agency in writing the Tribe's environmental codes but acknowledges that times were changing in Washington with the new administration."

"After President Obama, the Keystone XL Pipeline project was given the go-ahead immediately after Trump's inauguration," Mark offered.

"And First Americans not like this, Mark Gadarn? Oil is big money." Gints handed Mark another beer.

"Just that, Gints. To cross the Missouri River, the pipeline passes through sacred Sioux land. They are protesting that decision by Washington as a violation of treaty rights."

"When did you get so smart, Gorgeous Darling?" Rebecca said. "I love that 'First Americans' designation." She tried to tousle Gint's Marine high and tight but ended up rubbing his skull affectionately.

"You are not only one who is beautiful and smart, Rebecca. Gints no pouch."

I looked up from the computer to see Mark, Rebecca, and Scott, stunned to silence and about to burst into laughter. None of them was about to correct the muscle beauty's mistake. Yes, he was indeed no slouch. And his ah... pouch... well...."

I cleared my thoughts and said, "According to this, Jeron was reluctant to speak up. He kept his mouth shut, fearful of retribution. There is a personal annotation to the memo."

I looked up and said, "It seems there were some covert threats regarding his family."

Scott hastily remarked, "Like fuckin' mobsters. Oh, sorry."

Mark read over my shoulder, "There have been other instances where individuals have spoken up, and they have been kicked out, basically fired."

He concluded, "I would imagine the whole atmosphere around Red Eagle and Kriegston was pretty chaotic and paranoid at this time."

At the office window, Kayne raked the pesky bang off his forehead and spoke to the darkness outside, "There is something more here. I am convinced of it. Nick, we need more. We are facing an enemy who will do anything to satisfy their greed.

"They are up to something more heinous than simple murder. Besides, making a case against Kriegston based on environmental pollution will not get us the urgency required to stop them and save captive lives. There is a more evil power operating here."

I felt his anger rise.

"Bleedin' wankers!"

He shouted the derogatory phrase and slammed his hand on a credenza.

I looked up from sailing through the reports trying to bookmark essential passages and opening other folders, thinking we were both feeling the fatigue of the lateness of the hour. Kayne came back from his outburst looking withdrawn as well as physically and emotionally exhausted. He was having a tough time keeping his concern for his brothers from showing. Rebecca stood up and took her friend into her arms.

"Easy, Darling. We'll find him. We'll find them both. Kayne, you need to get some sleep. We have Susan's burial tomorrow, and then there's Ace. I suspect he will be quite a handful."

Kayne looked at his team, struggling for words.

"My friends, I want to let you know how much I appreciate your efforts to find my brothers. It is evident who the enemy is we face -- this group of greedy conspirators who show no limits to their criminal behavior.

"I feel I owe you an explanation for my procrastination. As frantic as I am to rescue them, I cannot risk my brothers' lives by behaving in an overly rash manner. Forcing the enemy's hand without controlling the outcome could be disastrous as they are capable, as you have seen, of murder most foul.

"The Sorensons are a bit of a handful, I will admit that. And yes, I am afraid the *paterfamilias* is his own type of crazy/eccentric. You're in for a treat, Mates."

"Fasten your seatbelts, Darlings."

Gints leaned in for a translation, and Scott said softly, "He means his father is bonkers."

Scott assured his boss' brother, "I got him, Dr. Kayne. Nine-thirty-five a.m. at the Aspen airport. Gints and I will get him settled in here while you all are at the funeral. I will have a good meal for him when he gets here to the Lodge."

"Thanks, Scott."

"Dr. Kayne, Matthew Strong Bear asked to borrow White River. Josh Walker's request, actually."

"Fine, Scott. You did spectacularly today. Thank you. One last assignment."

"Anything, Sir."

"Now, see if you can take care of all that horniness," Kayne waved a hand at the handsome, Latvian muscled boy. "I'm talking, a few world-class shags, lad. Think you can handle it?"

The boy blushed and beamed.

Gints bounded to his feet and gave Kayne a hug up. "We try not to make too much noise tonight, Big Doctor. Good night, Niko." The beauty leaned over and gave me a smooch before exiting with his adoring companion.

"Before the three of you Darlings, have a similar attack of midnight testosterone, I am taking this hot man. Furthermore, I make no promises on the noise level, Darlings. I scream; he roars." She gave Kayne and me goodnight kisses and started to the door. Mark patted me on the head and shoulder-bumped Kayne.

Looking into Kayne's eyes, Mark said with sincerity, "We got these assholes, *fy ffrind, peidiwch â phoeni.*"

Rebecca took Mark's hand and softly kissed his handsome cheek while hugging Kayne with the other arm, "Welsh is so sexy, Darling. Come on, I want some private lessons."

172

***

As the door closed, I yelped softly.

"Holy shit, Kayne. Look at this." I pointed to what I thought was a report filled with a mish-mash of chemical figures.

He bent over my shoulder, read the screen, gently squeezed my traps, and said, "Bloody hell, Mate. The socks are radioactive!"

Tribal Blood

Chapter Twenty-Three: Red Center
NICK SECHI'S JOURNAL

I held his shuddering, sweat-drenched body against me, his face lost in shadow, wet black hair spilling down on my face. His mouth was opened in a lustful struggle for breath. My release came next, intense – a full-body clench, matching his breathlessness with a gasp of primal passion into his ear.

I pulled Kayne tighter against me, legs and arms entwining. I wanted to possess him entirely, mindlessly, and utterly, an oasis of desire amid the quagmire of the events in which we found ourselves. One hand on the small of his back and the other on the back of his head, bodies pressed together, I was overcome with a longing to never separate.

Our sex talk had changed to post-orgasm babbling, slowly making some sense. Between breaths, I managed to say, "I love you, big guy. You and me, I ... Kayne, I can't tell you how... Ohh, yeah."

He covered my mouth with his and returned my body caresses, his panting chest against mine, his strong hands working my body.

"Nick, you are amazing, my love. We are quite a team. I need you... more...."

He gnawed my neck and shoulder and went back to some heavy kissing. We rolled over and began a second, more tender round.

✶✶✶

Kayne was standing naked at the sink and shaving. Since I first saw him naked, I remembered how much I liked the blue and black panther tattoo that snaked down the back of his left shoulder onto his back muscles. And then there was "dat ass"—a narrow waist that gave rock-hard gluteals with soft tan lines mounted on thick quadriceps and tapering calf muscles.

I tried to listen despite the sound of the shower and the distraction caused by my usual friskiness.

"Be warned, my love. He is the alpha prime in the hierarchy. Always has been. He is fiercely protective, highly assertive, and never a game player. Given the cards he has been dealt, Ace is deserving of much admiration. His sons and his business are his entire world. He cares little for anything else, I am afraid."

"I've handled a few alphas in my day, Kayne. I like that he gives no ground to 'arseholes,' as you blokes say."

He turned from the sink to add, "He thinks that Americans are batshit crazy. A bunch of bludgers, as he calls them. Never did like the fact that the four of us went dual on the citizenship thing. Mother's last gift before she left."

I stepped from the shower, and he handed me a towel and turned to splash cold water over his handsome face.

"I am looking forward to meeting him. Should be fun." I tried to keep the sarcasm out of my voice.

"Ace is as self-made as you can get, Nick. Former Aussie Marine. Never say 'ex,' by the way. He is passionate about his military service to the 'Lucky Country' and, like most of his comrades in arms, believes it is a vocation. He is very patriotic. Ace is a very passionate and vocal man."

This ought to be good, I thought.

As I toweled off, Kayne asked, "Know much about the 'Red Center' of Oz, Mate?"

I slipped my arms around him. "No," I said, reaching past him for the razor. *Clothing optional lecture on Australia's topography is coming up.*

"The Northern Territories is a very arid land with a confluence of three deserts right around Alice Springs – said to be the exact center of the country. The soil and the climate are iron-hard, as are the inhabitants.

"Ace grew up at a time when camel caravans still brought people and goods to Alice. Our family's cattle station is relatively big – 20,000 km². Almost the size of Belgium -- sheep, cattle, camels, and horses."

"Damn, Kayne. That is huge. American ranches are not that big."

176

"Australia is the second-largest exporter of beef in the world, only surpassed by Brazil. The Woop Woop... sorry, the Outback is so dry and the vegetation so sparse that it takes a lot of land to support the industry. My ancestors bought up a lot of territories and grew the industry.

"As an undergrad, Kick did a paper on our station. It was quite good. My family's style of ranching is very different from America's. The animals are mainly wild and have minimal human contact. Ace believes in no chemical treatments and, with great respect for the Aboriginal peoples, works hard to preserve the ecology of the land."

"Life must have been pretty isolated when you were growing up. I mean school and all."

"Isolated communities in AU have a government service called 'The School of the Air.' Historically, it started out as radio classes. Satellite television and computers took over when we were ankle biters... ah, children. During the last years of secondary school, three of us were sent to boarding school in Perth. Eric attended a military school in Europe, but that is another story.

"We had a 'govie.' That's a tutor who supervised our studies and tried to keep us in line. Ace had his hands full with the station most of the time. And was often away on musters. To be truthful, we went through three tutors – poor sods. As I said, we were quite the handful."

Kayne fussed unsuccessfully with his signature fetlock, trying to tame it into a more controlled look before giving up.

"A muster?"

"Yes, days and weeks when the cattle needed to be gathered in, branded, get their meds, that sort. Da has a small army of ranchers working at the station. It is a tough life, and he did not want any of it for the four of us. Although, it appeared for a while that Kick would end up back there. But Ace was dead set on the University of Notre Dame. He is an alumnus. His Da sent him to the US because he wanted to clear his son's lungs of the dust of the GAFA."

No words here, just an expression of WTF on my face that he observed in the mirror.

"Great Australian Fuck All – the Outback, sexy boy." He gave me a chaste kiss and a 'bad boy' ass swat, saying as he left the bathroom, "Get used to it, Kiddo. Bring your electronic translator."

Chapter Twenty-Four: Smoke

The sky had cleared over the snowy mountains and glistening buildings and tipis of the Nu Ci Village. Kayne, Rebecca, Mark, and I stepped out of our SUV some distance from the site of the funeral rites. We followed members of the Clan, many in traditional ceremonial dress. They wound up a steep path to a hilltop clearing marked by a tall pillar of smoke up against a high mountain ridge to the north. Below lay the sweep of the Reservation, hills, and dales covered in snow. Over the southern cliffs, the Aerie Valley unfolded against the horizon. Native Americans and other members of the Valley and Aspen community, including Earth Rae Jordan, gathered on the flattened tor to send the spirit of Susan Chipeta Walker to her rest.

The space around the funeral bier had been left open. Chairs were arranged in a circle for members of the grieving community on the north side of the hill. The body, wrapped in a simple shroud, was positioned so that the head was in the west and the feet to the east. The bonfire blazed behind the head of the deceased. A special section reserved for the family was on the south side. Blankets on the ground took the place of chairs.

The Walker family and the leaders of the Tribe were dressed in the traditional garb of the Ute branch of that ancient people, the Nu Ci Nation. Guests of the Clan, including members of other Native American Nations, were received by the Tribal Elders. A war-painted Matthew Strong Bear, in his police uniform but with his hair loosened and trimmed Native style, introduced us to members of the Tribe. We again expressed sympathy at the loss of their sister.

Joletta Golden Tree, Elizabeth Rising Lark, and those I took to be women of the immediate family arranged personal items around the body. These were meant to ease Susan's journey into the next world. Recognizing Kayne and me, the women stepped over to welcome us.

"We are honored by your presence, my friends," Elizabeth said softly. "Our daughter, sister, and wife..." she took the hand of Joletta as she spoke these words. "... will pass over from this world of tears even more peacefully knowing that friends of our people share our grief." Susan's three sisters and two brothers also acknowledged us in welcome.

Matthew led us to join the other guests. He pointed to the remains and said, "The body is oriented to face the rising sun as she is lifted up. As her soul leaves the earth, she will be guided by the spirits of the Tribe's ancestors who come forward during this time to lead the life force of the departed to paradise."

Mark asked, "I understand the Nu Ci would not allow an autopsy."

"My people believe Susan's spirit will leave us through our traditional ceremonies. The family and members of the Tribe must help her to cross over. Cutting open a body will not allow the proper release of the spirit after death."

The young Brave continued, "There is another matter that must be resolved if the soul of our sister is to find rest in the Sky World beyond the Northern Lights."

Kayne said, "*Lex talionis*?"

"Yes, Dr. Sorenson, the law of retaliation. The Christian Bible puts it as 'an eye for an eye.' For us, blood revenge is a private matter between the family of the victim and the assailant. In these times, revenge killing is not condoned. It is outside the law, but I am afraid that this weighs heavily on the spirit of the Red Cedar."

Earth Jordan asked, "Do all Native American people believe in an afterlife?"

Matthew Strong Bear answered, "It can vary greatly from tribe to tribe. Many traditions speak of the souls of the dead passing into a spirit world. These souls occasionally communicate through dreams or through the channeling of the shaman. Others have a different idea of the afterlife, often presided over by a god of death. I like the beliefs where dead people become stars or part of the earth or are reincarnated as new infants in the family."

A Christian priest, accompanied by four Native altar servers in white surpluses and black cassocks, came into the circle in the company of the Tribal Shaman, Joseph Brave Horse. The latter wore the elaborate dress of the Medicine Man. One server slowly swung a smoking censer.

Another had a bucket of holy water and an aspergillum to sprinkle the body. The third, a young girl, held high the pillar of a lit candle. The last child, almost smothering in his long cassock, lofted a pole capped by a Native-style Christian cross.

I asked Matthew for another explanation.

"Susan and her family have been Catholic for generations. They practice a mixture of our beliefs with Western faiths. Susan's burial will have elements of both her religious traditions. The children are Nu Ci, part of Susan's extended family."

Strong Bear continued referring to Josh Walker. "Josh has the strongest medicine here today. He has been prepared to be the Tribe's spiritual leader for his sister's burial. Brave Horse will guide him through the ceremony as a representative of his family and of the community." He pointed to the arriving Tribal Elder.

The assembly turned silent, and its attention turned to a horse and rider accompanied by a white dog who approached the ceremony from the west through the clouds of swirling gray smoke. Relatives and friends parted to allow the arrival of Josh Red Cedar Walker astride his stallion. They emerged through the smoke like a vision of grief, strength, and revenge.

Josh was dressed in black buckskin chaps and vest, biceps banded with leather strips, each with hanging red feathers. His long hair, now shaved to the skull on the sides and spiked on top, hung down to the center of his back. A lone red feather trimmed the end of his leather headband. Josh's handsome, stoic face was striped horizontally with black, white, and yellow paint.

The Warrior was accompanied by White River. The dog focused his full attention on his master. Her tail drooping between her legs, White River followed the ghostly horseman into the place of ritual.

As he dismounted, Josh removed his sister's spirit shield, which was attached to his saddle. With Joletta, his mother, and White River, the warrior walked to the bier, raised the emblem to the sky, and placed it on the body.

The dog sat at attention next to the bier. White River raised one paw up to the stretcher as if to say, "Can we go home now, Mom?"

Josh stepped back, raised his arms skyward, and sang a throat-sobbing, plaintive lament to his dead sister in the ancient language. His rich baritone rose and fell in heart-breaking lamentation. A lone drummer took up the hypnotic cadence until the last notes died on the cold morning air.

The priest began the Catholic prayers for the dead. The family members brought forward a large white pall embroidered with the Christian cross and Native images. With it, they completely covered the body. The attendants moved the spirit shield to rest on top of the covering below the cross. Brave Horse added charcoal from the bonfire to the censer, and the dense, sweet smoke of the incense rose over the assembly.

The priest sprinkled the pall with holy water and intoned, "With this water, we call to mind Susan's baptism. As Christ went through the deep waters of death for us, so may he bring Susan to the fullness of resurrection and life with all the redeemed."

He circled the bier, moving the smoking censer up, down, and over the deceased. He prayed, "O God, whose mercies cannot be numbered, accept our prayers on behalf of your servant, Susan, and grant her an entrance into the land of light and joy, in the fellowship of those who have gone before her."

Readings from scripture and native lore preceded a grief-filled elegy given by Joletta Golden Tree. The woman prayed that the assembly would be filled with the spirit of courage and fortitude of their dead sister in the face of all adversity. After memorializing her spouse's life, the grieving widow invoked the spirits of Chief Arapeen and the Ute Elder, Chipeta, Susan's namesake. She asked that they guide Susan's soul to the paradise of the south.

Drums took up again, and Strong Horse began to sing. Josh removed his vest and joined his brothers and brothers-in-law in a dance before the bier. Other voices joined Strong Horse as the family women moved forward to join the Braves but off to the side. Some waving smoking bunches of sweet, white sage.

Matthew Strong Bear stood, removed his jacket and uniform shirt, and joined the men dancers next to Josh. The entire assembly was wrapped in grief expressed in song, dance, music, prayer, and smoke. The sight, sound, and smells were vibrant, hypnotic, and intoxicating.

After a time, the ritual abruptly stopped. Entering the circle from the north was the Tribal Leader with an escort of five Non-Natives. I recognized one of them as the bodyguard, Sebastian Moran. Another was Officer Stefan Connelly and his deputy. Gray Wolf seemed to be looking for his place of honor in the assembly.

The funeral liturgy stopped abruptly. Josh strode forward and shouted in the Nu Ci tongue at the newly arrived men. Matthew Strong Bear pulled a ceremonial spear from the ground near the bier and walked to stand next to his brother Brave. Kayne and I moved to stand between the unfolding incident and Earth, Mark, and Rebecca. Mark leaned over and whispered to me. "That guy is the Director of Landrose. His name is William Carson. And the other guy you know, Renault from Kriegston. Interesting."

Josh took the spear from Matthew and continued with, "You are the reason my sister is dead. You are not welcome here."

Moran made a move, but Gray Wolf held out a hand to restrain him. He stared at the sweating, panting, and angry Brave who had disrespectfully called him out at an assembly of the Tribe. He moved his gaze from Josh to Matthew and spoke what must have been an insult as he pointed to the two of them.

Josh raised the spear threateningly but held back. Connelly's right thumb flicked the strap off his holstered gun.

Chief Gray Wolf said, "This is not finished, Red Cedar."

He looked over the gathering. The animosity of the group for the Leader was palpable. Gray Wolf turned and led his men out to the murmuring of the crowd.

Matthew touched his friend's shoulder and led him back to the ritual, which continued with more prayers and blessings. As the family members raised the pallet beneath the body to begin the procession to the place of internment, two women members of the family brought blankets for their brothers, Red Cedar and Strong Bear.

Josh came over to us and spoke in ceremonial style, using the ancient sign language to accompany his words.

"My friends, please join my family as we bring my sister to the place of her body's rest in preparation for her spirit's journey to the sacred paradise."

Kayne spoke, responding with the signs of the ancient language.

"Red Cedar does us a great honor. Thank you."

The cross-bearer and the Catholic ministers led the gathering, followed by the family bearing the litter, which contained the remains of Susan Chipeta Walker. The path wrapped around the hillside and had been plowed free of snow. No one seemed to be bothered by the cold. Once away from the bonfire, the air was bright and clear in the morning sun. Besides the priest, we five were the only Non-Natives in this part of the ceremony.

***

The internment at the burial caves was short and straightforward. The family added personal items to the grave after placing the body into a pine box on a low shelf carved into a niche of the vast cavern. More prayers and songs mentioned the return to the earth of the body and the soul's journey to the place of no sorrow or grief. Around us were the other gravesites of the Tribe in similar alcoves and recesses.

Elizabeth Rising Lark Walker and members of her family spent a few moments after the service at the grave of Chief Arapeen. Kayne wandered around the cave, observing the secret recesses and passages that extended deep into the mountain.

A small fire was lit before the cave's mouth, and the mourners began the walk back to the Village. White River broke free from the family and ran back to the mouth of the burial caverns. As departing mourners turned to watch, the faithful dog laid down in front of the opening. Then she sat up and raised her head heavenward.

Susan Chipeta Walker's final mourner that day was White River.

The dog broke forth in a pitiful howl.

Chapter Twenty-Five: Strong Bear
Nick Sechi's Journal

Gints stayed at the Aerie. I wanted some one-on-one time with Matthew Strong Bear, and Gints preferred to hang with Scott Iverson.

What was it that this young man kept buried in his heart?

The dogs were excited, especially White River, who needed to be distracted from her depression. I brought Chouko along, but he surrendered his lead dog status and deferred to White River's expert tracking skills. I wanted him along as another level of security. His breed excelled at defensive watchdog skills. I feared the 'Big Bads' were out and about in these mountains. Folks who were edging for a confrontation -- a fight or worse.

Matthew Strong Bear had an excellent rapport with White River. Up at the mountain road turnaround where Susan had met her demise, Matt showed the dog the plastic bag Susan used to transport the human remains and a sweater from Jeron's office. White River sniffed the items and thought about it for a moment before taking off down the hill.

Leaving Matthew's patrol car at the turnaround, we dashed behind the canine tracker. About three-quarters of a mile down the road, White River disappeared around a bend. The snow had been cleared from the road and shoulders, but the dog was nowhere to be seen.

Matthew called her, and Chouko barked. I said, "*Kanojo o mitsukemasu*, Chouko. Find her." The Akita dashed to a snowbank on the cliff side of the mountain road with his curled tail wagging.

White River wedged her head out of a gravelly hole in the snow and barked conclusively. Chouko danced around her and found the other end of the culvert to join her in her hiding place. We followed.

"This drainage system was set up to control water runoff from the road and the mountain slopes above on the other side of the road. You can see by the size of the conduit the water run gets very heavy.

"If we believe White River, she and Susan found the bone here. But there is no sign of additional remains, so...."

I joined in. "The bone most probably washed down from above. Let's start by tracing the runoff there." I pointed to the uphill opening.

We emerged and began our search.

The temperature in the afternoon sun had dipped slightly below freezing, and runoff was plentiful. A glistening sheet of water stretched across the asphalt further uphill to be gathered into the stone-lined ditch feeding the culvert. We backtracked the water stream and came to a cleft in the mountain rock. Snowmelt spilled forward and down. The runoff trench was steep but wide enough for the four of us to scramble up its dangerous rise. The dogs clambered up first. White River was taking the point with my "Beautiful Butterfly," Matt and I following.

Matthew was more sure-footed than I, despite my athleticism. In my favor, Florida is flat terrain. A few times, as I lost my footing and landed on my ass in the shallow water, he reached back to help me.

"There is a small volume of water here today. Not much force," he said.

"The weather this winter has been so erratic. Cold and snowy, followed by brief spells of spring-like warmth. We had some driving rain at the beginning of January. There have been some mudslides in this area with enough of a gushing flow to push a small bone forward among these pebbles to where it got caught in the debris in the trench below us."

Agreeing, I said. "Then we may find remains near the source of the stream."

As we continued up the steep slope, I found myself thinking about the dynamics at the funeral this morning. The burial rites of the Nu Ci people were a deep and sincere experience of their vibrant culture. Roles were clearly defined, and the tribe's grief management blended the spirit and sense of community of these ancient and wise people.

My thoughts explored the personal dynamics as we continued to climb. It was evident that the man ahead of me was crazy in love with Josh Walker. The way Matt looked at Josh at the services held deep respect and admiration – a robust, silent bond. The way he rushed to Red Cedar's side with the ceremonial spear in the face of adversity displayed an act of bravery and love.

I wondered if we would have the opportunity to continue our talk about his would-be rival, Kick Sorenson. I had a sudden thought, *If anyone benefitted by the possible demise of the frisky Aussie, could it be this man?*

It would be better, I thought, to let him bring up the subject of his competitor. It was essential to respect his quiet manner in the pressured atmosphere of so many fabulous extroverts of the Aerie crowd. I thought of the request of Elizabeth Rising Lark Walker to be a mentor to the Strong Bear.

The break in the mountainside narrowed a bit and then opened to a small slanting dale about 70 yards long and 30 yards wide. It was faced by sheer cliffs. Above and higher up at the far point of the basin, a little fall of water filled a shallow pool that eventually ran off down the opening through which we had ascended. The vale was snow-free on its eastern side. How we were going to continue following the stream beyond this spot was not clear. It was a dead end, and the entering water fell from a great height.

The dogs passed us, running ahead to drink from the cold mountain rivulet. Matthew and I sat next to each other on some boulders after drinking ourselves. Dog and dog lay at our feet, tongues dripping through panting mouths. Above us, a pair of eagles swooped and called out their annoyance at the human and canine invasion from below. There was a nest wedged in the rock about 100 feet up one of the cliffs. This was a very hidden opening in the mountains.

"These ranges are filled with spots like this, Nick," the Strong Bear said. "I like hiking to these secluded areas to think things over sometimes."

"What do you think about?"

"Stuff." He said enigmatically, looking away and then back at me.

The hell with waiting. I pursued, jumping in with both feet.

"Love's a bitch, Bud. Take it from one who has loved and lost a few gazillion times. Totally fucked up."

He shifted uncomfortably and looked away.

I added slowly and sincerely, "But I would not have wanted it any other way."

I stood up and walked into his line of vision.

"Matt, does he know?"

He stared at me and gulped. His secret was out. Reluctant to pursue the conversation, he said, "Yes."

He stopped, trying to formulate his thoughts. After a bit, he continued as if speaking his most profound feelings for the first time.

"I guess I have loved Josh since we were boys. He was a big brother in many ways, intimate ways. I have pretty much idolized him for just about forever. He takes my breath away, always has."

"And what does he feel? About you, I mean?"

Matthew Strong Bear stood up and turned his back to me. He shrugged his shoulders, saying, "See, that's the problem."

"Go on, Matt."

He turned and said, with a bit of emotion. "First, he is a man of few words. Next, Josh is in love with Kick, um, Mr. Sorenson. That's it. Pretty simple, I guess, and I just need to accept it."

He was at the point of tears but fought them back.

"Ahh, and you are sure about that?"

"The two of them are inseparable, Nick. They are sexing up all the time. I know that for a fact. Kick and Josh spend a lot of time together. Since Mitch died, Josh has constantly been at his side. Nights and days with him at the Aerie, not at the ranch or at the Reservation." He tossed some pebbles into the water as he spoke.

"Are you sure the relationship is love and not anything else? I am assuming you want no rivals in the bedroom, correct?"

"What else could it be, brother? And, of course not. Kick's a great guy and all, but I don't want Josh to think about Kick when he is with me. You ever make love to a guy and realize that he is thinking of someone else?"

Thinking back to the recent events in Florida, I felt a pang of guilt, but I decided not to respond.

He paused, attempting to sort it all out.

"Most of all, I guess I want Josh to feel about me the way I feel for him. I mean, Nick, how fucked up is that? He is totally in love with somebody else. Not into sharing, no way."

"No judgment, Kiddo. Just asking." I stood next to him.

"Matt, how are you about the gay thing?"

He looked at me but said nothing.

"I'm not talking about being 'out' as much as I mean in here." I touched his chest over his heart and added a tap to his head. "And here."

Strong Bear stared at the ground and answered. "Naw, coming out for me is too risky. My brothers will go apeshit. They are totally conservative – haters, you know?

"In some ways, the old ways of accepting the two-spirited folk were better, but attitudes vary in these times. Gray Wolf is a definite homophobe, and he is my boss. I'd be out on my ass. No job, no family, no...."

"No Josh?"

He looked at me and nodded.

This dude was coming apart. Only strength of spirit held him together, but as Elizabeth Rising Lark Walker suspected, his anguish was eating up his insides.

I ventured, "Man, you really think so? How about the Council?"

"Yeah. I'm good with most of the tribe's leaders. Susan and Joletta have been excellent friends along with the Walkers. But most things I keep private." He tossed another set of pebbles one by one.

Gently, I turned him to face me. "OK, here goes. Not my business, but in my family, we tend to spell it out."

He blinked.

I smiled.

"I can see you do not know many Italian Americans. So anyway… real friends always know, and they remain friends.

"Next, what matters most, Matt, is that you love the hell outta who you are. It all starts with that. The rest is major bullshit. Folks who disrespect you because they don't like who you are need to be marginalized big time. As that old song goes, 'Ain't Gonna Let Nobody Turn Me Around.' Know what I mean?"

"Yeah, I guess so," he said quietly.

"Take it from me, Bud. Law enforcement does not have a sterling record for us fabulous gays. You just say, 'fuck 'em,' know how to fight when called out and move on."

I started to get very preachy at this point but stayed the course.

"Harvey Milk is one of my all-time superheroes."

Matt nodded.

"Like him, I give no one the power to steal my soul, bro. And this…" I did a hand-sweep over myself.

"And this…" I waved the same hand to cover all of him.

"…is stuff to be proud of, bro. Don't let anyone, *anyone* tell you different."

In his big brown eyes, I could see that he was getting this.

"Now, let's talk about men."

Matthew shifted a bit but started to relax as I continued.

"We are hardwired for sex 'cause we're men. But I believe love and sex are two different things. Great when they combine, and ideally, they should, but a shag doesn't necessarily carry love with it or obliterate a loving relationship. Hence the situation of having a fuck bud is sometimes a good thing, I believe. Couples make their own rules, and it's all consensual."

The dogs started to stir, but I continued.

"The only way, and I mean the only way, you have a chance with Josh is if you communicate your feelings. Both of you. And Bud, that is hard as hell to do."

I thought of the struggles and stumbles that Kanye and I had with communication over the last three months. Nick Boy, do you really know what the fuck you are talking about? You are a great one to be lecturing on expressing one's feelings.

Regardless, I pressed home the point. "If it is Kick, then let Josh tell you that in all honesty."

Matt was engrossed in our conversation, but, at this point, he said few words in reply.

"One last thing, Matt. That strong-silent-type that both you and Josh are rockin' is sexy as hell but can lead to trouble. Make sure he knows what you feel in your heart. No male shame with the passion thing, bro. And *my* people know passion, I assure you."

A bit of a smile seemed to break. Matthew started to speak, but we were interrupted.

The dogs had run to the eastern wall of the canyon and, with eagles screeching overhead, were raising a ruckus. We raced over to investigate.

There was something there.

***

The afternoon light had crept up the eastern face above the shallow grave. Remains peeked out from the rocks that had been disturbed by mountain scavengers. Half of a broken and cracked skull was covered by mud and gravel.

I took photos with my cell phone, careful to remain apart from the body. I airdropped my pics to Matthew Strong Bear, who called into his Alpaska office. They would connect with Stefan Connelly's team and send a recovery crew outfitted with their best drones.

"So, the canyon gets flooded during an ice melt, and debris flows down and out, eventually ending down on the road and then going into the ditch. The gravel and dirt covering the body are washed away.

Matt nodded, took out a steel pen, and turned over some debris. A silver and turquoise chain hooked to some bone matter was among the rocks and pebbles still left on the pile.

With recognition in his voice, the Native police officer said,

"Nick, it's Jeron."

Chapter Twenty-Six: Radiation
MARK GADARN'S NOTES

Rebecca said what we all seemed to suspect.

"I thought we were in for a showdown, Darling. Josh was not pleased with Gray Wolf and his henchmen at his sister's funeral."

"Agreed. It was quite a tense moment. The opposition, in our case, seems to be headed for a major confrontation, one that will, I am hopeful, bring about the return of my brother and information about Mitch.

I stopped taking notes and spoke up, "Kayne, let's bring this to a head. Lives are endangered."

"Believe me, Mark, there is nothing I would like better. However, I am torn between immediate action and the risk that our foes have the resources to create further havoc and the additional destruction of innocents."

"What I don't get is the attitude of the local authorities on this. I did not have the opportunity to tell you, but last night, I had an interesting conversation with our friend, Stefan Connelly's deputy, Darling."

Kayne arched an eyebrow, "Go on, Rebecca."

Kayne had invited us to meet him at the Wild Life Preserve Station. The beautiful and informative Antionette Singe provided a tour and a tasty lunch in the private dining area.

By way of introduction, she explained, "We entertain prospective donors here. You can see that the view encompasses a few of the paddocks for our resident animals, including those recovering at our veterinarian facility. They need fresh air and space to run as they make what we hope is a full recovery.

"We are especially proud of our Aerie Raptor Rehabilitation Center. Dr. Mitch established it six years ago as a wedding present for his husband, Mr. Kick. The purpose of the Center is primarily educational, teaching members about area raptors and their plight as a potentially endangered species. We also care for injured and orphaned birds of prey, some from out of State."

Ms. Singe seemed to be accompanied everywhere by two small dogs, Lucy and Beau. She left us alone for a private conversation. Kayne had sent Nick on a special assignment, the follow-up search related to the murder of Susan Chipeta Walker.

Rebecca continued her information on the State Trooper situation, "The deputy's name is Jack Barberi, and he had quite a few questions about our involvement. At the time, I passed it off as friendly banter, but the more I think about it, the more I believe that there was a veiled warning in what he had to say to me."

I asked, "In what sense? Was there a threat in what he said?"

"You know, Darling. Yes, there was. I am paraphrasing, but he was telling us to back off and let the State Police handle the murders and disappearances. He also had nothing good to say about the FBI. He seemed a bit resentful of their requested involvement, which he attributed to us."

"Right," I added. "In that context, Kayne, I remember Stefan seemed to be in an animated conversation with Agents Kura and Ras. Looks like it was not a friendly one, from what I could tell."

Rebecca added, "When Nick spoke about the Sorensons having incrimination evidence against Kriegston, Connelly confided, 'We need to find those Excel sheets. Excel sheets? Mitch could have had tapes, physical materials like rock samples, legal documents, weapons, witness testimony... but Connelly knew there were incriminating financial reports and the exact format. Interesting."

Kayne responded, "Connelly is dirty, my friends. Not to be trusted. He is stonewalling with evidence like crazy and holding back resources. No Jeron and no Mitch after months? And his explanation amounts to Kick vanishing into thin air. There is not the slightest bit of evidence or in-depth follow-up on the death of Susan Walker. Not acceptable. He is working for the other side on this one; be assured."

"I am sorry to interrupt, Dr. Sorenson, but there are two people here to see you." Antionette Singe ushed US Marine Captain Robert Pauley and Special Agent Kristin Kura into the room. We exchanged greetings.

Captain Pauley said as he shook hands, "Mr. Gadarn, I want to say how much I appreciate your reporting from the Middle East. I didn't get a chance last night to say that I am a big fan."

"Thank you, Sir. Your men and women are doing a hell of a job out there."

Rebecca warmly acknowledged the Marine Captain as Kayne asked him to join us. "Thanks for coming, Bob, Special Agent."

"Dr. Sorenson, please let me express my concern for the disappearance of your brother. Anything the FBI can do to aid in the search, please do not hesitate."

"That goes for Clarion Base also, Kayne. Our resources are at your disposal. Drones, whatever you need."

"Thank you, both. I appreciate that."

The Captain continued, "And I want you to know, at a personal level, it will be great to see Captain Thomas Sorenson back again at the Aerie. When does Ace arrive?"

"My father got here earlier this morning. He is up at the Lodge. I have major muscle on him assuring that he does not single-handedly tear up the Valley."

The Captain could not help a small smile at the mention of another Marine and alpha dog.

"So, what is the latest on the investigation, and how can I help?"

"We were just getting to the heart of the matter. I need your impressions on the evidence I sent to you both."

Pauley spoke up, "Kayne, Kristin, and I were discussing those files on the way over. Those documents you shared are pretty incriminating."

Kristin Kura added, "The environmental officer had the goods on Kriegston for a while, and that report looks like it goes back at least eight months."

"Please fill us in, Darling."

The FBI agent continued, "There is no need for speculation here. Jeron produced documents and hard evidence, namely the radioactive petroleum sox, indicating that Kriegston has been mining uranium illegally from the Nu Ci nation lands. "

Rebecca asked, 'What are they doing with it?"

I jumped in, "Rogue nations."

Rebecca said, "Surely not weapons-grade. Wouldn't it be hard to disguise a refinery? Even amid all that oil equipment. Unless they have one hidden in the mountains somewhere."

Kayne continued, "Right, I expect they are selling unrefined uranium ore using their international connections through...."

Ever the teacher, Kayne paused to allow his students to finish the conclusion. I jumped in, "NEO. Well, I'll be damned.

Robert Pauley added, "Dirty bombs for terrorists. Homegrown on American soil. Kayne, we need Kristin and the Feds to move quickly on this.

"I agree, Captain, but I believe they have my brothers in a hostage situation."

"That's it, gentlemen. State Police Deputy Barberi's warning left it pretty much unspoken, but if we want to see Kick home safely, we need to back off. Holy shit, Darling."

Agent Kura said, "Dr. Sorenson, it appears NEO is up to their necks in this, no doubt. We represent an International Contract Corruption Task Force, which deals with overseas US government spending fraud when at war. We are talking about the Middle East here. I remember Mr. Gadarn's piece on them a while ago.

I said, "Yes, the Schlachtross boys in Afghanistan — bad business."

Kayne added, "Yes, Mark. Accusations of bribery, gratuities, contract extortion, bid rigging, collusion, conflicts of interest, product substitution, items/services invoiced without delivery, diversion of goods, and corporate and individual conspiracies at various levels of US government operations. It is an infamous list."

Agent Kura said, "We have been digging around these guys. Their suspected crimes go beyond the war effort to include worldwide Contingency Operations involving US military actions, foreign aid and development, and humanitarian assistance in any international region. Off the record, Schlachtross has friends in very high places."

The FBI agent continued, "Misuse of US funds overseas poses a threat to the United States and other countries by promoting corruption within the host nation, damaging diplomatic relations. It inadvertently supports insurgent activity and potentially strengthens criminal and terrorist organizations."

Kayne offered, "All this is your division's bailiwick, Agent Kura, and we need you on this. But there is more, my friends." Kayne was sizzling.

"Wait, wait, wait, Darling. I need a mid-lecture review. Kriegston is the Oil and Gas extraction company, right?

"Yes, my love."

"Renault, right. Very dirty."

"Yes."

"Schlachtross, a private security firm, military and law enforcement services, and humanitarian aid. Part of the NEO consortium. And they're dirty, also?"

I responded, "Pretty much so, Beautiful, Quite a few scandals resulting in company name changes and court cases... plenty of bad press."

Captain Pauley added, "I believe at one time they were doing business with the Defense Department in the order of $500 million."

"Small change for them, I'll wager, which most likely led to the black market uranium business," Kayne said. "Oh, yes. And that brings us to another branch of the NEO Family."

He counted off on his fingers. "So, we have Kriegston, Schlachtross, and…"

"Landrose," I said.

"Ahh, the prison folks. That William Carson guy from the Walker funeral. Holy shit, Darling. According to sources at the Resort, they are really hurting and neglecting those poor inmates."

"So the Aerie Valley is in a death grip with these shady folks," Robert said.

"Yes, and there is more. Kriegston is dumping the radiation waste on Nu Ci Lands."

"How did you come to that, Dr. Sorenson? There is nothing in those reports to indicate illegal dumping."

"Mark passed me some information obtained from an inside source at Landrose. And…" Kayne pulled up an app on his phone and put it on the table before us.

"Take a look at this -- the reading from the Nu Ci burial caves. Taken just two hours ago at the internment of Susan Walker."

"Darling, how did you get this? It looks like a report from a Geiger counter."

Kayne went into his pocket and pulled out a black cylinder about an inch long, resembling the butt of a cigarette. He snapped it to the bottom left-hand corner of his phone and brought his antique watch over the modified mobile. He turned up the volume. The phone began to click slowly.

I picked up the phone and scrolled through the readout, "Yes, high levels among the graves." I gulped and looked up.

"But not enough to do us harm, given the time we were in the area. Kriegston is taking precautions in packaging the waste. A bit sloppy, I will say, however."

"So, Kayne. How do we get your brother back?"

"Divide and conquer, Mark. We are fighting this on two fronts, Mate. Agent Kura, despite all this evidence, we cannot rush in with the feds. My brothers' lives are on the line. Just give me 24 hours to continue my investigation."

Kristin Kura said nothing. Kayne began to move the chess pieces in the dangerous game.

"I want a look around at Landrose. Can you get me in there?"

The Special Agent paused and then said, "Yes, Doctor, I agree we need to move carefully on this. Since Landrose is operating on a government contract, let's do a drop-in on Director Carson."

"Great. We must work quickly. Rebecca, can you get the oil and gas folks to the Lodge for a showdown? We will put Agent Ras there as Federal muscle.

Agent Kura jumped in, "I'll give Bill a call to give him a heads up."

"Yes, Kayne Darling. I'll make it happen. We need Mingan, Renault, and Connelly in the room."

"Mark, I am going to need you with me for the Landrose visit."

"You got it. But you said divide and conquer."

"We get Gray Wolf and Renault to meet with the FBI and Rebecca while you and I hit the prison. Bob, your involvement is on a need-to-know basis right now, off the record. And, Captain, if this all should go to shit, use those files I sent you to get those fuckers."

Pauley nodded.

"In this way...."

A somewhat familiar-looking, blustering, and overwrought man, followed by an exotic black woman, burst into the room, followed by Antionette Singe and her yapping dogs.

The man slammed one hand on the table and roared, "Where the bloody Hell are my sons?"

Kayne looked up and said, "Good to see you, Da."

Tribal Blood

Chapter Twenty-Seven: Earth

Nick Sechi's Journal

As a police officer, I dreaded these visits more than staring down the barrel of a gun.

"Please come in, Dr. Sorenson, Officer Sechi."

Earth Rae Jordan was visibly shaken as she opened the door to her home on the Aspen side of Aerie's southwestern pass.

"I am pretty sure I know what this is about. Won't you please sit down?"

Kayne took Earth's hand and gave her the bracelet I discovered among the newly recovered remains. The woman closed her fist at its touch.

She slowly opened what she found there and stared.

Kayne said, "I am very sorry, Earth."

No one said anything for a long time. Earth made no move. She just stared at her son's bracelet until tears fell from her eyes, hitting her hands and the treasure they held.

Finally, she drew breath from the depths of her grief, threw her head back, and loudly cried out in pain. The sobs and gasps that followed wracked her body with soul-deep anguish.

Kayne stood and pulled her into his arms, comforting the grief-stricken mother.

Phrases poured out between her crying. "Twenty-four... only twenty-four... finally had his life back together... loved his job... Oh, Jesus, no."

Earth Jordan continued to wail, and Kayne let her cry while offering his strong shoulder of support as a long-time friend.

"Where is he? I want to see him. Take me to him, please."

I spoke up, "No, Miss Earth. You see, the body is hardly recognizable. It has been in the wilderness for too long." I did not elaborate out of pity and respect. "Matthew Strong Bear has taken charge, and Jeron's remains will be brought to the reservation facilities for further investigation. This must be done carefully if we are to apprehend his killers."

Kayne said, "Earth, Joletta Golden Tree, and Elizabeth Walker are coming to see you to offer the rites and services of the Tribe for his final journey. Speaking for the Nu Ci Tribal Council, they consider your son one of their own. I believe they will stay with you for a bit."

Earth calmed down slightly and said, 'Thank you. That makes sense and will be most helpful. We really have no family, and they have been so good to us. Susan was Jeron's very close friend."

Earth broke away from Kayne and walked to the center of the room, her back to us. She focused on the pictures of her son on the mantelpiece. She selected one and gently touched it as if it could speak comfort to her aching soul. As she turned around to face us, she said with hands clenched, "Dr. Sorenson, you know who did this?

"Yes, Earth."

With red eyes and a murderous steel tone, Earth Rae Jordan said, "Get them, please. Make them pay, especially him."

She looked back to the picture and then off in a blank stare. Her voice dripped with hatred as she spoke.

"You get him, or I will."

Chapter Twenty-Eight: Ace

NICK SECHI'S JOURNAL

Commanding everyone's attention, the thickly accented and robust gentleman began the conversation.

"I trust you, Kayne, to get the job done. I will back off a bit and let you solve this. I have every confidence in you, my son.

"We can get back to the rescue plan in a tic, but first, I need to assess the players. My companion here is Ms. Darana Cooper, and I will return to her in a bit."

Thomas Michael Sorenson, Sr., was an imposing figure, and by that, I mean bigger than life. This is hard to believe since his two scions, Kayne and Thomas, Jr., aka Kick, are quite extraordinary on their own. Their strong personalities created an energy that ranged from electric to atomic. I could imagine how adding big brother Mitchell and the black sheep, Eric, to the mix would boggle the minds and emotions of us mere mortals. Again, I thought that growing up in the Sorenson clan must have been an experience beyond understanding.

Ace tended to make his points with a loud and noisy emphasis, suggesting a mixture of the personal quirks of a warrior and an Aussie hooligan at a football match. He seemed overly zealous about everything and never doubtful of his decisions or points of view. Strength of conviction was obviously a necessary feature of a successful business leader of the world's sixth-largest cattle ranch.

Kayne referred to his father's thinking as Ayers Rock hard-headed -- extraordinarily stubborn. Hannibal reincarnated, Ace Sorenson was the living embodiment of the Carthaginian general's motto, "I will find a way or make one."

He was in his mid-fifties and stood slightly under six feet while weighing in at about 190 lbs., a very fit, confident man and a genuine, former Marine. His face bore the marks of a man who had spent a lifetime in Australia's hot and dry interior. It was clear he was at home in the rugged outback on horseback, shouting orders to his ranchers. Additionally, Ace tended to hold nothing back in his assessments of what was going on, whether people, their interactions, or situations that demanded his attention.

"Come over here, lad, and let's have a look at the latest dingo my Kayne has brought home," he said with an Australian accent while shooting a wink at his very perturbed son. "With this one, it's one after another, eh? Like his Da, I will admit. We Sorensons are a robust breed."

He put one hand on my shoulder and thumped me on the chest. "Right solid and not bad looking." He turned me around and palmed my ass. "Good rump for riding, it appears."

I balked and pulled away, blushing down to my ankles. Kayne quickly drew into the space occupied by his father and me.

"Da, please. Have a care and a bit of respect."

"Look how this one goes red." Ace pointed and laughed loudly. "Matches his hair. It's just my style, boyo, no drama." He raised his fists playfully.

"Come on, you young bluey cop pup, show this old Hoolie what kinda balls you're swinging."

I segued from feeling appalled to getting the joke. I raised my fists and threw the tough soldier a few fakes and jabs, which Ace caught with open palms.

The former Aussie Marine smiled at the physical encounter and pulled me in for a bear hug. "This one will most likely stay around a while, eh, Son of Mine? Now, you do what you can to keep him a bit." He said to a flabbergasted Kayne.

"And you. Boyo, let me just say Sorensons are more trouble than a pack of mad dingoes. Hang on and keep him satisfied in the sack. For all his intelligence and la dee dah, my Kayne is one randy stallion. Runs in the family."

Seriously? Holy shit.

Rebecca laughed, and when Kayne shot her a look, she faked a jump back to a serious expression.

We had returned to the Aerie as the afternoon was growing late. It appeared that we needed a much bigger space for continued conversation. Ace's personality demanded large venues, indoors and out. Gints and Scott had picked up Ace and Darana at the Aspen airport. Apparently, the ride to the sanctuary had tempered them down to meekness in the presence of an Australian force of nature.

"Now you, my girl, I...." He was not able to finish.

Rebecca held up one index finger and, with a look that would halt a train, stopped the advance of Kayne's father. She turned gracefully and placed her Gint's-made Marie Laveau on a side table. She turned back to face her bestie's rather outrageous father with hands on hips.

I looked at Mark and saw the following expression on his face: *Nope, she is handling this one all on her own. She is quite capable.*

"Just watch yourself, Mate. I am nobody's *girl*, I can assure you. I am a *woman* and an extraordinary example of my gender. And I expect that you will behave like a gentleman, however unfamiliar you are with that way of conducting yourself. In other words, Mr. Sorenson, step back and do not piss me off."

She flipped her hair, adding, "Otherwise, I am delighted to meet you."

Stunned silence all around.

Ace looked around the room at the many dropped jaws from the spectators. There was one exception. Kayne had shot back his Hibiki, flopped into a chair, and held his head in his hands while emitting a soft moan.

Ace let forth with a boisterous laugh, and mock bowed to the commanding woman before him. Darana was beaming with admiration for the assertive Rebecca.

"I was merely going to compliment you, Ms. Quinto, on your appearance, manner, and choice of good-looking men." He nodded to Mark and raised his Foster's bottle. "Fine looker for a Welshie. Cheers, Mate."

Mark acknowledged with a return toast. "You call me 'Ace,' my beauty, and if I may, I will call you Rebecca. Never was one for formalities." He stepped over to his keening son and placed a hand on his shoulder that seemed to say, *Buck up, Boyo, it's just your ole Da, pay no mind.*

Rebecca retrieved her drink, "Good, we've settled that, Darling. Now I would like to know some backstory on this stunning woman." She turned her attention to Darana.

Ace started to reply but was silenced by two forceful looks from the women in the room who seemed to say, *No mansplaining, Bub.*

"I have worked with Captain Sorenson at the Inala Ranch for about three years as Director of Operations while serving as his personal attorney. My clan is the Napaltjarri people of Central Australia."

Mark said, "The Aboriginal tribe that owns Ayers Rock?"

Darana's black eyes glowed, "No. Mark. The Arrernte People have been given back Uluru, named 'Ayer's Rock' by the colonists. The Arrernte are cousins to my people, the Napaltjarri."

With immaculately black skin and the regal features of her community, Darana was a perfect foil for her Boss, soft-spoken and refined. One assumed that she was extremely capable of running Inala and that the partnership with Captain Ace Sorenson was a powerful one.

"We are here to add our efforts to restore Captain Sorenson's sons to the family."

Chapter Twenty-Nine: Scissor Hold

He was groggy but coming back to consciousness. There was little pain, considering the intense electroshock that caused him to pass out. The one place on his body that felt the most painful was his throat. The trauma was caused by screaming against the gag.

The prisoner's eyes roamed the cell as he tried to remember what he may have told his inquisitors. He was pretty convinced he had maintained silence and provided his torturer with little or no information. Standing up, he continued to favor the healing leg in its walking cast. Still, he wanted slowly to test his ability to walk steadily. Using the wall for support, he circumambulated the confines of his cell. Some pain, but considering the circumstances of his confinement, astonishingly better.

He was surprised to find the door to his cell unlocked. However, his hopes were dashed when a guard in a surgical mask entered with a sheet-covered gurney.

"Get on and lie down. Quickly."

***

"I have to piss, you fuck wads!"

The effects of his second capture had no lasting pain or mental confusion. He remembered the shock, the shortness of breath, and the instantaneous immobility. It took three guards to subdue and bind him. They left him in the tiny enclosure in only his underwear.

Kick yelled his urgent need over and over, facing the security camera. During the last supervised visit, He had surreptitiously shoved a roll of toilet paper into the toilet, disguising his movements as attempting to clean himself.

After what seemed to be an eternity of yelling and jumping around, a guard opened the cell door that contained the cage of his confinement. In the meantime, Kick continued to watch the camera's movements as its lens ball rotated to take in the breadth of the larger space. He carefully gauged the roll and scope of the lens.

"Hurry up, Dude, my back teeth are floating."

The guard opened the cage, uncuffed him, and led him to the toilet in the corner of the larger room. Kick used the facility and tried to flush the waste away. The plumbing responded by overflowing with gusto, a fountain of used toilet water. Kick backed away and faced the guard with hands raised.

"Ew. That's nasty. Didn't do nothing, dude. Time to call Roto-Rooter."

The guard moved in to inspect the mess. Kick slowly slid to the side and slammed an elbow into the guard's temple. The security officer spun and reached out for support as he went to one knee, holding his head.

Now, things happened very quickly. Kick scrambled up the grating of the cage and smashed the camera. In a lightning drop, the reluctant prisoner caught the rising guard with a crushing scissor hold between his legs. Kick reached between his legs and pushed down. The guard's head hit the wet concrete with an audible smack.

Confident that the man was unconscious, Kick very quickly stripped his victim and dressed in his clothes. He placed the guard on his bunk and covered him with a blanket. Kick carefully inspected the corridor before leaving and locking the door.

Moving quickly, he rounded a corner only to encounter a guard in a surgical mask wheeling a body on a gurney. He stopped and started to turn when a somewhat familiar voice called out, "Hey, Bud. Get over here quickly and help me get this body to the morgue." The guard who called out to him did not speak English, but Kick understood and ran to take up the other end of the pallet.

"Kayne!"

"Shhh. Brother dear, we need to be as inconspicuous as possible."

A guard held the elevator door.

Kayne addressed the guard. "Need to stay away, Man. Dead guy. Super contagious." The guard retreated quickly.

As they descended, Kick asked Kayne a myriad of questions in their private language. A voice from under the sheet said, "Would you two blokes stop the triplet gibberish, and let's get the fuck out of here."

In English, Kick exalted, "Mitch! For fuck sake, where you been, my man?" He lifted the sheet to hug and kiss his husband passionately."

Kayne said, "Later for that, my brothers. We need to move."

He handed Kick a surgical mask.

The doors opened on the lowest level to reveal a guard with a gun.

Chapter Thirty: The Falls
Nick Sechi's Journal

The FBI Agent halted the Facility Director's protests.

"No, Mr. Carson, I'm afraid that *you* do not understand. Unscheduled visits are part of the arrangement with the Department of Homeland Security and the FBI. They are designed to avoid any false appearances of your facilities or programs resulting from the knowledge that inspectors are expected at your facility. The purpose of our visit is to make sure that as a United States government contractor, the Landrose facility is complying."

Mark and I were accompanying Special Agent Kura acting as her subordinate agents. The trick was to distract the CEO of the Landrose facility. At the same time, Kayne scoped out the solitary confinement prisoners with the help of Danny Grant and Matthew Strong Bear. Mark's phone went off, and he checked the text message and whispered a remark to Agent Kura.

"Mr. Carson, I'd like you and senior security to accompany me around the facility. I want to start with the solitary confinement level. I understand that you use this special section of the facility to isolate uncooperative inmates. I want to see that and question them. Let's move out as time is most important. There is another blizzard coming through, and we need to get back to Washington."

The astonished Director stood up from his desk and led the way.

***

Behind the catering delivery truck, the Uncompahgre Falls roared against the cliffs, pouring a vast amount of the tumbling Palouse River into a deep gorge. The spring-fed waters also contained an abundance of snowmelt as the temperatures rose above freezing. The spray of mist from the falls rose high into the snow-covered cliffs, a study in white and gray in the winter air.

The rear enclosure of the Detention Center was a narrow yard surrounded by a chain-link fence topped by concertina wire. Beyond

Landrose's sentried, rear gate was a road that dead-ended into the facility near a loading dock. Nearby was a lot holding three semi-tractor trailers that backed up to the gorge. The far side of the road had no significant barrier against the steep canyon but a snow-banked shoulder and a guardrail.

The guards in the sentry hut had received a complimentary lunch from the Resort caterers. Security was in the habit of waving through the usual lunch delivery for Director Carson's office on the occasions when he had guests. They were aware that the FBI was on the premises. Danny had produced the order from the Resort for inspection. He, Matt, and Kayne dressed in parkas emblazoned with the Resort'sservice crew insignia. He rode easily into the rear of the compound.

They made a show of carefully unloading the food and drink for the guard on the loading dock. Kayne took the first supplies up, changed into Danny's old guard uniform, and stashed the food. Matt sized up the space and turned the van around for a quick escape.

Danny said, "They never change the passcodes for the floors, Dr. Sorenson. The place is shady and very shabbily run. And, the guards are so freakin' dumbass they can't remember a lot of changes to the keypads."

Thanks to Danny Grant, Kayne had everything he needed to get inside the solitary confinement section."

The game was on.

∗∗∗

Arriving at the morgue level, Kayne addressed the guard through his mask.

"Get back. Another case of Ebola. Orders are to send this one into the pit ASAP."

They moved quickly to the doors to the loading dock.

Matt popped the hood and faked a problem with the van. As Kayne and Kick exited, Danny hurried to help load Mitch into the back of the vehicle.

Kayne stopped them.

"Kick, take a look at this." He had stepped closer to the semis next to the van.

Kick joined Kayne and excitedly said, "Kayne, what the fuck? We have to get out of this place pronto, brother."

Kayne moved his enhanced mobile along the side of the truck, against its rear doors and underside. The ticking was loud and rapid.

"The nukes, Mate." He pointed to the chains that once secured the rear doors of the massive vehicle, which now lay coiled on the ground.

As he punched his phone, he pointed to the slope leading down to the chasm and said, "They are dumping nuclear waste into the gorge right where we're standing. This one is ready to go." He scanned the drop-off.

***

The stairwell door opened, and six men emerged onto the loading dock. Director Carson took in the scene and asked, "What is going on here, gentlemen?" He was shocked to see his long-time prisoner, Mitch Sorenson, about to be assisted into the open van with the help of his recent prisoner, the Spider-Man. He began to understand.

Three other guards joined the Landrose men, bringing the late-arriving news that the Sorensons had escaped.

Carson drew a handgun and addressed the escapees.

"I'd like you all to move to the far side of the road. Keep your hands in the air. You also, Dr. Sorenson. Your leg is not that bad and will soon be the least of your problems. Agent Kura, if you please."

Carson motioned with his gun, and Kristin, Mark, and I joined the rescuers.

"It's over, Carson," Mitch challenged. "Too many bodies will end up missing. And I'd wager that woman is a legitimate Fed." He pointed to Agent Kura. "Guaranteed, backup is ready to pounce, arsehole."

"Oh, my dear sir, so much can happen when a storm, such as we are about to have, hits these peaks. Death is inevitable. It will not be a problem in the wilds of these mountains to dispose of a few bodies with no evidence of foul play. Been done before, I will say."

As we were lined up close to the gorge, facing the security guards' guns, Kayne tried to stall for time.

"As the other Dr. Sorenson, Mr. Carson, that fact being quite inconsequential, I would like to know how much uranium waste you have dumped into the Palouse with your partners in crime from Kriegston, endangering thousands of community lives. I wonder about increases in the rates of cancer and congenital disabilities among the people who live here -- the families of your own guards. A purely academic concern. "

"You are as meddlesome as your twin is crazy, Doctor. I hope you realize that measures will be taken to minimize your involvement in our operations.

"But to answer your questions, we are about to dispose of our first load. We ran out of room in the caves, so over it goes today. An ingenious way to solve our Indian problem, wouldn't you say? It occurs to me that we also could cover a few bodies that will never be recovered. Ready to glow in the dark?"

Turning to Mitch, Carson continued, "Of course, if you were to return the socks and the files with an assurance that...."

Kick spat, "Rot, you fat fuck!" He seemed to shudder with energy, ready to explode.

As Carson looked at his one-time prisoner, a leering smile crossed his face. "Ahh, literally the fly in the ointment. I would have enjoyed the opportunity to explore your resistance to intense pain and, how shall I put it, extreme behavior modification, Mr. Sorenson. Such a strong and energetic boy."

The Director snapped his fingers, and one of the guards clambered into the first semi with the orange and green logo of Kriegston Gathering, Inc.

I detected a few strange looks among some of the guards at the mention of past and pending crimes of Director Carson. I threw into the mix, "So when Jeron wanted to blow the whistle on Kriegston, you had him killed and hid the body up in the mountains."

"Not me. That was Renault and the Chief. They hired the goons to take care of that. Moran is Kriegston's big muscle for those kinds of activities."

Kick was fidgeting like crazy, and Kayne put a hand on his brother to calm him and said something indecipherable. Kick responded in their secret language. The semi fired up and rumbled next to us.

Mark called out, realizing the tactic that Kayne had put into play, "What about Susan Walker, you miserable shitbag?"

"No, that was also Renault and the Tribal Leader." He nodded to two guards. "She was getting too close to our 'operations,' am I correct? NEO likes to keep things private."

As one of the guards patted me down and removed my Glock, I sensed the loyalty of prison security was starting to disintegrate at the thought of murder for hire and mass death. The truck bed of the semi began to rise, aiming its dangerous cargo at the canyon opening.

Just then, all hell broke loose.

Kick dropped his hands and began to move like a man possessed, spitting while tearing at his hair, shouting, and screaming gibberish. His eyes rolled, and he flopped on his back, throwing massive full-body spasms. He pounded the driveway with fists and heels. Mitch moved forward, but Kayne held him back with a whispered remark.

The crowd was astonished.

Kick sat up and spoke loudly to the Director, making little sense.

"ARRACK! I come... the Angel of the End Time... uhhh... listen to the words I speak... "

Kick jumped up and spread his arms, flapped them, and spun. He pointed and shrieked, "Your doom approaches... the terror has arrived... resistance will cost you everything. Fasten your seatbelts... babies... uhh, uhh... dim all the lights, sweet Darlin'...."

He raved and danced like a madman, spit and foam spewing forth. With a one-handed summersault, he spun on, hitting the ground in a splat. He tore at the confines of the stolen uniform.

He screamed, "ON JUDGEMENT DAY, WE WILL ALL BE INSANE!"

Carson and the guards were mesmerized. Landrose security stopped patting us down to watch the psycho, who flopped again on his back.

Next, the horn of the idling delivery van went off like the noon whistle, loud, sustained, and echoing over the din of the falls. Matt exploded through the van's rear doors, heaving a loaded catering rack into the midst of the guards. He raised his firearm.

Carson shot into the melee as the bodies moved together in offensive and defensive tactics. Kristin Kura fell to the ground. Kick did a kip-up, going from supine to standing in a flash. He landed on his feet, narrowly missing the crashing food rack, his demons instantly gone.

I grabbed the frisking guard and held his body in front of me. The dude took Carson's second round, which was aimed at me, and I tossed him away. Danny jumped from the van wielding a sturdy steel serving tray and nailed an attacker who collapsed unconscious.

Confusion reigned as Landrose security scattered.

Mark flipped the gurney on its side and pulled Mitch to the ground behind it. The journalist was checked by a bullet and fell face-first into the snow. I rushed to the wounded Mark, reaching him before the scrambling Mitch. At the same time, I hauled out my phone and made a 911 call. Mark was bleeding out on the snow. Mitch helped me to apply pressure to the fallen correspondent. Danny did what he could for the fallen Agent.

Matthew made for Carson, who ran for the road and down toward the safety of the sentry gate. The villain was screaming for help. Kick leaped up to the semi's cab and yanked open the door. Containers slid to the rear as the doors started to open as he battled the driver.

One of Carson's henchmen flew at Kayne and grounded him with a clumsy tackle. Kayne broke the hold and swept his attacker into a whirlwind of MMA moves that took the man out with exceptional speed.

Rather than continue after Carson, Kayne went to the rear door to prevent the spill. As the trailer bed rose, he scrambled to secure the chains that hung from the rear. He hastily made a crisscrossed web to restrain the opening, fastening the ends in solid steel hooks on the edges of the doors. As the angle steepened, Kayne clung to the back of the truck just inches from the drop-off.

Kick tossed the driver head-first from the cab, slammed the lifting lever into the down position, and jumped to the ground. Kayne rode the reverse action to where his feet almost hit the ground.

In seconds, the *Supaidāman* covered the distance between Matthew and the Director. They were struggling near the edge of the precipice. Carson had the police officer by the throat and struggled to raise his gun in the space between them.

Hitting the ground next to them, Kick somersaulted, bringing his feet down on the head of the Director as he crashed into them, sending all three into the gorge.

Chapter Thirty-One: War Party

Rebecca had invited the suspects to the Aerie for a meeting of the minds regarding the missing Sorenson brothers. She also asked the State Police representatives, Connelly and Barberi, to join them. She leveraged her clout with the FBI to get them to the Lodge.

Her first impression that this sting was going south was when Connelly dismissed two other police officers in the entryway of the Aerie. She watched through the glass wall as the second squad car descended the mountain.

Agent William Ras opened the conversation, addressing his guests. "We have discovered among Dr. Sorenson's files, reports, and materials we find very incriminating regarding your operations with the oil and gas business on the Alpaska Reservation."

Josh Walker had arranged that Tribal Chief Gray Wolf join Albert Renault and his bodyguard, Sebastian Moran. The latter accompanied the CEO with two additional very thuggish-looking confederates.

Agent Ras continued, "Specifically, gentlemen, the FBI has recovered documentation from Red Feather's Environmental Officer, Jeron Adobo Jordan. I have many questions and some initial offers related to what will be a sure conviction.

"Concerning the accounting procedures for the collaboration between Kriegston Gathering and Red Feather Oil and Gas. The reports in our possession show that Kriegston has not lived up to the agreement with the Nu Ci Tribe. And we would like to know where the funds are.

"Also, we have obtained from Dr. Mitchell Sorenson's possessions evidence that covert uranium mining is happening. The extraction and distribution of uranium are of interest.

"My offer for your consideration, gentlemen, is for full disclosure before we move this forward on a prosecutorial basis. Your cooperation in this federal investigation is paramount as the consequences for your company's actions will be grave."

Renault said nothing, but Gray Wolf responded, "You are asking us to confess to a series of crimes without the presence of counsel?"

"You are free to call your lawyers, but we hoped to get some information about the disappearance of Mr. Sorenson, the death of Susan Walker, and what appears to be the death of Jeron Adobo Jordan. If you have nothing to say, I will ask Officers Connelly and Barberi here to take you and your men into custody at this time."

There was silence. Renault looked at the state troopers and the security people in his entourage. He spoke with very measured words.

"As vital as you think it is for us to cooperate with the FBI, I believe you should know that this is a set up by Aerie Properties, Inc. Their hold on the Valley and the Nu Ci Tribe is a land grab for their own interests. They greatly opposed the setup of the Landrose Detention Center, a government-approved facility. The only uranium is the ore they have planted to incriminate our industry.

"I suggest you start with the Sorensons. They are hiding out somewhere out there. The rest of what you suggest is speculative at best. Sorenson reach is deadly -- bribes and payoffs. They are not even Americans. You look into that."

Ace started across the room with fists clenched. Gints and Earth intervened to stop his advance on the oil company executives.

He struggled around the hold of the Latvian muscleman. "You fuckin' liars. Where are my sons? For your sake, they had better be safe."

He strained at all efforts to calm him, including Darana's soft-spoken remarks.

"Look. You can see the insanity of the foreigner behind all this. We have nothing more to say to you. What you have in your possession is of no interest to my company or me. It is fake – false information." Renault said, indicating that it was time to leave.

"Officers," said Special Agent Ras.

Stefan Connelly looked a bit perplexed but said to Mingan and Renault, "Let's go, gentlemen. I am placing you under arrest. We have my squad car parked out front in the portico."

Ras said, "Officer Connelly, I will forward these documents to your office and the office of the State Attorney General."

"Put the bloody cuffs on them," Ace insisted, still held back by a formidable Gints and Darana.

The State Trooper and his assistant cuffed Gray Wolf, Renault, and Moran. The other two were trusted to come along of their own free will.

***

Josh was the first to say it.

"Something's not right here."

Scott called out from the third-floor landing, "Mr. Walker, you need to see this." He pointed through the glass wall to the driveway below.

Josh crossed the living room accompanied by Earth. He opened the doors to the second-floor patio and rushed to the rail.

Below, the state troopers had taken the cuffs off their captors, got into their cruiser, and drove away. Renault checked his Rolex and gave some instructions to his goons. He pointed to four places near the base of the Lodge and then to the upper stories. Then, with Jake Gray Wolf Mingan climbed into the company's Mercedes. Moran and his guards followed as both cars sped down the slope away from the Aerie Lodge.

Josh turned to Earth, "You in this?"

She knew exactly what he meant. "Let's go, Josh."

They returned to the house, grabbed coats, rushed out the front door, ran down the steps, and raced into the lower-level garage. Rebecca watched from the second-story patio as two Birds of Prey screamed out of their paddocks. The snow fliers flipped over the road's snowbanks to descend the slopes crisscrossed by the switchbacks into the valley in pursuit of the fleeing sedans.

"This is not going as planned," Rebecca said to the group in the living room. "I believe we have been duped, Darlings."

She punched in Kayne's number, but his mobile went to voicemail.

Agent Ras was on the phone with the local FBI office. He paused in his conversation and said to Rebecca, "You were right. Local law enforcement is very implicated in these wrongdoings. I was a fool not to have another backup on this. My guess is they will flee the state by company plane."

"Bloody hell!" Roared an irate Ace.

He was not able to finish his tirade when the world exploded.

Chapter Thirty-Two: *Supaidāman*
NICK SECHI'S JOURNAL

Leaving Danny and Mitch to staunch the wounded Mark, I sprinted to pull Kayne to secure footing as he struggled against the banging doors of the settling trainer. We ran to the edge and watched helplessly as the three men tumbled into the abyss.

The screams from Director Carson were literally drowned as he broke free from the clutches of the other two and plunged headfirst into the raging waters and the rocks 200 feet below the edge. His body slammed into the sharp rocks surrounding the basin and disappeared beneath the boiling whitewater.

Kick managed to guide the spinning pair of himself and Matthew Strong Bear so that the first few yards of their descent wedged them against the sharp outcroppings and naked brush of the canyon walls. Grasping the police officer with one arm around his chest and kicking against the chasm walls, he slowed their fall as a unit. Midway to the bottom, they hung up on a combination of rocks and branches protruding from the sheer cliffs. Kick's right arm and shoulder straddled an outcropping placing his back against the wall. With the other arm, he pulled at the body of the struggling Matthew.

"Easy Mate. I got you. Go slowly."

We ran to the loading docks for ropes. Using the front bumper of the catering truck as an anchor, I lowered Kayne into the abyss with a second line attached to his belt. As Kayne went over the edge, a second, third, and fourth pair of hands joined mine on the ropes.

Damn, we are so screwed, I thought in a panic.

Unbelievably, the guards who poured out of the back of the Detention Center in response to an alarm were not set on our destruction. They began to assist my efforts to save the three men dangling in the depths of the falls. It seemed that they had been released of their loyalty to crime and murder as their boss went to his death. The spell of evil had been broken.

Kayne repelled to the side of the impaled men. As Matthew slipped lower and lower down the body of the Kick, Kayne looped the second rope around the police officer's chest under his armpits.

Matthew fell, but only a short distance. The police officer was jerked to a stop as the slack of the second rope was taken up by the weight of his descending body. The police officer arched backward. As he was hauled back up to the level of the other two men, Kayne rotated Matt's limp body and slapped the man into consciousness. A bruised Matthew raised his hands to the rope and engaged his feet and legs to assist in his ascent. We hauled him up so that he breached the edge of the chasm.

Kick appeared to be slipping forward as the rocks and branches cracked and crumbled beneath his weight. Five feet away, he slid below his brother, increasing the distance between them.

Kayne pushed off the wall and to the right just as Kick lost all support. In an instant, I slackened Kayne's rope, so he dropped down just as his freerunner brother kicked against the rock face and shot forward and up. Kick made a successful catch on the moving body of his brother and jammed onto the rope at Kayne's waist with his left arm.

Kayne twisted in his rope to grab his brother. The combined weight strained the lines. The impact caused both brothers to spiral into a pendulum spin, dangling above the treacherous rocks and water below.

On top, we managed to send the second rope into the opening again. There was an awkward and painful catch-and-secure, but our efforts resulted in Kick, rope around his waist, being pulled up to the edge of the cliff.

Below, Kayne was in trouble.

The impact of his brother's hard catch and quick tie-off on the second line loosened the ropes on his body, causing him to slip out of the hastily made harness. He fought gravity and ended up clinging to the rope with one hand dangling wildly above the abyss, frantically trying for a full catch with his free hand.

We had four men pulling on the rope, but a fast pull would shake the dangling man free. I quickly drew the line off the gasping Kick, tied it around my waist, and scrambled over the edge, repelling down to Kayne guided by the belayers on the cliff above.

When I came alongside him, the men above pulled my rope tight. As I reached for him, they introduced more slack into the system. I managed a soft catch, pulling him into my arms. Somehow, we ended up with him on my back as we were pulled up from the dangerous drop to the safety of the ledge above.

I joined the identical brothers Sorenson, lying on our backs on the landing before the roaring falls. We recovered a bit, gasping in huge gulps of cold air, and moved into a colossal hug-up.

Sentries opened the gates for arriving vehicles responding to the 911 call. Members of the Native Police Force and medics rushed to attend to the fallen. Matthew's injuries were cuts and scrapes, with one broken wrist. Mark was in shock, bleeding from the shoulder wound.

Kick's right shoulder and arm had been dislocated, and he had gashes and bruises on the back of his head, neck, and shoulders.

"Take hold of my wrist, Mate, tight. Now. Fucking do it. Hurry up." Kick ordered a young paramedic. As the man obliged, Kick jerked his body back and then forward. He shrieked. And fell into a ground roll. Sitting up, he looked at his astonished audience and said, "Reset!"

The paramedic fainted.

Mitch left the medicos and Danny to tend to Mark and pulled the fallen Kick into his arms. They clung to each other in an emotional embrace that consisted of unfinished sentences, tears, and passionate embraces. Kick grabbed his husband with a force that begged for safety and protection.

Wincing, Kick pulled apart and said to his long-lost husband, "About time you showed up, handsome. I was about to take up with innumerable suitors just to assuage my grief." They both grinned, but each of their smiles dissolved into sobs of relief and happiness as they hugged up again. This time, with less desperation, respecting Kick's shoulder and Mitch's leg.

I pulled Kayne to me with relief and joy that he was safe and unharmed. "Thanks, Kiddo. I knew with a strong boyo like you at the other end, I was not gonna land in the drink." His bravado vanished, and he pulled me closer. A shudder seemed to wrack his body. We both touched at the tears rolling down our cheeks.

Abruptly, Mitch held the amused Kick away from him and looked the man over. "*Kick Insane* was an award-winning performance, Boyo. But, wait a bleedin' minute, if you have been missing, what is it three days?" Kick nodded. "Why are you not really mad as a wet Tazzy Devil?"

Kayne, somewhat recovered from the after-effects of his rescue, wiped his face and said, "Make that *madder* than a wet Devil. We know he has always had a few kangaroos loose in the upper paddock."

He moved closer to his brothers and continued, "I was wondering that myself, given your incarceration and your aversion to taking your medication."

Kick smiled with wicked intent as a different medic wrapped his shoulder and another bandaged his head. With one hand, he boldly opened the front of his pants. "Care to take off my jock, husband? Now, don't be shy. How about you, big brother?"

"I will pass, Lil Tommy. Our family cannot afford any more public improprieties at this time."

Mitch examined his husband's privates and emerged from the cotton pouch with a small container of white capsules. Kick was giggling and basking in the attention of the open-mouthed group that surrounded him.

I piped up, "And here we thought that was all you straining that pouch." I raised my right hand and looked around as I continued. "Anyone else totally girth-disappointed?"

Kick was jubilant at the laughter at his expense. He flipped me the bird and juggled himself in a comic attempt to correct mistaken impressions. Mitch gently calmed his antics.

We surveyed the injured. Agent Kura was in the direst of straits. State troopers and Aspen police officers began an interrogation of the Detention Center staff. Mark was loaded up on a stretcher. He had slipped into unconsciousness.

Danny rushed up to the Sorensons and me as the snowfall, and the wind started to increase. He pointed to the valley to the southwest and the lights through the white whirlwind. It appeared to be a massive blaze.

Mitch shouted, "It's the Aerie Lodge!"

Chapter Thirty-Three: Tribal Blood

Onboard the Osprey with Earth following on the Kite, Joshua Walker crisscrossed down the slopes between the switchbacks. The snowmobiles soon caught up to the three cars headed down the southeast slope of the mountain that anchored the Aerie Lodge. By running before and between the speeding cars, they were able to cause the confused drivers to stop and repeatedly skid on the icy, twisting mountain road.

Earth set the Kite directly in front of the other sedan as soon as she saw an opening. With Josh out in front, the speeding group approached a steep downward turn. As the car behind her bore down, Earth swerved off and to the side.

To avoid rear-ending his Boss' car, the driver slammed on the brakes just as the road turned sharply to the right and down a steep grade. The result was a high-speed skid that sent the second security vehicle and its passengers airborne into the valley below. The car tumbled against rock and precipice until it landed upside down on the road below.

Now, Josh flipped the Osprey to the side, jumping up and over the roadside snowbank. Traveling parallel, he allowed the first car to pass him. With a sharp turn of handlebars, the avenging Brave sent his charger directly at the fleeing sedan. The Osprey vaulted up and over the snow pile and bounced off the hood of the speeding car. Walker held on and rebounded into the cushion of new powder on the opposite side.

The car's driver, harassed by the speeding Kite at their rear, never saw the catastrophe coming until the Osprey fell directly on top of them. The impact obliterated the windshield and pancaked the hood, exploding the motor.

The acrobatic collision produced a momentum that caused the smashed getaway car to careen up on two wheels and flip into a steep ditch. There was a tearing of steel on rocks as auto pieces and occupants of the vehicles were hurled over the roadside terrain.

Earth and Josh halted the Birds and ran to the scattered bodies. Josh tossed his helmet as he raced forward through the snow like a savage warrior pursuing his prey. The occupants of the first car were crushed. Moran had been thrown from the tumbling vehicle as it descended. His body was perched on the rocks on the steep side of the road. He did not appear to be conscious.

Not far from his confederate in crime, Renault lay on the right side of the road pinned under the wrecked Kriegston VIP car. Miraculously, Mingan had been thrown clear.

Renault began to scream. Josh squatted before the man who put the death order on his sister. The Brave studied the situation as if in awe of what lay before him. He cocked his head from side to side like a raptor inspecting the dying throes of his prey.

Earth ran to his side as he slowly drew a hunting knife from his snow boot. His visage seemed to change menacingly in the headlights of the parked Birds, catching one side of his determined face. He seemed to grow more primal and insanely murderous. His body was a coiled spring ready to pounce.

As he dropped to his knees next to his mortal enemy, Josh drew the flat of the blade against the throat of the hysterical Renault. The corrupt businessman began to lose consciousness as his would-be executor started an eerie chant in the Nu Ci language.

Josh pulled the head of the crushed CEO so that the man faced him. Beginning a deadly ritual, Josh held the knife in an upraised arm, held skyward over the emaciated man. He chanted in the ancient tribal language as the storm boiled around the bloody horror of what was about to happen.

Earth threw down her helmet and ran to her friend, grabbing him from behind. She held onto his back with frantic desperation.

"No, Joshua. Not like this."

Josh seemed to speak from a trance, slipping further into madness. With a mesmerized expression on his face, he shook her off and vocalized to the protesting Earth with a dream-like cadence.

"It is our way... part of what holds us together. Blood revenge has been a battle ritual of our clan structure for centuries. It is a sacred obligation. I must free the spirit of the White Singing Bird."

He pulled off his jacket and shirt as he rose in a killer stance. The Brave both of his muscular arms skyward and threw back his head, a savage warrior bent on revenge. The wind whipped the mane of his long black hair in a wraith-like swirl. Eyes bulging, he looked down at the dying Renault, his victim, stretched before him.

The ruthless avenger shouted into the heart of the storm, "This is my right. His blood will flow."

Around the murderous specter, the snowstorm raged with an apocalyptic intensity. Snow and ice spiraled in a whirlwind around the crash. The ground shook, and thunder seemed to fill the Aerie skies, exploding and echoing across the valley.

Josh raised a wild scream to the blackened, snow-filled skies.

"IT IS TRIBAL BLOOD! AHHEEEEYAHHH!"

He began to bring down his knife-wielding arm for the kill strike to vindicate the murder of his sister. Before he could stab, Earth grabbed the upraised arm.

"No! He is no longer your foe, Red Cedar. See, death has already embraced him. Susan's spirit is free. The evil he has done has come home to roost. Your blood feud is finished."

The Director's eyes flickered, rolled back, and half-closed. His chest, partially pinned under the wreckage, stopped its frantic heaving.

The Master of Horse and the Mistress of the Skies were frozen in their stance over the dead Renault. The storm raged like a beast around them, carrying souls away to judgment.

***

They could hear sirens approaching from the mountain pass and valley below. Lights cut through the gale as the trucks and cruisers rounded the lower switchbacks to find that the crashed cars halted their advance.

A bloodied hand reached up to Earth and pulled her back as Josh retreated from the dying Renault. The lower part of the Tribal Leader's body was twisted and faced backward, away from the front. He looked down at the backs of his legs. Mingan's back had been broken, and his pelvis smashed in the crash. Mangled but conscious, Jake Gray Wolf looked at Earth Rae Jordan, crouching next to him.

"Help me, please." He feebly tore at the ground between them.

Earth stood up, brushing the mud, snow, and blood from her clothes. She spoke quietly against the raging wind.

"You have sold the heritage of your people like a cheap pimp, Gray Wolf. You disgraced your office with greed and murder."

Her voice sounded a terrible verdict. She knelt, bringing her face close to the Tribal Leader. Her hand brushed the debris from his agonized face.

"Tell me, is this how he pleaded, Jake? With your last dying breath, tell me. What were the last words of my child as your men took his life? Did they tell you after they followed your kill order, or were you there to see him die?"

More thunder seemed to shake the valley. Earth lowered her face inches from the fallen Chief. "Tell me. Tell me of the murder of the son you never acknowledged. My dead boy."

She spat.

Unable to move, Gray Wolf turned his head away and began to sob.

Renault was dead from his injuries, as were his two confederates in the first car. White River had run down from the Lodge following Red Cedar and was barking excitedly. Chouko joined in her distress, howling and racing about the mangled ruins. The arriving emergency vehicles screamed to a halt before the wreckage that blocked the lower road. First responders jumped from the trucks and SUVs, talking to communicators to bring in extra equipment.

Red Cedar and Earth Rae Jordan looked at the troubled white dog and her bigger companion. Their eyes traveled to the bluff above and behind the scene of the wreckage. It was not thunder they had heard. It was the exploding and burning of the Aerie Lodge.

Chapter Thirty-Four: Conflagration

Scott leaped from the twisting stairway as the front of the Lodge exploded and broke away down the driveway. He rolled into the living room area as timed explosions ran down both sides of the building, crumbling the second-floor balcony throughout the circumference of the Lodge, including the rear of the building. A circle of flames and wreckage reached upward and outward to the top two stories as well as into the interior of the Lodge.

Darana ran back through the kitchen and returned quickly. She yelled over the melee, "The rear stairwells are blocked. No elevators."

Ace and Rebecca ran in opposite directions down second-floor corridors, searching for a way out. A falling, flaming beam trapped Rebecca in the library. Using a Native blanket torn from the wall, Gints beat away the flames to bring her back into the center of the living room.

As beams began to explode and fall into the great room, cries went up, questioning why the sprinklers failed to engage. Flames poured out of adjacent rooms on the perimeter of the building and had begun to come up through the cracking floor. Dense smoke was everywhere.

Darana called out to Ace, who returned, his clothes in flames. She pulled him to the floor and extinguished his conflagration by slapping and rolling him. Gints grabbed those he could muster to group within the shelter of the large fireplace as the front of the upper story collapsed into the vestibule and half of the living room.

A pit to the second floor opened before the fleeing Ace, who launched Darana into the open fireplace just as he began to fall into the inferno.

Scott began to scream at the top of his lungs.

Chapter Thirty-Five: The Prodigal
NICK SECHI'S JOURNAL

Commandeering any vehicle we could, we headed away from the Landrose facility on the northeast rim of the valley. We raced down and across the Palouse River and up the southern slope, taking the back mountain road to the Aerie Lodge. The drive was treacherous due to the snow and ice on the steep two-lane highway. In the distance, our destination, the exploding Lodge, erupted against the black and white night sky, burning with a doomsday intensely.

Searchlights trained on the fiery mass of the burning building. A snowy fog of light and snow crystals enveloped four fire trucks. The company of firefighters caked with ice poured fountains of water onto the burning lodge. A pump drew water from the nearby river. Water spouts arched up over the remains of the blazing architectural wonder that had been the Aerie.

The explosions had made for immediate destruction. The top two stories had collapsed. Leaving the six chimneys and four piers naked and black against the mass of flames, smoke, and blizzard. A mound of flaming debris filled the lower level and spilled down the mountainside. Thankfully, the wind seemed to come to a dead stop.

White River raced through the humans and the trucks appearing and disappearing in the swirling snow as she barked incessantly. I thought I saw Monica and Nathan from the Resort with Luke and a few of the staff from the Horse Palace come to watch the destruction of the Sorenson mansion. Kayne called out to Josh Walker, who stood with Earth Rae Jordan a bit back from the smoldering beams. Earth arranged his parka around the stunned Brave as they gazed into the fire.

"Tell me you got them out, Josh. Where are they... where? Josh!" Kayne had Joshua Walker by his coat and clutched him with a passionate entreaty. Kick, Mitch, Matthew, and I followed, our eyes searching the gloom for family and friends. I saw tears on fire-reflected faces as Mitch watched the home he had designed for his one true love come crashing down in an explosion of flame and smoke, his father and friends inside.

As if transfixed, Josh's strong face was etched against the cold mist that swirled around the last of the blaze. Matthew Strong Bear, with care for his wounds, moved in to wrap an arm around his friend. Josh looked over Kayne's pleading face into the smoking wreckage that had once been the Aerie and spoke.

"Kayne, please...." I tried to pull my man back from the trance-like sentry that was Josh Red Cedar Walker. White River took up her mournful howl.

Finally, Josh spoke in a monotone. "No one has gotten out, Kayne. They are gone. Everyone."

A gasp went through each of us as Kayne collapsed to his knees in the snow and mud, burying his face in his hands. I tried to gather him in my arms, but he was not to be consoled. He pushed me away in a rage, his face contorted with agony. Through his anguish, Kayne said over and over, "No! I should have saved them. Oh, God, no! No!"

I joined him on the ground, fighting to alleviate his physical and mental fury.

"I did this all wrong. WRONG!"

He was inconsolable.

Mitch and Kick were in an animated but inaudible conversation, disagreeing about something. "Yes, Mitch, I am sure of it! It must be that. Listen to me. Please!"

Kick broke away and ran up to a firefighter to yank an ax from his backpack with his uninjured arm. A man who knew no fear, he vaulted over the burning barricade and disappeared into the smoldering ruins. Twisted and burning furniture slid off broken floors above to create a curtain of fire and destruction behind the dashing athlete. Mitch's grandfather clock, scared and smashed, tottered over the edge.

"Get your men to follow him, Captain," yelled Mitch, and he hobbled over to the place where Kick entered the somewhat smoldering ruin, attempting to follow. Chouko leaped on top of a pile of the building's foundation in what seemed to be an attempt to rescue a human. Still, a renewed rush of flames, following Kick's wake, deterred the dog's brave efforts.

Josh came out of his trance to grab Mitch, preventing him from entering the blaze. He said over and over, "No. No." Earth joined her boss, holding Mitch back.

We heard pounding and a great disturbance from where the Lodge's ground floor had been, now encased in fallen and burning timber. The firefighters trained the hoses on the area that had swallowed up the fugitive Kick. Men and women of the force used grappling hooks to clear a path into the interior.

Two bulldozers with the Aerie Ranch logo moved piles of the burned mansion to the sides, opening a way to the interior. This was the same machinery that had pushed the wreckage of two cars from the main road below to make a passage for the fire engines ascending to the burning Aerie. Luke and his staff had cut across from the Palace and up the slopes surrounding the steep drive. They rumbled up to the wreckage in the heavy earth-moving equipment.

The heat from the blaze drove us back. Now, the flames and crashing beams near the center area of the Lodge seemed to abate against the copious water spray and efforts of the two bulldozers to clear the wreckage. There was no sign of the erratic Spider-Man.

The fire chief approached us. "You folks need to step back and let us handle this. In that conflagration, it is not likely...."

As we watched in stunned horror for what seemed like forever, phantoms seemed to move forward through the intense smoke from the interior of the wreckage, stumbling and falling to be quickly assisted by the firefighters. Six soot-covered Hell's escapees coughed, yelled, stumbled, and staggered as rescuers covered them with blankets and led them from the fire.

White River barked loudly as her pal, Chouko, bounded over a pile of smoking wreckage and landed next to her. Excited and a bit traumatized, they moved off into a chase, up and down the soot-covered, snowy slopes. My Beautiful Butterfly finally flopped at my feet and jumped up for some face licking.

I loved up my dog and then commanded the Akita to stand sentry a distance from the action with his pal and ran to the group emerging from the wreckage surrounded by paramedics. We embraced the survivors, blackened, wet, and shivering in their blankets.

Kayne was barely able to speak. "How?"

"Try answering your fucking phone, Darling. Although I suspect that service is limited in a panic room amid all this exploding mountain shit." She gestured to the wreckage.

"It is Scott who saved us, Big Doctor. He was guide through office to the safety room below. Secret stairway."

Entwined in the fatigued Matthew's arms, Josh raised his head in the direction of the one solitary figure amid the smoke and snow. He watched as Mitch gazed into the corridor of wreckage for the lost Spider-Man. Kayne and I moved to his side. A crash brought the last of a hanging mass of burnt building across the opening. Mitch wavered as if he would collapse. The rest of us cried out in horror.

Just about when all appeared lost, an object came hurtling out of the wrecked pile, landing near my feet. It was a very battered briefcase.

Next, a flying gymnast jumped and somersaulted between crossed beams. Our crazy-assed hero misjudged the last few moves and landed on his ass in front of a stunned Mitch Sorenson.

"Holy shit, that hurt," Kick exclaimed from his pratfall. His right arm was still in the sling. He was totally blackened, his shirt and pants torn and burnt. "I thought you would want the incriminating papers, handsome. And I broke the fuckin' ax. Oh well, I'll just...." He turned to the firefighters.

Mitch pulled him up into his arms, lifting his husband. "Jesus! C'mere, you. Just when I found you, I thought I had lost you again. Kick... oh, Kick..." The big man was overcome with emotions.

Kick pushed back and grinned, "So, maybe it was my turn to get lost for six months, big man, but then I thought, nah." He buried his dirty face in Mitch's chest, giggling and twisting.

Mitch tousled his smoky and grimy, short hair and said, "Kick Boyo, this time, you really are one hot mess."

"Kayne, where's...."

240

Kayne turned to his best friend. Her clothes and body were covered with dirt. He placed his arms around her and spoke with reassurance.

"He's fine, Rebecca. They took him to the hospital. He was conscious, and he will pull through. The bullet went through his shoulder, out again, and...."

Rebecca made the sign of the cross. "I am going...." She dashed off in search of transport. Danny ran after her and caught her not far from the Resort's catering van.

"Hop in, Miss. I can take you there."

Ace stood apart, giving directions to the firefighting crew with expressive hand gestures. At the same time, a relatively calm Darana held out some water for him. With one arm, Ace pushed a First Responder away who was trying to take the Aussie's vitals. Draped in blanket coverings, they moved over to where we were standing. I stepped back and let Ace share some loving with his lost, prodigal, and arrogant sons.

He pulled out of the man hug after exchanging a few words with his progeny. Kayne had been speaking words I could not hear and directed Ace's gaze to me.

The bear of a man approached me and smothered me in an embrace.

"Thank you, Nick. My family and I are in your debt."

He continued with much tenderness, "There is a Chinese proverb, 'If you save a life, you are responsible for that life.' Sorensons are enormous responsibilities, Boyo. I am here to tell you."

I fuckin' lost it.

I held on to the older man, buried my face in his shoulder, and cried like a baby. A somewhat bewildered Ace brought an arm up and around me. He spoke some words of comfort like a father. Then, Kayne was at our side, saying nothing but my name over and over as he ran a hand over my back.

Ace shook off his own tears and emotions. He turned to his youngest.

"My boys, listen to your Da because I have a few things to say."

Kick whispered, "Shit storm coming, bros." He tried to duck behind his formidable husband.

Darana moved to Ace's side.

"First off, that shelia, Rebecca, she saved your ole Da's life. Along with my Darana here. Reached into the fiery pit of hell to snatch me back. Your Gints-bud serving as the anchorman on the play. A bleeding rippa, to be sure."

I thought, *This was a day for falling Sorensons.*

Looking at Darana, he added, "When did girls get so strong?"

She jabbed him gently and said, "I believe it all started with Eve, Captain."

Ace continued, very sternly and very angrily. "Now, Master Thomas Michael, step forward, lad."

The Marine Captain made as if to remove his thick belt. "You have a few things to answer to your Da for, you crazy-arsed young hooligan."

Kick hung his head as Mitch suppressed a smile reaching back, pushing the imp forward.

"Do as Da says, Mate."

Holding the belt, Ace folded his arms across his broad chest. And began in a disciplined tone.

"How many times have I...."

He never finished.

Kick looked up at his father. The boy/man laughed, smiled, and rushed into the arms of his ideal man. The big Aussie rancher blubbered into the neck of his youngest.

"I am so proud of you, Son."

Chapter Thirty-Six: *Après-ski*

NICK SECHI'S JOURNAL

One week after the fire at the Aerie Lodge, the Sorenson family and friends began to relax a bit. We were ensconced at the Resort in the Owner's Suite and its five luxurious bedrooms. Mitch had commandeered the rooms usually reserved for heads of state and other dignitaries who found their way to the Aerie Valley searching for relaxation, recreation, and solitude.

Ace decided to throw a ski party to celebrate an end to the troubles. Those of us who could hit the slopes. Rebecca and Monica agreed to teach Darana to ski. I was fascinated to watch Ace trying to take over the lessons. He was as much a commanding presence on the mountains as he was in the Outback.

Gints and Scott hit the Black Diamond slopes.

The muscle man beamed, "As boy in Latvia, this is mere foothills to Gints." He waved at the surrounding ski slopes. "You never catch me, Scott boy. Gints remains champion in and out of bedroom."

"I call BS, studly. When I do catch your ass, you will agree to be my slave, and we are gonna do that thing that makes you crazy," the boy jeered. He dashed after his crush.

"I'm telling you, Mitch. I *can* board with a bum shoulder. It is practically totally healed. See?" Kick tried to conceal what was most assuredly a sharp pain as he attempted to raise his right arm above his head."

"Kick, stop being so fuckin' wiggly, lad. Your doctor said at least four weeks. *It has been seven days.* Come and sit with your husband, who missed you so much, and we can have a quiet conversation."

I thought, Yeah, like that's gonna happen.

Mitch turned to us and said jokingly, "It's like loving eight guys at once. Always has been – nothing stops his perpetual motion."

It was easy to see how much Mitch adored the frenetic Kick. Kayne, for one, was glad to have Mitch back in the picture as the stabilizer of the "Hot Mess." He was able to free up a lot of energy, and I was happy to attest to that.

The hyperactive freerunner's abduction and confinement, followed by the rescue and his superhero-like intervention in the burning wreckage opening the blocked panic room, was directly from a Marvel Studios script.

For three of the four nights, I jerked awake from a horrific dream of Kick and Kayne dangling over the abyss at the Uncompahgre, twisting, shouting, reaching, falling. I pulled the startled Kayne to me, hoping the nightmares would end, each time finally falling back to sleep in his arms.

Shortly after the pieces of our lives came back together, Mitch pulled me aside and began a sort of delayed introduction. "You know of me, Nick, but I am just learning about you, and I feel like I need to say a few things. Thank you for saving the life of my brother and my husband. I can see that you and Kayne have an amazing connection. Kayne needs that, Mate. Bottles up too much, my brother does."

I remember thinking as we began our first one-on-one, *Jesus, these Aussies were handsome as hell.* Mitch is also 6'2". There must have been a rivalry among the Brothers Sorenson about who was physically the most superhero gorgeous.

He is also "fit as fuck," as we say in the gay boy Mecca of Wilton Manors, with striking blond hair and a gorgeous smile. (I imagined Kayne saying, *Use the big head, Nick, not the little head.*) This left Ace as the smallest of the clan, but the size of his gruff personality made up for the 5'11" stature of the former Aussie Marine.

Mitch seemed to be a man of honor, integrity, and strength. When it came to presence and personality, he was a calming influence on relations with the blustery Lord of the Inala Ranch, his "Da." As the eldest brother, he easily reassumed the role of the pack-builder. His profession in psychiatry helped bring a rational dimension to his energetic husband and the challenges of Kick's disorder.

As a business leader and Monarch of the Aerie Empire, Mitch smoothly retook control of the family corporation meeting with the

Lodge's Board, the staff of the Resort, the Horse Palace crew, and the rangers of the Wildlife Preserve. Kayne had cautioned him to leave off meeting with members of the broader community until his leg improved. Mitch deferred this for next week but, amid protests, accepted a position by way of his honorary Nu Ci membership on the tribal commission to investigate the Red Feather/Kriegston scandal.

Here on the patio, Mitch said, "Kayne told me of the *Seed Blood* murders and the troubles. Sounds like it was an intense experience. How are you doing with all of that?" Typical of the family, Mitch was easily physical with folks he liked. He put a firm hand on my shoulder.

I butched up my reply, "No signs of damage, man. My body has recovered quickly, thanks to my addiction to tough training and exercise." After I said it, I couldn't believe how bullshit macho it sounded.

Sensing my remaining internal turmoil, Mitch let his dark blue eyes meet mine. "And in here? If you don't mind my asking. Able to let go?" He touched my temple and waited for a response.

"Any day now, Mitch. Any day now." I looked off to the group assembled on the Resort's patio, watching the swooping of the descending skiers. I searched for Kayne amid the animated conversations, cocktails, and quasi-arguments that set our group off as the most wild-assed of the *après-ski* guests.

Kayne accepted a drink from Danny as Kick carried on an overly demonstrative conversation with his forbearing brother. Kick was no doubt looking for an ally in his quest to show off on the slopes, slinged arm notwithstanding.

From across the patio, Kayne glanced over at Mitch and me and shot an array of body language.

First, he did his signature Kayne Sorenson forelock sweep, pushing back his pesky right-side-of-the-forehead forelock.

Next, he popped a shrug and nodded in the direction of his excited and fast-talking brother. Kayne silently said, *I am listening to this harangue, but I am far from present, Mate.*

Kayne's smile and wink suggested, *Isn't my brother Mitch as impressive as he appears? Glad you two are hitting it off.*

Finally, he seemed to add a longing look that said, *What do you say we slip away from this party and spend some time together, alone?*

Mitch followed my gaze over to Kayne. He picked up on the feeling and passion I had for his brother. "He is quite something, Nick."

I stammered, "I got no words, Mitch. I got it bad as far as Kayne is concerned. Used to think there for a while; it was just lust-on-steroids, however... and I know it hasn't been very long, but... I only want to be by his side all day and night."

I felt my usually intense blush rising from my socks to the tips of my ears.

Mitch smiled and gave me a manly hug up. "I want to know more about you, Nick. You impress me as a pretty amazing bloke — a bit of the hero type yourself." He alpha-thumped my chest. He added with sincerity, "I am grateful you are in Kayne's life and hope he will continue to share you with the rest of us. You are welcome to the Aerie at any time."

"Thanks, Bud." I returned some affectional contact. Damn, a definite Aussie-American Chris Evans, only hunkier, if that is possible. *Like, man, don't you have to get back to filming the next Avengers sequel?*

He smiled, "Please excuse me, Nick. Those folks are the team who are rebuilding the Lodge, and I promised to review some preliminary plans." He indicated the arriving group of four professional-looking men and women.

"Sure, Mitch. Let's talk later."

Halfway to the architectural firm team, Mitch turned and retrieved his husband from the very patient Kayne.

Kick was thrilled to be a part of the consult. The group exited the patio to a nearby conference room. I glanced through the window and just caught the designers queuing up a presentation on the room's media.

***

Released from his sibling's captivity, Kayne started in my direction, carrying what I soon found out was his own Hibiki rocks and my Negroni. As we met, we wordless clinked glasses. We were intercepted by the arriving Special Agent Ras. He was pretty much recovered from the escape from the burning Hell of a week ago. A bandage on this forehead was the only hint.

"I am sorry to intrude, Dr. Sorenson, but may we have a few moments?"

"We are at your service, Special Agent. I spot a private space on the other side of the fireplace. Will that be acceptable?"

As we moved off, I remembered the official interactions after the events at Landrose and Aerie Lodge five days ago. The FBI and the local law enforcement departments had taken statements from just about all involved in the death of Special Agent Kura at the Landrose Detention Center.

"Please allow me to again express, on behalf of my family, our sincere sympathy at the death of your comrade, the late Kristin Kura."

"Thank you, Dr. Sorenson. Services were held at Quantico yesterday. The FBI is again indebted to you for your involvement in this case. I believe our united efforts saved a few lives and will put the criminals behind bars."

Danny came by to take the drink order of the three agents who were officially off duty.

Nodding to his team, "Yes, this meeting is just an unofficial summary for your information."

Ras continued, "Under the leadership of Special Agent Mary Chaffee, we have mounted a full-scale investigation on the operations of the Landrose facility. It is being closed. It presently detains 800 undocumented men, women, and children, 200 more than its design capacity. Injunctions have been filed against the NEO group, which has yet to release a statement. Curiously, they seem to have disappeared off the map, but we are following up."

I noticed the oddity of a few guests who looked out of place, a bit tough and rawboned. They seemed to be observing Kayne and the members of our party. I bookmarked it and thought nothing more of it at the time.

Kayne continued the conversation, "Increasingly strange. A situation that holds the potential for all sorts of evil, I'll wager. We have not heard the last of NEO or whatever mutation of the company will follow because of this series of crimes."

"We are making some international inquiries, Doctor. It may take some time, but we will get them."

We were joined by Mark Gadarn. The reporter looked a bit wan from the recovery process and favored his injury beneath his ski jacket worn over his broad shoulders.

"Guys, I am bored spitless, waiting for Rebecca to complete her runs, and a bit jealous. You mind if I join you?" He pulled up a chair and placed his bottle of Guinness on the coffee table.

"Mark, what say we get you and Kick on the bunny slopes? Two gimpy goofballs getting knocked off by the kiddies out of the way down." I joked.

Mark responded in kind, 'Don't make me take you on, Officer, remember the poisoned pen of a member of the press can whomp your red ass along with these." He attempted to raise both fists.

"Ow!"

Kayne, Mark, and I roared. The FBI dudes did not know what to make of us. Kayne introduced Mark, another hero of the battle of the Uncompahgre Gorge.

Kayne said, "My brother Mitch mentioned that the Nu Ci Tribal Court has called for an official review of the activities of Chief Jake Gray Wolf Mingan. That group will turn over to the FBI their findings on the money laundering, embezzlement, racketeering, kidnapping, and murder-for-hire. The Jeron Adobo Jordan papers represent key evidence in the case against the Tribal Leader. You will have those."

Ras responded, "Yes, Red Feather Oil and Gas operations have been suspended. However, with re-organization and proper financial and environmental oversight, their oil business can begin to bring much-needed revenue to the Tribe. The Council is in the process of passing legislation that prohibits Tribal members from owning private interests in the industry and its subsidiaries."

I added, "Good move on their part. I understand Josh Red Cedar Walker was appointed Interim Leader. It is a sure bet that he will clinch the election next month."

Ras continued, "Kriegston is also under Federal injunction. Their offices are under lockdown as hordes of our agents and local prosecutors examine data, hard copy, and electronic files.

"Sebastian Moran has survived the crash and has recently regained consciousness. His response to criminal charges has been to cop a plea in return for turning state's evidence.

"A critical piece of evidence turned over to the FBI was retrieved from the safe room. Dr. Mitch Sorenson had stowed a leaden chest in the Lodge's vault containing the oil socks given to him by the Tribe's environmental officer, Jeron Jordan. All Kriegston mining operations have been shut down."

Mark asked about the uranium.

Agent Ras explained, "There is ample evidence that Kriegston had set up a covert ore refining operation on the Nu Ci land disguised as part of the oil and natural gas industry. Depleted uranium was being sold in the Middle East and Africa. The process involved fusing uranium ore with metal alloys to create bullets used to penetrate enemy armored vehicles. They also had plans to develop armored plating for mega-war weapons.

"All of this was being done in collaboration with Schlachtross. Their research division had developed an unmatched tank killer weapon capable of destroying any fielded armored transport. The facility here was a prototype for a much more significant operation headquartered in the Caucasian Mountains of Azerbaijan.

"We are looking at the damage to this environment with the Tribe. Initial readings seem to indicate it is relatively minor. Still, these studies will take years involving cases of radiation-related health issues."

Mark said, "US forces used depleted uranium in the Gulf War, Bosnia, Operation Enduring Freedom, Operation Iraqi Freedom, and Operation New Dawn. Many of our fighting men and women may have been exposed to DU munitions. This is deadly stuff for warriors and civilians. Depleted uranium --all supplied by Schlachtross Security Operations."

Kayne said, "I am familiar with a report from a Harvard study on the fallout of depleted uranium contamination in the Gulf War. That study underscored the extent of the damage related to the use of such depleted uranium weapons and the intended concealment, denial, and misleading information released by the Pentagon.

"The study shows the incidents of cancer and congenital disabilities among the Iraqis since 2004 is tantamount to the civilian damage to Hiroshima and Nagasaki in 1945."

Mark mused, "It is unconscionable that the Western nations are outraged to the point of calls for intervention and retaliation when Syrian civilians are the victims of chemical weapons. However, the US and our allies have appeared to ignore the use of DU weapons that are equally vicious."

I asked, "Agent Ras, is there evidence that Kriegston was refining any other nuclear material — for energy reactors or warheads?"

"We believe that it was among their long-range production goals. It is hard to disguise large-scale nuclear refineries here, but we have indications that the parent company...."

"NEO," Kayne interjected.

"Yes, Dr. Sorenson, NEO — is selling uranium ore to developing nations to be processed on foreign soil to high-grade nuclear weapons material."

Kayne looked around at the group. "There is great evil here, gentlemen, and I fear we have just scratched the surface."

***

Rebecca came within feet of the low retaining barrier, spinning to the side in the last seconds to shower Ace with a sheet of powder. Ace yelled and vaulted over the wall at the beautiful skier, who placed an index finger at the tip of her chin that teased, *Opps, my bad.*

"You will pay for that, my girl." Ace stopped a few feet from her to gather handfuls of snow and propelled them at the dark-haired Snow Queen.

"You mind yourself, you big bruiser." Rebecca popped her skis and took up ammunition, firing at the blustering Aussie. Darana and Monica skied up into the fracas and joined in the battle. The snow flew, landing on heads and torsos and sending icy slivers down collars and into open jackets.

Ace roared, "Come on, blokes, your Captain is outnumbered here. *Semper Fi!*"

Mark, Kayne and I left our Feds and jumped the wall, scooping up snow and hurling it at any and everyone. The battle was on.

"Hoo Rahh!"

Hearing the hoopla out on the patio, Mitch and Kick dashed from the conference room to witness the escalating snowball barrage. I heaved a snow missile at the unsuspecting Kick and nailed him in the crotch. I whooped with delight.

Kayne shouted, "Now, you've done it, Mate, messing with the *Supaidāman*. You will pay for your folly."

We watched as Kick recovered quickly from iced nuts and ran, arm still in the sling, to the wall of the Resort.

The dude actually *ran up the wall*, flipped, and landed feet-first next to me. He grinned at my amazement.

"Hah Haaaa! Surrender to my power, puny man!"

He scooped snow and, with one hand, washed my face in the icy, wet mass. I flopped on my ass in hysterics.

Mitch raced to his side and, with a bit of mischief on his face, began to make snowballs for his one-armed husband to fire at the combatants.

Mark came up behind his lady love and pulled her from the fight.

"Let's go, Wonder Woman. There is a Marie Laveau over on Danny's bar that has your name on it."

The Ice Princess surrendered at the mention of spirits and kissed her Welsh Prince. Smiling and quite mischievous, she flipped the bird to her Aussie opponent and headed to the bar.

Ace lost interest in the snow war without his Amazon nemesis. He captured his Darana in a hug, saying, "You were bewdy bonza out there. I am very proud of you, my girl."

"You have no idea of the unleashed powers of all of this, Captain," She indicated her fabulousness with a twirl. "Buy me a hot drink, please. Lace it with a bit of spirits, Soldier. And we can take it from there."

Determined to wage the battle even without confederates, Kick landed a few ice bombs on the newly arriving Gints, who followed a victorious Scott to the finish line. They made a few return shots on defense. Before Mitch declared a truce.

Doffing their skis and poles, Scott rejoiced, "And your ass is mine, Latvian boy!" He jumped on the broad back of his big buddy and then bounced off at a run. Gints declared defeat as he chased the victorious boy onto the patio and towards the bar, clunky ski boots notwithstanding.

I pulled Kayne into a snow wrestle and ended up making out in a snowbank with my gorgeous-looking professor man. Mitch, settling on the patio wall, pulled Kick into his lap. He called over, "Come on, you two, it's way too early for the spring thaw. Let's not melt the slopes. Aerie Valley, Inc. needs the revenue."

Chapter Thirty-Seven: A Tom Waits Lyric
Nick Sechi's Journal

As darkness settled over the Resort and the night, ski lights flooded over the slopes, a much subdued and somewhat inebriated Sorenson party gathered around the central firepit of the nearly deserted patio. It was all laughter and friendly jibes when a pair of new arrivals joined us.

An impressive Josh Walker and his no less striking brother Brave, Matthew Strong Bear, joined us around the roaring fire. In the last four days, both had recovered remarkably well from the Battle for the Aerie Valley. Dressed in winter outerwear, they each sported the trimmings that distinguished them as the Nu Ci Nation leaders.

Both sets of shoulder-length black hair were tied back with leather headbands and plaited with subtle decorations of beads and a few feathers. Their boots bore the markings of expert Native American artisans. The few occupants of the bar were transfixed by the presence of these two gorgeous Braves. *Again, I noticed the weird guys on the watch. Hmmm.*

Ace said with a bit of macho swag, "Well if it isn't the Tribal Leader, himself, and the head of the Nu Ci Police. Welcome, friends of my family. We are delighted to see you." It was easy to see he was sincere.

"Mr. Sorenson, we would like Ms. Cooper to have this as a token of our Nation's esteem for you and your family."

Josh presented Darana with a turquoise and silver necklace.

"As a remembrance of your visit to our people."

Darana was ecstatic as Rebecca placed the jewelry around her neck. The metalwork was highlighted by the deep black of her coloring. She modestly thanked Josh and Matt with a shy kiss of gratitude. Ace beamed.

"Mitch and Kick, I regret that I must resign my position as Master of Horse, at least temporarily until the installation of the next Tribal Leader."

"Which is him, no doubt about it. It did not seem possible, but the Tribe has grown in even more respect for Red Cedar." Matt clapped a hand on the shoulder of his man, who looked at his young partner with affection.

"Speaking for Kick and myself, I want to say how appreciative we have been for your years of service and your continuing friendship."

They both moved close to shake hands and do a shoulder bump with the two Native leaders. As Kick took each of their hands, he joined them in his. He spoke softly, but we managed to overhear.

"You will both come by occasionally for a ride -- the horses, I mean."

Kayne did a spit take, waisting a mouthful of Hibiki. Rebecca let out an appalled, "Oh, Kick Darling!" Gints was signaling bewilderment to Scott, who made a silent side-by-side rubbing of two index fingers, trying not to be noticeable. Gints got the idea.

Like many of us, I was speechless but looked to see the reaction. Matt and Josh smiled at the terrible *faux pas* but gently hugged the shoulders of the impish Prince of Aerie.

"Let's go, Kick Boy. We need to roll this one way back." Mitch pulled his husband out of the mix as Kick protested, "What? What'd I say?" No one, for an instant, believed he did not know the meaning of his comment. He had this habit of lowering his head and smiling as he devilishly gazed through his eyelashes at the crowd's reaction.

Kayne wiped up his mouth and said, "Please join us." He pointed to two empty outdoor chairs near the fire.

Josh looked up at the night sky and heaved a sigh. Then, his face shining in the firelight, he smiled and said, "Thank you, but I need to do something first."

No one made a move for about fifteen seconds. Then Ace said to the somewhat conflicted Brave, "Do it, Mate. The time is now. No going back." He stood up and moved back to stand behind Darana and give Josh a bit of space.

Josh dropped to his knees in the firelight and stared at the flames as if hypnotized. Rebecca gasped with emotion and reached over to Mark. She also knew what was about to happen.

Matthew, a bit perplexed, looked down at his hero and his love as the beautiful Brave used his right hand to struggle in his pocket and remove a large silver ring.

On his knees, Joshua Red Cedar Walker turned to face Matthew Strong Bear. I remember thinking that the expression on Matt's face was that of a man on the knife edge of wonder and realization.

Josh took Strong Bear's hand in his and spoke with love and conviction.

"Matthew, all my happiness is yours. All your sadness will be mine. May the whole world be yours if only you will be mine. From this day forward, your spirit shall not walk alone. My heart will be your shelter, and yours will be mine. My arms will be your home, and your arms will be mine."

There was absolute silence.

Josh held up the ring. "Please say, 'yes,' Matt."

Matt pulled Josh off his knees and into his arms. He kissed him with years of unleashed passion in a moment of absolute freedom from shame and doubt.

Pulling back but not releasing the dazzling Chief, Matthew said, "Yes."

Red Cedar let out a loud whoop and placed the ring on Strong Bear's finger. The kiss that followed was a true expression of love's triumph.

The result was an uproar that tossed our crowd into jubilation and ecstatic congratulations for the happy men. Guests emptied into the patio to find out what the excitement was.

Kick did a series of no-hands flips, somersaults, and cartwheels, hooting and cheering in a freerun celebration of joy over the happiness of his friends. Chouko and White River raced around, bounding and barking like they were part of the acrobatic act.

"How did you know, Captain?"

Cuddling up, Ace replied, "Darana, a man only gets that look on his face when he is about to do something monumental, my girl. Your Ace reads the heart, my Shelia. You just realizing that? Fair dinkum, and Bob's your uncle."

Mark commented on the action to the practically swooning Rebecca, "Never love anyone who treats you as ordinary, my girl. Oscar Wilde."

Holding on to the strong arms of the man I so deeply loved, I started to speak. Kayne placed an index finger against my lips. It was one of my favorite intimate gestures from my adorable beauty. He looked around, shot his black locks, and whispered my favorite Ingrid Bergman line,

"A kiss is a lovely trick designed to stop speech when words become superfluous."

He replaced his finger with his lips, and I was 'all in,' as they say, body, mind, and spirit.

After a heavenly eternity, it was my turn to quote. Unsuperfluously, I whispered to Kayne, "It was a hubba hubba, ding dang. Baby, you are everything."

Chapter Thirty-Eight: Moonstruck
NICK SECHI'S JOURNAL

Later that evening, Kayne and I had a chance to be alone. We took one of the Resort's snowmobiles and headed up to the Horse Palace. Kayne phoned Luke and asked if we could go on a night ride. He met us by the light of a full moon at the Palace with Black Shadow, an impressive stallion, and a regal two-year-old Appaloosa with a black, gray, and white Grulla blanket pattern.

"This is Aerie's Legend. She is a spirited Appaloosa but does not suffer from night blindness as many members of her breed do." Luke explained as he handed me the reins, and I mounted up into the saddle

Kayne looked like a Tartar Lord astride the Black Shadow. His long black hair and slightly almond-shaped eyes gave him a pagan warrior cast on his mighty charger. I was lost in the thought of coming back in the summer and riding bareback and naked into the woods with my fantasy crush.

Damn, this dude made me so fuckin' frisky.

"Officer Sechi? Hello."

"Oh, sorry, Luke."

"I was saying to you both that when you return, phone me, and I will put the tack and the horses up."

Kayne said, "Not necessary, lad. We can put them away. I remember how. We may be a bit late. It is pretty warm, so the horses will be fine. Not thinking of running much. Just a walk around. Is the code for the keypad still the same."

"Yes, Kick's birthday... Oh yeah, it's yours, too. Sorry, I forgot."

I smiled as the Legend backed up and did a slow circle in the courtyard. We were getting used to each other.

Black Shadow reared up, and Kayne held his seat. It was as if they were figuring out who would be the master on the midnight jaunt.

Tribal Blood

"There's the cabin back in the hills if you guys want to, ah…."

"I think we will pass on that." He looked over at me. "If it snows again, we may not get out for days."

"Actually, that sounds good to me," I joked a bit lasciviously.

Luke rolled his eyes and let us be on our way. The horses were anxious to take us out along the moonlit trails, glistening with snow and ice crystals.

We walked our mounts down the ranch's trails and headed north up the Valley. We trotted through fields where the snow was not too deep. Near the forest edge, we got into a good, short run. After about an hour, we entered a pine glade and moved slowly between the trees.

Kayne dismounted. "I need to rest my arse a bit, Mate. I haven't been astride in a lifetime, it seems."

"Did you wear proper gear?"

"Oh, yes. And I hate when I am trussed up like a Christmas turkey." He did a man-equipment adjust.

We tied the horses to the brush, and I pulled my sore-balled rider to me against a tall pine.

"Some vacation, eh, my love?" he said. He passed me his hip flask of Hibiki- an excellent warm-up.

"You know how much I love big, loud families, but it is good to get you alone with me. I am so thankful we all got out alive. I mean the battle at the prison and the destruction of the Lodge. Now it's over, Boss." I hugged him close.

"Yes, poor Agent Kura, though."

He added, stumbling a bit, "I will never let anything harm you, Nick. I can't tell you how much you, um… how much you mean to me."

I looked into his sky-blues, shaded but catching a glint of moonlight every now and then.

"Try."

I was so in the mood.

He paused, swallowed, and said, "OK. I have been thinking of this for a while now. I hope it makes sense.

"When I spent a bit of time in Japan a few years ago, I became acquainted with a remarkable custom. I hope you don't think this is weird."

He pulled me close and whispered, pointing to the sky through the trees, "*Kon'ya wa tsuki ga utsukushīdesu ne?*"

Knowing that my Japanese was limited to commanding my Beautiful Butterfly, Kayne translated, "The moon is beautiful tonight, isn't it?"

He kissed me and said, "In Japan, the one who speaks these words does so with a sense of shyness. The sentiment expresses gratitude to the beloved as if to say, 'You've opened my eyes and my heart to the beauty of life, my love.'"

He caressed my cheek with one gloveless hand. The horses moved softly nearby, almost as if they respected our intimacy. A soft night breeze brushed snowy branches overhead, sending a delicate cascade of light snow into the moonlight around us.

"Nick, I am so hopelessly in love with you. You make me happy and bring to the chaos with which I often surround myself a saneness and a strength. My beautiful Nick...."

"Wow." I smiled and said softly, "I thought sentiments of love tongued-tied you as much as it does me, but I was wrong. You are awesome, Kayne. You leave me breathless." I kissed him for what felt like an eternity.

He chuckled and turned me so that he hugged me from behind. "Or, more simply put, your crazy matches, my crazy, kiddo. But I am amazed at what's happening to us in some very insane situations -- quite remarkable."

The light, the horses, the snow, the trees – all so exotic, I was spellbound and snowbound. Rather than just think it, I said, "Let's see this through, beautiful man. I am starting to be unable to think of a life without you. With you, it holds more wonder."

We stayed that way for a while in each other's arms, exchanging words of love. As the night grew colder, we mounted up and turned the horses toward the Palace.

Chapter Thirty-Nine: Shadow
NICK SECHI'S JOURNAL

The lights were on in the old horse barn.

Strange, I thought. It was after 2 a.m. *Who works this late on a ranch in the winter?*

We had stabled the horses and put up the saddles and tack. We were walking back to the snowmobile to return to the Resort.

"Let's check this out, Nick. Could be Luke has insomnia."

The opening through the double set of large barn doors was unlocked and partially ajar. A shaft of light spilled out over the icy driveway from the interior. Kayne examined the snow that let up to the partially opened door. There were no footprints.

As we stepped over the raised threshold into the interior of the old structure, the vastness of the open space was captivating. Originally designed to hold rows of stables, the area had been gutted to provide a performance and auction arena for the Aerie breeds. Tiers of seats banked the two side walls. Together with the large sliding barn doors at the rear of the arena, the set-up suggested an area that held the horses up for auction before they were brought forward into the arena staging area.

The barn ceiling was open all the way to the underside of the roof. Massive rafters crossed the open space, and ten wooden piers, sunk in cement bases, five to a side, supported the weight of the roof and the heavy snow in winter. Long chains ended in large, white, circular metal lampshades. Their curved surface reflected the substantial lighting elements across the area. Only three were illuminated. The result was a series of light shafts descending into the darkened space.

I called out, "Who's in here?"

Somewhere in the back, there were horse sounds. Into the last circle of light stepped a man dressed entirely in black. A full-length coat dropped to the top of shiny leather boots. He wore a long scarf and gloves but was without a hat. As we approached cautiously, I saw that the man had albinism with a brush of snow-white hair worn in a tight crew cut. He wore dark glasses and spoke with a slight sibilance and a foreign accent. He held his hands in front, palms pressed together as if in prayer.

"Ah, Dr. Sorenson, the man who has cost me a fortune."

Kayne and I were thunderstruck. We stopped our advance, and I made sure that I was slightly off to Kayne's left, my cop training kicking in.

I sensed there were others about, somewhere in the back. A man with the military bearing of our unexpected guest would not travel alone. The shadows at the rear of the barn were too thick to make out much detail. A set of doors stood open, but the space beyond was entirely black.

"I am afraid, Sir, you have me at a disadvantage."

"That is as I intend, Professor."

The specter removed his dark glasses and squinted before opening wide red eyes, gazing at his two apparent captives. As I moved to outflank the stranger, he warned, "Careful, Officer Sechi. We dare not repeat past mistakes, eh? Your exploits are well known to me.

Furthermore, I am sure that the two of you are unarmed. There is no place for guns in a romantic, moonlit forest. So much passion, gentlemen. Quite disgusting."

He paused to let his point sink in.

"I assure you that my comrades...." He gestured behind him, " ... have you in their crosshairs, shall we say?"

I thought of the mysterious-looking men at the Resort party.

Again, the stirring of horses in the dark behind him.

"I will stay just a few minutes more. However, before I leave, a word of warning. Your interference in my activities is about to end, Doctor. It would be disingenuous of me to say that I regret the dire consequences of your annoying behavior. In truth, I have looked forward to it."

"I am afraid I do not recall our direct association, but I can draw inferences, Mr...?

The white man in black said nothing. He let the question hang in the air of the arena.

Finally, he replied, "I am Ragheb Karadžić."

"Ahh. Your brother is Radovan Karadžić, the Butcher of the Balkans... the Bosnian War."

The man clicked his heels and made a small nodding bow.

He hissed, "I, too, have a very, shall we say, interesting family, much like yours, Dr. Sorenson, and yours, Officer Sechi. My my, all those women, Nicky."

At the mention of my family, a chill went down my spine. I also became aware that the door behind us had closed. The sound of a bolt had snapped in place from the outside.

"We came close to spending time together in Hungary a few years back, Dr. Sorenson. Your very scandalous and carnal affair resulted in quite a bit of somewhat embarrassing trouble for a significant operative in my organization. I believe you referred to him as 'my Golden Hussar' in your many romantic communications.

"Regrettably, your Magyar prince had to be removed as my special 'liaison,' shall we say, after his dismissal from a very vital position in the Hungarian Government.

Kayne said nothing.

"Seriously, Doctor? Public nudity on the Danube Promenade while fleeing an overzealous lover? The people of Budapest are not as liberal as, say, the communities of Alice Springs or the Bronx."

Again, he paused. This last ludicrous remark informed us that he knew each of us in much detail. This is a man with considerable information and a network of informers.

Kayne, as if transfixed, spoke one word, "Ádám."

"Very good, Doctor," Karadžić leered. "How ironic that Major Haagen's last word as he died was a pain-filled single word: 'Kayne.' As always, you make quite an impression on your men, clothed or unclothed."

The albino's mocking laugh was high-pitched and terrifying.

"And then there was the imperial affair in Japan. Your interference cost me substantially. My interests needed to be relocated because of your intrusion."

"You could not blackmail the third in line to the Chrysanthemum Throne once I convinced him to admit his sexual orientation. And, Karadžić, your mafia assassins are complete hacks, then and now. No match for the Osaka Brotherhood. They and the Imperial State police were able to clear out your organization admittedly with my considerable help-- quickly and completely."

"You will address me as General Karadžić, Doctor."

His voice had attained a new intensity verging on the manic. He pointed accusingly at Kayne as he began another charge.

"I was growing the perfect psychotic in Ft. Lauderdale when you and your Watson here decided to play your little Sherlock game. You destroyed my enterprise in a very wealthy and strategically positioned community. The mentally unstable have always been useful to me. They are easily guided to create the most delectable chaos. The opportunity to work with your brother, or should I say, 'brothers,' continues to be a delicious prospect."

He drew closer but stopped. I looked across the broad, empty space for something I could use as a weapon. The empty arena space offered no such opportunity.

"And now..." he hissed. "Now, you have destroyed a major arm of my industrial operations here in Colorado. It may interest you to know that Colonel Sebastian Moran passed away a few moments ago, to be exact. One of those dreadful hospital mishaps, it appears."

He paused and smiled before continuing.

"Jake Gray Wolf Mingan will be found dead in his hospital bed by morning. Many will express surprise as he appeared to be on the road to recovery. Taking an unexpected turn for the worse. So unfortunate."

General Ragheb Karadžić now stood inches from Kayne. He deftly lifted a revolver from his coat, dramatically raised it to the ceiling above his head, and slowly lowered it. Gun in hand, he extended his arm to the side and pointed the weapon at me. His eyes never left Kayne's face as he spoke.

"Ahh. Such a lovely boy. Young Nicky. Are you in love again, Dr. Sorenson? I would strongly advise against it. You do not do well with intimacy, and the danger that surrounds you is vast."

I could feel, across the space between us, Kayne's cold, ticking rage. Starting off slowly and quietly, the Bosnian Monster threatened, "If you continue to frustrate me, Dr. Sorenson, I will begin with this fine specimen and…."

His words seemed to trail off in a whisper. But suddenly, the wraith finished his threat by screaming with a deranged ferocity.

"… I WILL FEED YOUR FLESH TO PIGS!"

The insane General drew out the last phrase in an echoing scream of anger and frustration, a fine spray of spit accompanying his rant.

Kayne started for the gun, but Ragheb Karadžić moved back with lightning speed, flapping his coattails like the wings of a horrifying dragon. He returned to his calm, cold state and aimed now for Kayne's chest.

"No, no, no, Doctor, Sorenson. Maintain your position, please. Harm me at your peril."

The movement of armed men in the dark increased as the two of us stood frozen. I heard firearms click in the near darkness as safeties were removed. The General spiraled into the night but not before turning and facing us once more with a hateful, red-eyed stare.

There was no sound for a second. Then, a black horse appeared under the light shaft that had previously spotlighted our nemesis. The mighty beast stopped and raised his head to look at us with large, dark eyes. It was a surreal image that seemed at once beautiful and foreboding.

Shouting and gunshots erupted from the back of the barn.

"Run!"

The stampeding hoard rushed from the blackness and made directly for us. I followed Kayne's example and shouted and raised my arms, fending off the panicked equines as they raced to the front of the barn, only to turn back and swirl around the open space.

Drivers in black appeared for a short time to keep the mob rushing in our direction. I fell to one knee as I rebounded against the side of a massive beast. I fought to reach the safety of the arena's seating area. The last I saw of Kayne, he was moving with the horses stampeding towards the entrance doors. He reached up and grabbed the mane of a steed slowed by a pile-up of its companions.

I covered my head and tried to dash under the belly of a charger. No good. I came out and smacked my head against the skull of an enraged stallion. As I crashed into the mass of horseflesh whirling around me, I knew that if I fell, I would die.

The stampede continued in the dim arena. The frenzied swirl of the horses grew denser as they kicked up dirt. The yelling from the drivers ceased, and the lights went out. One after the other, screaming juggernauts -- 1,300 pounds of frightened animal knocked me around like a ping-pong ball in the dark. I managed to reach one of the seating area walls, pressing myself against the boards. Careening mustangs made it impossible for me to heave myself over. I tried to move to the front of the arena, where movement stalled as the horses reversed their direction.

Suddenly, Kayne, astride a black mount, reached down for me and hauled me up behind him. I grabbed his body, slumping into him. Moving horses mashed up against our legs, and the mass began to reverse its direction yet another time.

As the darkness of unconsciousness began to fill my brain, I felt a blast of cold air shoot through the barn. I heard yelling and screaming from the front of the building.

"Cooee... cooee... mook, mook, mook."

The stream of frightened animals turned and raced through the newly opened doors. Torn, bruised, and bloodied, Kayne lowered me off the side of the stallion and dropped next to me. His horse followed the herd in the direction of the stable. I slumped into his arms.

"Nick, are you...?"

I managed to stand on my own, staggering against the wall of the gallery. I assured Kayne I was not seriously hurt.

The last of the horses streamed to the wide, opened stable doors. Reaching out to him to steady us both, I asked Kayne, "Are you OK?"

"I feel like the only defender in a very rough footy match, Mate." He managed a weak smile and winced at pressure against his bad shoulder.

We turned to our rescuers, who were outside herding the chargers across the paddock and into the open doors of the Horse Palace. With arms raised, Luke and a few of his staff shouted the poor beasts home. The crew had been awakened by the shots, and animal screams echoing through the ranch compound.

"Da! Well, what the bloody Hell? Shoulda recognized the herding call of an Aussie rancher."

"My son, you are not the only Sorenson seeking some moonlight-loving tonight." He and Darana pulled us close.

She smiled and said, "Do not be fooled. The Master of Inala Ranch had a yearning to be near some livestock. We have been too long, too far from our own paddocks. Are you both uninjured?"

I said, "Nothing broken but badly bruised. Ow."

Kayne hugged his father. "It would appear we both will survive. You both know how to herd a mess of horses. You saved our lives." Ace stroked his loving son's hair and spoke softly to him.

"One of them clipped you good, Nick," Darana said, examining my skull. "We need to get you both checked out."

Abruptly, Kayne pushed out of his father's grasp and raced around to the rear of the building. He held his shoulder at an unusual angle as he ran with a slight limp. I yelled after him,

"Kayne, no!"

I managed to dash after him with Darana. Ace sprinted ahead.

The headlights of a speeding vehicle were disappearing around the back road to the ranch, climbing into the mountains.

"Fuckin' bloody hell!"

Chapter Forty: Exquisite Butt

MARK GADARN'S NOTES

Rebecca jumped back into bed and pulled the blankets up above her breasts. She had arranged my pillows so that I was sitting next to her and did the same for her side of the bed. She wore one of my white dress shirts, a look that always got me going.

She swatted the tented space between my legs.

"Put that thing away, Darling. We can make *bumsen* all morning long. Breakfast with my gays first."

I lamented my frustrated male condition.

"Mark Darling, a bet is a bet, and we won." She pointed at the slowly shrinking evidence of my ardor. "And that will just send the wrong message to these frisky boys. You know that it will."

I guffawed as a knock came on the door of our bedroom.

"Come in, Darlings."

Wearing only catering aprons, the losing teams of the snowmobile race entered from the living room of the Owner's Suite with bed trays and trolleys of breakfast fare.

Kayne acted as the *maitre d'*, directing the feast. Gints brought a standing ice bucket of champagne, carafes of orange juice, and iced flutes. Nick poured the coffee, and Scott arranged the Eggs Benedict before the beaming couple.

There was naked man-ass everywhere.

I said, "Looks like our own male strip show at one of them...."

Dead silence and all action stopped. All eyes shot to me.

Nick teased, "Yeessss? Please go on, Mr. Hetero-Gadarn."

Rebecca's expression was the priceless visage of a woman waiting for a car crash.

I cleared my throat and stammered, "Oh, come on! Well, so I am told... um, yeah, and well, I've seen movies and...."

"Movies? Gints is familiar with same. We call it gay porn in Latvia."

"No, no, no... I mean... ahhh... so, not exactly that kinda...."

"Mark? Mark. Stop talking, Darling. Shhh now. There's a good boy."

Rebecca shot back a glass of the bubbly. I felt a "Nick Sechi blush" of my own.

"Kayne, be a darling, Darling, and bring me my slippers. Yes, behind the chair."

"You are as subtle as a flying brick, my girl. You just want to see my hot Aussie arse."

Nick grabbed some Kayne buns and said, "And gorgeous ones they are."

We both raised our glasses.

The scene was interrupted by a late arrival who flipped onto the bed, straddling the lower part of my legs.

Kick's version of the "caterer's apron only" dress code was a navy-blue dinner napkin tied with an extra-large shoelace at his narrow waist. The resulting loin cloth was barely enough to cover his flopping privates.

He joked excitedly, "I brought the Tequila, fellas. Let's flip this straight, babe. What say?"

I roared and tumbled the jokester off the bed. He toppled to the floor without dropping his bottle. Rebecca threw a slipper at the giggling, just about naked, "Hot Mess."

"Yo, no ravishing, my man, you frisky little devil. Leave the hot, straight men for the real girls, Darling. Warning, I am deadly with shoes."

"Why am I never invited to the party? Could it be that I most assuredly outshine the rest in the jaw-dropping physique department?"

Mitch stood in the doorway with yet another trolley. This time, more champagne and flutes surrounded by chocolates and strawberries, enough for everyone, filled the trays. He had respected the dress code, rocking one magnificent, ginger, muscled body complete with a breathtaking jock butt.

"Get in here and show that Sorenson arse, Darling."

Laughter all around as Mitch poured out the Dom, exaggerating his "bend over" a bit.

"Who is blaspheming the honor of my family?" Came a booming voice from outside the bedroom door.

Screaming with laughter, Rebecca pulled the napkin to her face, expecting to see a semi-naked head of the family. Ace and Darana joined the troupe modestly clad in their dressing gowns. Mitch handed them filled flutes and strode to the window wall.

"Put ya knickers back on, lads. There are ladies present. Did I not raise ya better, ya brogans?

Kick half-stepped behind Mitch, saying, "Na, Da, ya didn't." This brought laughter from each of us.

As the aproned group assembled before the glass, Rebecca and I got a full view of some of the most muscular male glutes in the state of Colorado. She squealed beside me and clicked my glass with hers.

"I am in straight-woman heaven, Darling."

As we scrambled out of bed to join them, Mitch, one arm encircling Kick, raised his glass to the mountain cliffs across the Valley. The beginnings of a spectacular building site rose against the side of the mountain.

With bright enthusiasm, he led the toast,

"To the new Aerie. Cheers!"

Tribal Blood

Chapter Forty-One: Cava

Nick Sechi's Journal

I shot my cuffs. The tuxedo jacket was a bit tight in the shoulders but tailored just right at the waist. I appraised myself in the mirror. I let my scruff grow out a bit in the last month. I sized up my attempt at a stronger, more masculine, and less boyish look.

Not bad, Nick, my man.

I called across the sitting room of our suite, "Ace and Darana arrive OK?"

"Took 'em two days to make the Bush. Ace was as cross as a frog in a sock. Not that he isn't usually. He spit the dummy at having a stopover in Brizzie. Made it far worse. Hates the cave toads."

I scratched my head comically and said, "Kayne, bring me the 'Strine dictionary, please. I have no idea what you just said."

He laughed, heaved a fake sigh, and smiled, "The 'Bush' is the Outback. You know that one."

"Yep."

"Brisbane is the capital of Queensland, Australia -- Brizzie. Folks who live in Queensland are referred to as 'cave toads.' The reason for that is shrouded in the mists of legend. The rest is just colorful metaphor."

"Too bad the Ozzies never learned English."

Kayne came up behind me, nuzzled my ear, and gave one a sharp nip as punishment for the snide remark about his countryfolk.

"You know, you resemble those good-looking men on the red carpet, my love. Who's that gorgeous golden boy from PBS' *Grantchester*?" He snapped his fingers, trying for a name. "Plays the crime-solving country vicar."

"James Norton. Damn, you think so?" I smoothed my hair." He is crazy hot, dude."

"Ohh, yes. Fair suck of the sav, lad. But I love *your* beard, you ginger hot bastard." He traded an Aussie exclamation for an American one and rubbed my scruffy cheeks.

"You know, we need to do a 'Sexy Curate meets the Hunky and Very Hony Grounds Keeper' session real soon. Where do you suppose we can borrow a Roman Collar?"

I laughed and tried to calm his ardor by swatting him away. Giving in a bit, I kissed his sexy mouth and said, "You clean up pretty good yourself, Big Man, but underwear and pants are in order here. Who would ever attend a wedding going commando?."

We laughed and said together, "Kick."

Kayne was in his socks, an unbuttoned tuxedo shirt, and an untied bowtie, looking very handsome even though he had yet to finish dressing. He had picked up my boutonnière from the bar, smoothed the shoulders of my jacket, and turned me around.

"Here's your lapel thingo, Handsome. The red-tipped feather indicates that you have been injured in battle." He carefully pinned the small red feather and sprig of white sage to my left lapel. "But, Nick, I have been wondering why young Matthew asked you to be his best man."

Dramatic pause. With wicked delight, I smiled and faked unzipping my fly. "Here, allow me to show you why boy." I made like I was ready to haul out my junk but stopped.

Kayne laughed loudly, "I walked right into that one, Mate. You are a rippa, Nick. Funny, sexy, and all mine." He hugged me with care for my formal wear. He smelled of clean soap.

"Seriously, I think he has just about no one. His brothers aren't even coming to the wedding. Also, I think Matt hit a turning point after opening up. That was when we were up in the mountains searching for poor Jeron. I think I represent his newfound authenticity, to be honest."

Kayne's ice-blues looked deeply into my green eyes. "You are a good man, Officer Sechi." He smiled wryly. "I don't care what they say." He stepped into his briefs.

I cuffed him, and we raised up for a mock fight.

"Let's go, Darlings. You can do slap and tickle after the wedding."

Kayne mocked, "Girl, do you *ever* knock?"

"No, Darling. Just think of the things I would have missed."

She looked beautiful in an Ines Di Santo stunner – cream filigree lace from collarbone to thighs and a silk skirt flaring to her ankles. She wore her hair up in a tight bun set off by a bejeweled hairpin that matched her only other accessories, her turquoise earrings – gifts from the Nu Ci.

Mark followed, looking like a Welsh-American 007 in his black tux – a dirty blond Sean Connery of the *Dr. No* era. He also sported a red feather and sage boutonnière.

They had flown back to Ft. Lauderdale and returned for the Easter wedding. Rebecca was knee-deep in the planning stages for the new exhibit at the Fritcher Museum, *Tribal Blood*. She predicted a lavish opening in two years and a return to Aspen to continue the curating arrangements.

Mark had picked up a *60 Minutes* with his astonishing exposé reporting on the murder-for-hire scandals surrounding the Kriegston scandal in the Aerie Valley. Anderson Cooper's questions highlighted Mark's military connections and sources in the Middle East to reveal the global scope of the corruption. He was working on a book that expanded his coverage, poking around for more intel on NEO's crimes and their government connections.

"I think the next time we will all be in formal wear, Mate, will be when you get the Pulitzer for your journalism," Kayne said. He poured four flutes of Cava, and we toasted our friendship.

"We saw Mitch and Kick on our way in, Darlings. Mitch looks as nervous as a Christian Scientist with a severed artery. Are there a lot of issues with the construction?" Her voice took on a faked innocence, disguising her actual knowledge of Mitch's uneasiness. This was not lost on her three escorts.

I offered, "Oh, no. Mitch is there around the clock. Everything is going along as best it can be. He told me Kick is actually focused and helping with project details. It was his idea to bring in Bob Harper, the fitness guru, to design their exercise rooms and the pool."

Kayne agreed, "And Scott Iverson is very excited about being allowed to plan the kitchen facilities, the security, and the technology of the new Aerie Lodge. Mitch was talking about giving him a new title within the organization."

"Gints?" Mark switched gears.

I responded, "That boy's got it bad. If I did not know he was Latvian, I would have said he got hit by the Italian American thunderbolt. Flat-out stars in his eyes every time Scott wiggles his cute little butt."

Kayne agreed, "He falls fast and intensely, that boy."

"Yes, that you should know through experience, Darling."

Kayne stuck his tongue out at his best girl as he upended his glass and slipped on his jacket. He wagged an index finger at his best gal bud.

"Rebecca, why are you so naughty this morning? You are up to something, my girl. I know that look."

Rebecca shook her head and again did a burlesque of the innocent ingenue.

Mark asked, "Think he will be going back to Florida anytime soon?"

"I expect an announcement on that any day now," Kayne said. "You have got to see him in his new suit. That boy's physique drove the tailors absolutely mad."

Kayne next addressed the previous issue, "No, Dr. Sorenson, the psychiatrist, is sweating bullets because he has to stand up as Josh's best man. He is a hotter mess than the real Hot Mess this morning."

Everyone laughed. Rebecca jumped on it, seeing just the opening she needed to dish.

"Ohh Kayy. Now, let's break this down, shall we?" She began to imitate a society columnist. "Mitchell Andrew Sorenson, M.D. served as best man today for his Master of Horse, Joshua Red Cedar Walker, and occasional lover of Dr. Sorenson's husband, the notorious Thomas Michael Sorenson, aka...."

Mark, Kayne, and I interrupted her by saying the exact same thing at the same time, "He thought Mitch was dead!"

"I'm just sayin'." She brought her flute up to her lips but rolled her eyes over the brim as she took a sip.

She smiled wickedly and added one more jab, "A bit nervous? Darlings, I would be shitting bricks."

Kayne made as if to chase her around the suite.

"You absolute cat! You are Maleficent to the teeth."

Rebecca laughed and dodged the oncoming Kayne but did not get far in her gown.

"Oh, no, Darling." She now held Mark between them. "This Evil Queen was invited to the wedding of our two Beauties."

Mark stepped aside with hands raised as if to say, "Have at her."

Kayne hugged and tickled while commanding, "Promise you'll behave. Promise."

"Kayne, no! Stop." She wiggled and squirmed at his touch. "The gown, Kayne! OK, OK. I promise. I promise. There, OK? Family loyalty, my ass."

She gave him a lighthearted smack, "It's Ines Di Santo, you Outback hooligan." She cuffed him again, reversing his forelock sweep, which descended over his left eye.

"Don't make me report this to Ace, Sweetie. He will take you over one knee. Haute couture or no haute couture."

Mark's and my turn to eye roll.

"The man's a Neanderthal! You know he met his match with all of this." She did a fabulousness twirl. "Although, I would say Darana has him leashed up well."

Kayne straightened up a bit and appraised himself in the mirror, shot his forelock into its correct place, and pulled me into the frame. "Damn, we are a gorgeous pair of man hunkies, Officer."

I mugged with him and said, "Hubba hubba ding dang, Professor." I palmed his ass.

Rebecca attempted to push us away to recover her look from her high jinks with Kayne when her phone pinged. "Mary Chafee text... Holy shit."

She swept from the text from the FBI Agent through the link.

Two bodies found along the banks of the Palouse River had been identified as the missing Colorado State Troopers, Connelly and Barberi. Foul play is suspected.

Kayne looked as if a shadow had passed over his grave.

I looked at him and said, "Damn, more investigations, and I was hoping to leave. Blow this town and get onto some true vacation."

Mark finished his Cava, set the glass down, and addressed the group, "Enough. No crime fighting today in honor of our two illustrious grooms."

He put out his hand. "Cell phones, please." He gathered up the four amid some protestations. Still, in the end, we all agreed that honoring Matt and Josh with food, spirits, music, and dancing was the order of the day. No sooner had he placed them on the coffee table than they began to ping and chirp like baby chicks.

"I'll get the car, my lads, and fair Bond Girl. Meet you downstairs." He dashed as we three crushed the last of the sparkling wine.

Chapter Forty-Two: Joining Earth and Sky

NICK SECHI'S JOURNAL

The Alpaska Reservation's community gathering space was filled with the most eclectic crowd I had ever seen. Ranchers, cleaned up and finely dressed, sat side-by-side with law enforcement officers from all departments, including the Alpaska police, in their respective uniforms. Members of the Aerie Resort, the Wildlife Preserve, the Horse Palace, the Eagle's Nest Airstrip, and the staff of the Aerie Lodge filled another section of seats along with dignitaries from the greater Aspen community. The community joined with the Nu Ci Nation, arrayed in colorful Native attire to honor the marriage of their newly elected Tribal Leader and his Chief of Native Police.

As in every celebration, a fire pit dominated the center of the space. The entire area was decorated with cultural symbols, ribbon-festooned banners, and spirit shields of the grooms and their ancestors in the bright Easter sunshine. I recognized the insignia of Susan Chipeta Walker next to Josh's. I remembered thinking that her spirit had attained a new level of peace on this day.

Guests were seated in a circle surrounding the open area. Joletta Golden Tree and Elizabeth Rising Lark held their heads high as Kayne ushered them to their places in the front near the glowing brothers and sisters and other family members of Josh Walker. Matt's family was not in attendance.

The music was Native traditional, and the procession began with drums, flutes, and beautifully dressed Native dancers entering the space from the four cardinal directions. They whirled, jumped, and sang throughout the ceremonial expanse swooping poles trailing long ribbons out over the assembly.

The best men, Mitch and me, were escorted to the front by a pair of dancers and two children dressed in white. The youngsters served as acolytes throughout the ceremony holding our ritual objects until called for by the rite. As I walked next to Mitch, who looked like Captain America in formal wear, I noticed the distinctively exotic smell of Hibiki whiskey – Kayne and his trusty flask.

More colorfully dressed Natives danced around us with rattles, flutes, and smoke pots, calling forth spiritual blessings of peace, joy, and love. Two Elders led the grooms, one from the north and the other from the south, into the circle.

Matthew Strong Bear and Josh Red Cedar were dressed in white, fringed buckskin with matching boots, representing their new journey of happiness, fulfillment, and peace. Their cuffs, boot tops, and jewelry held splashes of vibrant color on their immaculate attire. Each warrior wore a folded blue blanket on their right shoulder, a symbol of the old ways. More richly colored ribbons completed their wedding regalia.

The grooms' headdresses symbolized their status in the Tribe. Josh's black, red, and white trailer war bonnet descended in double tails of eagle feathers, reaching all the way down his back to his heels. Matthew's was a smaller "halo" war bonnet but no less magnificent in turquoise blue, white, and black. Matt had been made a new Chief of the Nu Ci three days before the wedding by a unanimous vote of the Tribal Council.

As they approached the fire pit, elders of the Nation joined Pastor Irene Mendoza from the Aspen Metropolitan Community Church and the Tribe's Shaman, Joseph Brave Horse, as the entire clan began to chant.

The Medicine Man prayed in a voice that carried throughout the assembly.

"Red Cedar and Strong Bear, now you will feel no rain, for each of you will be a shelter for the other. Now you will feel no cold for each of you will be warmth for the other. Now, there is no loneliness. Now, you are two persons, but there is only one life in your shared journey. May your days be good and long upon the earth."

Elizabeth Rising Lark Walker stood beside her son, holding gifts of food and cloth. Joletta Golden Tree Collins stood beside Matthew, holding corn and a tanned buckskin.

Mitch and I stood behind the marriage group as representatives of support and responsibility for the new family should one of the partners die. We each held a red and black cloth belt made by Matt and Josh for each other. We also bore hand-crafted silver and opal wedding rings.

Reverend Mendoza asked God as the Great Spirit to bless the union and prayed for a long and happy life for the couple.

Josh fastened his belt around Matt's waist. He lovingly took the right hand of his life-long friend and partner in love saying, "I add my breath to your breath that our days may be long on the Earth. I give my life to you that the days of our people may extend to the far horizon of time. I join my spirit to yours that we may be as one person, that we may finish our journey together."

Matthew took his belt from me and tied it at Josh's hips, saying, "You are part of me now. You caressed me with your enchanted gentleness. Your lips are kind and full of truth. Your eyes glow with life. I rejoice that you have touched me. You are part of me now. We will never be parted in this life or the next."

As the couple exchanged the rings, Elizabeth and Joletta presented their gifts. Each unfolded their son's blue blankets and wrapped them individually. Josh and Matt joined the coverings by knotting the fringe, symbolizing the couple's mutual support.

Together, Reverend Mendoza and Brave Horse handed the grooms a ceremonial drink from a double-sided vessel. The couple toasted east, west, north, and south, declaring their union to the whole earth. Finally, they raised the cup to the sky as Brave Horse called upon the spirits to bless the marriage. The chalice was dashed upon rocks to seal the wedding vows. The broken fragments would be buried to return the symbol to Mother Earth.

Mitch and I carefully replaced the two blue blankets with white ones. Mitch carefully lifted the train of Josh's headdress over the portion of the covering that enclosed his back. The couple circled the fire clockwise as the sun circles the earth, taking seven steps together while reciting a prayer of devotion at each interval.

"Now we have become one completely. I offer my total self to you. May our union last forever."

"All these promises I have spoken with a pure heart. All the spirits bear witness. I shall love you forever."

Family and friends linked hands in a circle around the fire. Kayne took my hand as we joined the Native family members. His blue eyes were shining. I looked across to Mark, Rebecca, Gints, Scott, Luke, and Earth, who danced in the celebration of true love and a sacred way of life. Kick and Mitch pulled in next to us, and Kick added a few unique jumps and leaps to the circle dance. A young Brave mimicked his acrobatics with his own.

The mothers and the priests stepped into the center of the circle with the newly married couple. They prayed together, "God in the sky above, please protect these Braves. We honor all you created as we pledge our hearts and lives together. We honor Mother Earth and ask that their lives be abundant. May they grow strong through the seasons."

As the ceremony drew to a close, the two acolyte children broke into the inner space and jumped into the arms of Josh Red Cedar and Matthew Strong Bear. White River bounded in to secure her place in the new family with a cheerful bark.

Chapter Forty-Three: Generations

NICK SECHI'S JOURNAL

Kick crossed the reception area space, holding one of the wedding party children in his arms and leading the other by the hand.

"These are Matt and Josh's children, Blue Sparrow and Running Fox." He dropped to one knee and told the children, "You guys were sensational." After the introductions, he released the youngsters, and they investigated our group with wide eyes. They were especially fascinated with Rebecca and Gints. Blue sparrow touched Rebecca's dress with fascination.

"You will be big Chief of Tribe," Gints said, patting Running Fox on his head. "Grow big and strong like Gints." Coatless now, he threw a double bi-shot and bent over. Each of the children grabbed a bicep. As he stood up, Gints lifted the giggling youngsters off the ground."

"And you will grow big and strong too, Darling. And very stylish," Rebecca said, lowering Blue Sparrow to the ground. "Just like Wonder Woman."

The children laughed, gave the cross-arm salute of the Amazon superhero, and raced back into the party.

I watched as their new fathers swept them up into their arms, setting each on a strong shoulder.

Mitch enlightened us. "These children were orphaned when their parents were killed in an accident at Red Feather Oil and Gas Company. The Walkers took them in. Josh and Matt asked Blue Sparrow and Running Fox if they would like to join their new family.

Kick thought a moment and then said, "Hey, Mitch...."

"Don't even say it, love of my life. I would go completely bonkers." The handsome older brother turned to us and said with a stage whisper, "When people ask me if I have children, I say, 'Just the one.' If you catch my meaning."

He grabbed his wiggly husband and said, "C'mon, lad, give us a pash." Kick obliged, going from a pout-face into a husband-kiss.

"So much flagrant homosexuality," Mark mocked. "What's a poor straight boy to do?"

"After the party, sexy Darling. I talked Josh into lending us his war bonnet."

Mark faked a lustful beast response, 'The Savage Brave and the Innocent but Insatiable Quaker Missionary?' Count me in."

"I was thinking more of 'The Warrior Maiden and the Temporarily Impotent Calvery Officer,' Darling. The storyline is he needs some coaxing and the very talented maiden, well, she's quite good at...."

Mark growled.

Rebecca laughed and gently pushed him away. "Later, Darling. Come with me. The Tribe is beginning the ribbon dance."

Epilogue: Unforgettable

NICK SECHI'S JOURNAL

We walked away from the celebration to an isolated spot beneath a budding aspen tree. As spring settled into the Aerie Valley, we could see the snow clinging to the high elevations from where we were in new green meadows. The first wildflowers braved the sun's warmth and carpeted the slopes in yellow and green.

I pulled Kayne down beside me on flat rocks beneath the greening tree. We loosened each other's bow ties and slipped off our patent leathers.

"Impossible footwear," Kayne remarked. "Absolute torture in shiny black."

I chuckled, "Rebecca would say something like, 'I sacrificed comfort for fashion years ago, Darling.' Suck it up, sport."

"Nick, you did not sleep well again last night."

I shrugged my shoulders and looked away.

"Another nightmare."

It was not a question. I looked up at the cobalt sky and then back down to meet Kayne's eyes, an overwhelming journey of shimmering blues.

"Yep."

"Karadžić?"

"Kayne, it's nothing. Just a stupid dream. They always pass."

"No, my love. You were bathed in sweat and screaming again."

Kayne continued, "He is the criminal mastermind that casts his shadow over us and those we love."

I thought, *No fear today.*

Eager to change the subject, I stood up and walked a few steps. Kayne's words hung in the air as I interjected.

"Too bad we can't see the site of the new Lodge from here. I think it's ...."

I was pointing out to the valley but stopped. I turned back to Kayne and saw him looking at me with tremendous sadness.

"Nick."

I faked again.

"Kayne, you worry way too much. Um... Earth told me that Ace and Darana invited her to visit Inala. She needs to take a break from all of this. So many reminders of...."

I stopped talking. Kayne continued to look at me for a long time. It was a look I hoped never to see. He took a deep breath before saying to the ground.

"Nick, maybe this may be a good time to take a break. You and me, I mean. Maybe we are going too fast at this. We have not really known each other all that long and...."

He was unable to finish. This time, his words died in the mountain air.

Stunned, I thought, *What the fuck am I hearing?*

I waited, hoping to calm down, feeling the blood rush to my face. My hands clenched and unclenched.

It took a lot to keep control of my voice as I said, "So, without even acknowledging the fact that you are attempting to break up with me at a wedding, let's analyze this bullshit."

I was losing it. I walked over to Kayne as he stood up and turned.

"Look at me."

He raised his eyes to mine. I read a deep, cold resolve in his gaze.

I smacked him roughly in the chest— harder than I intended.

"So, what is Australian slang for being a total asshole or arsehole, or whatever the fuck? Because that is what you are right now.

"Shit! Kayne, I am not stupid. At least give me that. You and I both know that this is real. What we have. Do you hear what you are saying, man?

"Of course you do. I so get it. I do. You are trying to protect me, and that is totally fucked. Yes, Karadžić is out there, and he is coming for us. *Us*, Kayne. Us."

He stepped away and succeeded in turning his back to me, looking off to the mountains.

I tried to calm down and struggled, as I always do with deep emotions. Well, the hell with trying to be the strong and silent type. This was not going to happen.

"Dr. Sorenson, I am a seasoned police officer and can hold my own and am trained to protect others. You need me by your side... for innumerable reasons, Boss. So that's the logical answer.

"But more importantly, here is what my heart says: Oh, yeah, and it *has* been a short time. I agree. But I have fallen in love with you so quickly and with such an intensity that it knocks my socks off. I know you feel this too."

I said in a hushed voice, "Or else everything you said to me—the moonlight, the snow, the horses. All of that was a lie."

Unbearable pause.

"When my nightmares come, I reach out for you next to me and know everything will be all right."

Nothing.

"Kayne, every time we touch, it's like...."

My turn to leave words on the wind.

He said softly, "You and your bloody thunderbolt. Time to be realistic, Nick. There is danger in this. Evil of the utmost dread. Talking legions of psychopaths. Can we go the distance?"

I turned him to me. "Kayne, you never walked away from a fight in your life. Neither have I, Boss. We can take this bastard, Kayne. Together, you and me."

Silence.

His eyes were wet as I pulled into a hug. His arms hung at his sides. I felt like I was losing him. *No, No, please.*

He pushed me off and raised an index finger to my lips.

"You are so wrong, Nick."

Oh, shit!

"You are *not* a seasoned officer of the law. You are brash and passionate and take many risks. You are exceptionally intelligent, but you follow your heart more often than makes sense. You need guidance and...."

I started to continue my protest. Kayne continued very slowly, "... and I am the one you are stuck with, it seems."

I blinked.

He looked at me with his ice-blues, and I felt the terror leave like someone had hit the release valve, sending my fear of losing him into the bright mountain air.

Kayne added, "I... I can't let you go. Although it makes all the sense in the world, it would appear that we belong together. And we do. We do Nick. You are everything I ever...."

He reached up to caress my head and shoulders.

"Nick, I don't know where this is going, but I am becoming convinced that we belong together despite my fears that the worst will happen to you. That is my nightmare, my love."

I felt the fear leave me as he gently hugged me with reassurance.

"I feel the same way, Kayne. This is beyond anything I know or have experienced of love and devotion. Who knows what will happen? Gotta take the risk, Boss Man."

He kissed away my tears. I whispered, "I'm staying, Kayne. You're stuck with me. Play your cards right, Big Guy, and it could be a long run we're talking about here."

Kayne stepped back, took my hands in his, kissed them, and then moved up for a full-on "pash."

I stammered, "Forevermore."

We walked back to the party as two singers began the opening notes of *Unforgettable*, the Nat King Cole/Natalie Cole version. The musicians played the romantic strains of Matt and Josh's favorite love song.

I swept my wonderful man into my arms, and we joined the wedding couple with other guests, including Gints and Scott, on the dance floor. Rebecca swirled in the arms of Mitch but kept looking with amusement over his broad shoulder at her "rival."

The irrepressible Kick had scooped Mark Gadarn into his arms and was floating in his embrace.

Eyes dancing, Kayne hugged me close and whispered into my ear,

"Yes, my love. Forevermore."

The End

Acknowledgments

Tribal Blood is a work of imagination. Folks who inspired my creativity, taught me to be human, and enabled me to see a world of wonder through my mind's eye are many, but my family comes to the front of the line.

My parents, Viola and Orlando-- your beauty, love, humor, and self-sacrifice are an inspiration for the exceptional qualities of my protagonists. My heart senses you in so many things and misses you both.

I would like to thank my big brother, James Severino, for teaching his younger brother, me, about Cowboys and Indians, watching westerns on TV, and building snow horses in the winter.

My dear sister, Janet Neary, very generously taught me to read starting at age four. This love of literature has remained with me all my life, for which I am very grateful. This strong and tender woman has filled my life with caring and determination. I was a pain in the butt growing up, but she took an interest.

Mary Owens, my baby sister, is a life-long inspiration for humor, love, and family. I cherish her gifts and am thankful for the times we had going back to our childhood and the reminiscences we share today. (Her baby piano had painted-on black keys, and her dolly looked like Nikita Khrushchev! N.B. she just "dropped book" laughing.)

My understanding of the magic and admirable qualities of women begins with the valuable gift of knowing my much-loved nieces, Angela, Monica, Donna, Kristin, Lee, and Jill. My cousin, Michele Tabbano, has been a loving and gracious woman who I have appreciated all our lives.

My husband, Anton Wallner, sister-in-law, Liza Wallner, and father-in-law, Tony Wallner, have opened my heart to new horizons of love, generosity, and imagination. Tony, my husband, served as my editor, and Liza as one of my "first lookers." I appreciate your keen eyes, expert insight, and interest in my writing, as well as your perspectives on life and its living. My father-in-law is everywhere in the story, wherever admirable and loving men are depicted.

My forever buds, Fr. John Costello and Robert Siccone, have kept me loved and laughing for more than 50 years. I am humbled by your gracious friendship. Memory Lane is indeed a golden road. (The "Kiss and Tell" *is* in the works. We'll talk.)

Others who helped with the manuscript are Irene Mendoza, a dear friend, and my niece, Jill Severino. Thank you for your encouragement.

I believe that life is a journey, and along the way, we discover companions to accompany, encourage, and challenge us. My dear and loving friend, Gerry Iacullo, is such a hero and comrade. Our adventures along life's road have been hilarious, sometimes sad, but always full of wanting to become worthy of the love we share. Thank you, GJI. You are a fantastic educator and comrade.

Appendix: A Note on Diversity

The characters of The Sorenson Mysteries are many-layered and richly composed. They represent a broad slice of the spectrum of the human family, i.e., many cultures, languages, and worldviews.

Whereas the stories are fantasy, the backgrounds of the folks inhabiting the world of Kayne and Nick represent the reality of a richly gifted, inclusive human community, some heroic, some in need of support, and some representing the most insidious evils that beset humanity. All provide distinct and sometimes very unique perspectives.

Crime-fighting in the stories attempts to resist evil on many levels. The most obvious is the malevolence that drives the plot. The underlying abominations of discrimination, exploitation, and marginalization of our fellow humans exist as a subplot throughout the series.

The protagonists resist the terrible effects of intolerance, namely prejudice and disenfranchisement of minority groups, which create death and destruction, diminishing all of us. An incipient madness is contained in this hatred that results in hate crimes, false religious rhetoric, and ethnic violence. Kayne, Nick, Rebecca, and company fight against these atrocities, which, in reality, are increasing around us.

The characters pose an essential question. Why should anybody be considered an enemy because one is different? The heroines and heroes of this series, with their allies, encourage us to recognize that in the other, we see ourselves. The characters confront bigotry and "call BS" to attitudes and expressions of bias against our fellow humans, beating back the forces that threaten the destruction of universal justice and care for those most in need.

Kayne Sorenson and friends represent an exciting celebration of all that is human, all that brings us together and tears down the walls of division. They are the author's fervent prayer for a world with more respect, understanding, and love, my *Nella Fantasia*.

Intolerance sucks. Diversity rocks. -- Kick Sorenson, Freerunner, and One Hot Mess

Afterword

Thanks for reading Tribal Blood: A Kayne Sorenson Mystery. I hope you enjoyed it. Please review it on Amazon.com and like my Facebook page (Thomas Paul Severino). Also, please visit my website, www.tomseverino.com, to find out more about The Kayne Sorenson Mysteries.

Are you ready to join Kayne and Nick in Europe for more adventures? Keep reading for a preview of Book Three in the series, Stage Blood: A Kayne Sorenson Mystery, available soon.

Stage Blood

A Kayne Sorenson Mystery

Thomas Paul Severino

Tribal Blood

Prologue

The tutor roughly deposited the battling boy on the tack room floor. The boy tumbled into a sprawl. His father stood with arms crossed, incensed at the behavior of the seventeen-year-old.

"Where did you find him?"

"It was as I said. He was at the airport."

The boy stood up and brushed the dirt from his clothes. His father walked to him and stood within an arm's reach. He refused to meet the man's searing gaze.

The tutor rubbed his shoulder, where the boy had clipped him. The kid was a superb athlete, and it took all he had to bring the boy here, including a restraining rope.

The man said nothing, studying his errant son. He knew the boy's brothers were hiding out in the lofts of the adjacent barn, observing the scene below from knotholes through the shared wall. It was a secret they shared and one they thought their father was unaware of.

"That will be all, Mr. Logan. I will take it from here. Thank you."

He surreptitiously gestured to the wall up and behind him and softly instructed, "See if you can do something about that, please."

Alone in the room, the silence between the man and boy bespoke of an isolation that began years back. The man could not call the boy by the name he had given him at birth. Too much had happened between them for the boy to address the man as 'father.'

The man turned his back on his son, who only then raised his eyes to take in his father. With a surly boldness, he addressed the man.

"So, is it to be the strap again?" He looked at the equipment on the walls. "Like so many times before?"

There was no response.

"Or the paddle. That's always been your favorite."

The man was silent. Then he said quietly, "He's dead. By his own hand."

The boy said nothing. He hung his head but felt no sorrow, only a cold numbness.

"You did this thing. I told you not to continue. I told you to stop."

The man spoke softly but spun around and pointed at the boy, taking a step toward him. His rage was palpable.

"But you would have none of it. You tormented him even after we all knew."

"He was mine. You will never understand what he meant to me. Never."

The boy's eyes were filled with rage.

"Yes!" the father yelled. "He was your toy, your plaything. You tormented him just the way you destroyed your other amusements, your brothers, schoolmates, everyone. You delighted in making him suffer from that first time. You are a monstrous cat toying with your victim. Even in the throes of death."

He stopped as words began to get away from him.

"You are missing some vital pieces of a human -- inside of you."

The boy smirked, "If I am incomplete... whose fault is that? You made me."

It was an accusation.

The boy changed the expression in his voice to fake a juvenile tone, "Anyway, I am a minor. I am not responsible for..."

His father raised his hand to strike his son but froze.

The boy lowered his eyes into menacing slits and taunted, "Go ahead, Big Rancher Boss. Do you think it matters? You know it stopped hurting a long time ago."

Unable to resist the taunting, the man caved in.

"YOU *ARE* RESPONSIBLE. YOU COULD HAVE STOPPED."

Broken, the father covered his face with his hands and waited to regain his composure before speaking again. This was a man who despised weakness in himself and others. That the boy had caused him to weep would be remembered for a long time. There was no forgiving this.

"I am so ashamed of you. This is beyond words. He had a wife and a small son, and you took him from them. You persisted and would not break it off. He could not face the consequences."

"And what else?"

The young man's tone lent a Satanic dimension to the whole scene, evil and perverse, taunting his raging father. He toyed with his father.

With his back to the boy, the man brought two strong arms up and slammed his hands down on a sturdy work table.

The overwhelmed man roared, defeated by rising emotion. When next he spoke, it was soft and pitiful.

"He was my friend."

The boy whispered with a frighteningly victorious quality to his voice. "I know."

Two men entered the tack room and stood next to the door, silently and with folded arms.

With perceived difficulty but with the discipline of a soldier, the man struggled to switch into a role he knew well, that of a business administrator.

"I am sending you away to school. You need to be away from the authorities for your own good and away from the rest of us if we are to regain some sanity in this family. I will send orders for your next steps upon your completion of secondary school."

He now commanded with even more authority in his voice, "If you bolt, you are on your own, and I will make no attempt to find you or protect you. I will deny you completely.

He finished, "You have brought this crisis upon my family, and it cannot be fixed as long as either of us is alive."

The emotion of what was happening returned. Anguish in his soul prevailed as he addressed the boy for the last time.

"You are no longer a part of me. We share no parts in common. I deny you."

He signaled to the men.

"Take him. I will not see him again."

The men led the boy from the room.

www.ingramcontent.com/pod-product-compliance
Lightning Source LLC
Chambersburg PA
CBHW030314200626
46816CB00006BA/1787